A leprechaun must have seized her mouth, because surely, *surely* she had never meant to say that. Why, those words hadn't even so much as crossed her mind!

Thank goodness there was almost no light left, because he couldn't see her fiery blush. Or if he did, it could be blamed on the dying ruddiness of the sunset.

Suddenly her gentleman friend turned back into a pirate. She could see that wicked grin even in the night.

That grin was coming closer . . . closer. . . . Then she nearly jumped when she felt his hand cup the back of her neck, sliding so smoothly beneath her hair. The brush of his warm fingertips sent chillls of sheer pleasure running down her back. Her heart almost seemed to stop.

SUE CIVIL-BROWN

Breaking All the Rules

AVON BOOKS
An Imprint of HarperCollinsPublishers

AVON BOOKS
An Imprint of HarperCollins*Publishers*
10 East 53rd Street
New York, New York 10022-5299

Copyright © 2002 by Sue Civil-Brown
ISBN: 0-06-050231-2
www.avonromance.com

First Avon Books paperback printing: September 2002

Avon Trademark Reg. U.S. Pat. Off. and in Other Countries, Marca Registrada, Hecho en U.S.A.
HarperCollins® is a registered trademark of HarperCollins Publishers Inc.

Printed in the U.S.A.

10 9 8 7 6 5 4 3 2 1

1

Richard Haversham Wesley, III, Esquire, sat in front of the judge and made a personal argument that never would have been allowed in a courtroom. But he and Judge Dipshot had looked at one another across a lot of courtrooms over the years, and they had shared more than a drink or two. In fact, they had shared so many drinks that, on more than one occasion, Rich had wondered if Freddy Dipshot had been arguing with two of him. This was one of those occasions. Because they were in chambers, and because he felt he could blame whatever happened on the other Rich the judge was seeing, he could let fly a bit. No court reporter was there, and there had to be some advantage to the judge's just having a three-martini lunch, paid for, of course, by the law firm of Richard H. Wesley, III, P.A.

"Freddy, you know why that jerk Linus Todd wants his aunt declared incompetent."

Freddy belched. Gently, of course. He dabbed his cheek, then his chin, before finally locating his mouth with a tissue, then excused himself. "Crab never sits right, for some reason."

"Freddy . . ."

"Look, Rich, I've read his motion, and your client sounds wacko. Hiring a Flying Fortress to bomb the beach, for the love of Pete! My wife got pregnant on that beach."

Rich arched a brow, and Freddy answered the unasked question. "Yes. By me. I'm sure."

Freddy paused for a moment, as if waiting for the room to stop spinning, then continued. "And when you think about the value of all that land the Todd woman is sitting on, and how much of it is undeveloped, you really have to wonder. She could be on easy street."

"She's already on easy street, Freddy."

"And all that land is being taxed at its highest and best value. It's insane not to develop it. I mean, just the lots across from her house are being taxed as if they had *hotels* on them."

Rich shrugged. "That's a decision she's free to make. And she's been paying the taxes."

"Doesn't mean she's sane. All it says is she pays her bills."

"All it says is she likes her ocean view." Rich uncrossed his legs and leaned forward. "You're being snookered, Freddy."

Freddy snorted, then loosed another belch.

"Remind me not to have crab the next time you take me out to lunch."

"Consider it done." Not that Freddy would listen to the reminder.

"I'm going to be belching all the way through my hearings this afternoon. Doesn't make a good impression."

Freddy didn't make a good impression in general, but he *was* the judge. The black robe bought him a lot of leeway. And the gastronomic theory of law had never been entirely a myth. Freddy wasn't the only judge for whom complex legal questions often hinged on the quantity and location of his stomach acid.

"Freddy . . ."

Freddy then did something so unusual that Rich found himself wondering if the judge was getting some kind of payola from Linus Todd.

"Look," the judge said sternly, or as sternly as any man who appeared to be the offspring of Humpty Dumpty and a Weeble could appear, "this conversation is crossing the line and you know it. You'll get your chance to argue in court. And my suspicions about motives aren't grounds for my ruling."

Rich was startled at first by this change of tack, but not for long. He was a good trial lawyer, which meant he was as quick on his mental feet as his cat responding to the sound of his electric can opener. "Your suspicions *are* grounds, Judge, and you know it. That's why you're the finder of fact. If you think someone's lying . . ."

"What I think is that old woman is crazy and ought to be locked up. She's lucky I don't Bacon Act her."

"I believe it's the Baker Act," Rich said dryly. Then added, "Your Honor."

The Baker Act allowed people to be committed to mental hospitals against their will. The Bacon Act, by contrast, described the judge's breakfast activities, judging by the stains on his shirt. Rich had a really ugly feeling just then, substantiated by the fact that Freddy was never loathe to let a lawyer buy him lunch, even if he was sitting on a case in which that lawyer was involved. Today being a case in point.

But Rich knew better than to pursue that suspicion. He opened his mouth, but Freddy cut him off.

"You better have one hell of an argument in court, Counselor. Because I *am* going to make sure she never hires a bomber to make a run on a populated beach again."

Hell, thought Rich. *Hell's bells.* He left the judge's chambers a minute later, after playing up to Freddy's ego enough to be sure that things wouldn't get any worse for Mary Todd. Freddy even shook his hand, after only three tries. Rich headed for the courtroom to get ready for the hearing—not that he had any doubt now about how it was going to come out.

And the thought sickened him, because he would have done just about anything on earth for Mary Todd. Anything legal. He loved that dear old woman.

Miss Mary Todd, social doyenne and all-around troublemaker of Paradise Beach, Florida, was waiting for him at the defense table. A woman in her eighties, Mary had a crown of beautiful white hair, a surprisingly young face for her years, and a backbone of Toledo steel.

But this afternoon, as she watched her lawyer stride out of the judge's chambers and make his way over to her, she could see the handwriting on the wall. Even if it was her own handwriting. Of course, letting anyone *know* this was her own handwriting would spoil the entire effect. Instead, she visibly sagged a bit and didn't quite meet Richard's eyes as he sat.

"Bad news?" she asked in a monotone.

"Well, let's just say I have my work cut out for me," he replied.

More than you know, my dear boy, Mary thought. *More than you know.*

"All rise!" The bailiff's voice was, well, a *bailiff's* voice, Mary thought. Stentorian. Self-important. "The Sixth Circuit Court for the State of Florida is now in session. All having business before this court, draw near and you shall be heard. The Honorable Frederick J. Dipshot, presiding."

Mary merely straightened in her chair, her hands folded over the end of the ebony cane that she held between her legs.

"Stand up," Richard whispered.

"I'm old and frail," Mary whispered back.

The judge waddled in, fixed Mary with a glare, and sat behind the high wooden bench. He shuffled papers for a moment or two, leaving everyone standing, then glanced up. "Be seated. Let's get started. *In re: Mary Maxine Todd*, on a petition filed by Linus Todd. Petitioner?"

Mary judged Linus's lawyer to be a smooth-talking, fast-rising, greedy little so-and-so. He methodically worked through his opening statement, referring to a thick file folder, which, from what she could see, consisted of dozens of sheets of carefully typeset notes, complete with bullets and indentations. Mary wondered if he had to wipe himself after using the bathroom, or if he'd trained his bottom to wipe itself. He definitely put the hyphen in *anal-retentive*.

Linus took the stand, and the lawyer led him through his prepared spiel. *Blah, blah*, Mary thought. There was more drama in watching mud dry. That these thoughts also projected the disinterested image she wanted to portray was an added benefit. Linus's lawyer finally finished, and Richard rose for cross-examination. This, she thought, should get fun.

"Mr. Todd," Richard began, "you seem to be very concerned about your aunt Mary."

Linus smoothed an imaginary wrinkle from a thousand-dollar navy blue suit and gave his best attempt at a sincere smile. A blind man in a fog bank could have seen through it. "Yes, of course I am. We all love Mary."

"Yes," Richard said. He took a moment to turn through his own notes, then looked up. "And it's your deep love for her which led you to file your previous six petitions to have her declared incompetent."

"Objection!"

"Sustained," Dipshot barked. "Mr. Wesley, you know the prior petitions are irrelevant."

"Of course, Your Honor," Richard said. "I apologize."

This made no sense to Mary. When it came to getting what she wanted, anything from Plato's *Dialogues* to the latest unfounded rumors was relevant. Never mind that in most cases she had started those rumors herself.

Trust the law to get things backward.

Richard continued. "Now, Mr. Todd, have you made contact with a certain Timothy Herschfeld of the High Lights Development Company?"

Linus gave Mary a how-did-you-know-that glare. She felt not the least bit guilty. If the boy was stupid enough to leave his appointment book on her coffee table when he used her bathroom, well *of course* she was going to look through it.

"I don't see where . . ." Linus began, at which

point his lawyer seemed to catch up to the pro-
ceedings.

"Objection! My client's business contacts,
whatever they may be, are irrelevant to the issue
of Miss Todd's mental condition."

Judge Dipshot looked over to Richard and
belched. "I think he's right, Counselor."

"This goes to the issue of bias and his credibil-
ity as a witness, Your Honor."

Mary could tell Dipshot wanted to go with Linus on this one, but apparently something held
him in check. "I'll allow it, but keep it brief, Mr.
Wesley."

Richard made a slight bow. "Thank you, Your
Honor." He then turned to Linus. "So, have you
or have you not been in contact with Timothy
Herschfeld of High Lights Development?"

Linus squirmed in his seat. "The name sounds
familiar. I talk to many people."

"Let me refresh your memory," Richard said.
"Didn't you meet with Herschfeld on six occasions, in January and February of this year? I
can give you the dates and times if you need
them."

Linus glared at Mary again before finally looking at Richard. "Yes, I guess. That sounds right.
As I said, I meet with many people."

"Businesspeople?" Richard asked.

"Yes, businesspeople."

Mary was watching a shark at work. Win or
lose, and she fully intended to lose, it was nice to

watch Richard tighten the noose on that little turd of a nephew.

"Development business?" Richard asked.

"I dabble in a lot of things," Linus said.

Dabble is right, Mary thought. Because the boy lacked the initiative or intelligence to do more than dabble. And he'd been longing to dabble in her estate for years now.

"But Herschfeld is in the development business, isn't that correct?" Richard asked.

"Yes."

"So with him you were *dabbling* in the development business, isn't that right?"

"Obviously," Linus answered with a smug smile.

"Now," Richard continued, "your real estate holdings are not substantial, are they?"

For the first time, Linus seemed to sense that he had walked into a trap. "I don't understand."

"Well, do you own property overseas?" Richard asked.

"N-no."

"Do you own property in other states?"

"No." Linus thrust his chest out a bit. "I was born and raised in Florida. I'm a native."

Not bad, Mary thought. Dipshot's campaign literature had emphasized his third-generation Florida roots. Linus was at least not totally stupid.

"So your real estate holdings would be in Florida?" Richard asked.

"Yes, they would be."

"If you had any," Richard said, leaving the unspoken words coiled like an angry cobra.

"Yes," Linus said.

His lawyer has drilled him well, Mary thought. When in doubt, give a one-word, yes-or-no answer. Richard had gone over the same tactics with her that morning.

"Except you don't have any, do you?" Richard asked.

"Your Honor," Linus's lawyer cut in, "do we really need to explore my client's financial situation?"

Dipshot looked at Richard, who simply met his gaze. The judge looked something like a deer caught on a railroad track. He knew where this line of questioning was headed, and he couldn't stop it. "Overruled. Continue, Mr. Wesley."

Damn, Richard was better than even she had expected. He just might find a way to win this case, which wouldn't do at all. He pressed Linus relentlessly.

"You don't have any real estate holdings, do you?"

"Not currently, no," Linus conceded.

Richard thumbed through his file. "In fact, given your financial situation, it would be impossible for you to buy any real estate, wouldn't it?"

"I wouldn't say that," Linus said.

"No, of course you wouldn't," Richard replied.

He held up a sheaf of papers. "But your credit report would."

"How did you? . . ." Linus snapped.

"Objection!" his lawyer added.

"It's routine discovery, Your Honor," Richard said calmly.

"It's also personal information," Dipshot cut in. "Mr. Todd is not on trial here. I see no reason to bring his credit report into evidence. Sustained."

"I had no intention of doing so, Your Honor."

Richard was pouring on the suave now. Mary had to suppress a chuckle as she watched him work; chuckling would not be the appropriate image here. Oh, no. But he was good. Damn good.

"Mr. Todd, isn't it fair to say that the only development deal you could possibly explore, the only deal which would justify *six* meetings with a nationally known high-rise developer, would be regarding your aunt's land in Paradise Beach? Wasn't *that* the subject of those meetings?"

Linus's lawyer shot out of his chair. "Objection! Compound question, Your Honor."

Now it was Richard's turn to bristle. "It's the same question in different words, Judge."

"Overruled."

Richard turned on Linus. "Wasn't that why you met with Timothy Herschfeld? To discuss development of your aunt's property?"

Linus's shoulders slumped. "Yes, it was."

"And this was back in January and February, *long* before Mary's alleged involvement in the incident with the bomber on the beach."

"As I said, I was exploring possibilities," Linus said. "We never reached hard negotiations."

"Of course not," Richard snapped. "You had to get her declared incompetent first!"

"Objection!"

"Sustained!"

"I withdraw the question," Richard said impatiently. "I have no further use for this witness."

It was, Mary thought, a virtuoso performance. The question now was how to torpedo it and still lose. Well, she'd always been her own best ace-in-the-hole.

Erin Kelly watched from the front row as Richard returned to the defense table and sat next to Mary. For the first time since Linus had filed this silly petition, she felt hope. Mary's lawyer had driven Linus right into the wall. That he'd looked so damned sexy while doing so was something she didn't want to think about. He did cut a fine figure in a business suit, though. Tall, his face a blend of studious and rakish, eyes that glinted with the glee of battle. It wasn't hard to imagine him at the helm of a privateer, ordering his crew to hoist the main and set off after a treasure galleon on the horizon.

Stop that! she told herself. He was a lawyer. A good lawyer, yes, but still a lawyer. Lawyers fed and thrived on other people's mistakes and miseries, and their concept of truth was elastic at best. The pirates of old at least had their own necks on the block. Richard Wesley would go back to his comfortable practice, with his comfortable office, and his comfortable desk chair, and his comfortable home, whether Mary won or lost today. He wasn't a pirate. He was just a lawyer.

Linus's lawyer had not been able to find a single other witness who was willing to testify against Mary Todd. *This should come as no surprise*, Erin thought. Mary was more than the grande dame of Paradise Beach. She was a living legend. Her reputation for good-natured mischief was woven into the very fabric of Paradise Beach. She took meddling to an art form. But she meddled with a kind heart, even if she had orchestrated a UFO abduction a few weeks back, not to mention the B-17 that "attacked" the beach. She'd never hurt anyone, not that Erin knew of, anyway. She'd burst more than a few bubbles, and nudged more than a few people into doing things they should have done for themselves. But she'd never hurt anyone.

And now that Richard Wesley had exposed Linus's real motive, she ought to be home free.

Judge Dipshot announced a recess—he called it a "comfort break"—which is to say he needed to use the little judge's room. Richard turned to Mary.

"Now it's your turn," he said.

"No, I won't testify," Mary said simply. "You've done all we can do already."

What is she thinking? Erin wondered. Yes, Richard had set the stage. Now all Mary needed to do was take the stand and explain herself. The judge was obviously leaning her way.

Erin bit back the urge to reach across the rail and say something; Mary had given her explicit orders to stay out of it. There were times when Mary's tutelage was almost insufferable. On the other hand, Mary had taught Erin more about human nature than Erin had imagined possible.

"But you have to testify," Richard said. "All I've done is set Dipshot up to listen to you. Now you have to take the stand."

"The way that judge looked at me, he'll never listen," Mary said, her voice gloomy. "He sees me as a doddering old woman. No, I'm not going to open myself up for the kind of grilling you just gave Linus. I just won't."

When Mary set her mind, that was that, and Erin recognized that particularly stubborn set of Mary's chin. Richard, either out of sheer stubbornness or sheer stupidity, continued to argue with her, to no avail. In the end, when the judge returned to the courtroom, Mary had not budged an inch.

"Does counsel for the respondent have any witnesses to present?" Dipshot asked.

"No, Your Honor," Richard said, his voice brisk and clipped with tension. "We have no witnesses."

The judge looked at Mary. "You realize that I can't evaluate your competence without hearing from you. All I'll have to go on is the motions and your nephew's testimony."

"I have nothing to add," Mary said.

No! Erin wanted to scream. What was Mary doing?

"Very well then," the judge said. He paused to review some papers for a moment, then looked up. "The petitioner has shown that Miss Todd has done some bizarre things. I've heard a lot in my time on the bench, but a bombing run on a public beach? Even as a joke, Miss Todd, that was very dangerous and showed an absence of judgment. And while Mr. Todd may have explored development of your land, all that shows is that he has a better appreciation for its economic value than you do. You've given me no reason to think the land is serving some greater purpose in its current state, nor have you denied or provided any explanation for the insensible acts which Mr. Todd has attributed to you. I'm sorry, but this leaves me no choice but to declare you mentally incompetent to manage your own affairs, and appoint your nephew as your legal guardian. So ordered."

Dipshot brought down his gavel.

Erin's heart sank. Well, this would not do. This would not do at all. If Mary wouldn't fight for herself, Erin would fight for her.

It was time for her to put Mary's teachings into action.

2

Feeling stunned, Rich left the courthouse with Mary Todd on his arm. He couldn't believe this. All he had wanted from the very start of the case was to defend Mary and get her nephew off her back. Instead she had hamstrung him every step of the way, refusing to let him call any of her friends and neighbors to testify—although, in all honesty, the thought of what most of them might say, all the while intending to be kind and loving, was the stuff of his worst nightmares as a lawyer.

But as if that had not been enough, Mary had put the last nail in her own coffin by refusing to speak for herself. If he hadn't loved the woman so dearly, he might have shaken her until her teeth rattled.

But worst of all was the order Dipshot had handed down. Richard couldn't believe that, either. He simply could not *believe* the order that Dipshot had written. As Mary's attorney, he should have been one of her trustees, able to keep an eye on the management of her assets. Instead, that idiot Freddy had given full control to Linus and *his* attorney. Which, to Rich's way of thinking, left Mary completely vulnerable.

He would file an appeal, of course, and a motion to stay Freddy's order pending the outcome of the appeal. It might be a year or more before the appellate court would issue a ruling. And if there was one certainty in Florida law, it was that Freddy Dipshot would know all six judges of any three-judge appellate panel. He couldn't believe this.

And Mary . . . she'd understood fully what had just been done to her. He had seen it in her eyes when the judge had read the order. She knew that Linus now had full control of her life and her money. There was no spark of life left in her. She hobbled along beside him like a zombie.

Rich couldn't believe this mess. Linus would have the property carved up into condo-sized slices within a month, and it would be all but impossible to challenge that if Linus could demonstrate that he was enlarging the fortune. Unfortunately, in this day and age, a beach view didn't seem as important as the money that could be made by selling land to a hotel chain. Linus could make a wreck of everything Mary had sought to preserve simply by pointing out that he was making her money.

No, he couldn't wait on an appeal. He'd have

to rack his brains and see if he could come up with a good reason for Dipshot to rehear the case. Maybe even defy Mary and get some of her neighbors to testify on her behalf. Something inside him cringed at the thought, but he reminded himself he could pick and choose among the best. Of course, if he thought it necessary, Linus's lawyer could pick and choose among the rest. He had to find a way.

Then his heart turned cold as Mary spoke.

"I should kill myself."

"Mary, don't say that!"

"I should kill myself. Everything would go to my great-nephew, and he and I don't see eye-to-eye on my property."

"Don't think that way. I'm not done yet. Where *is* your great-nephew, anyway?" If he could make a motion to get another family member involved in the trusteeship, that might help considerably.

"I don't know. Tobago. Botswana. You'd have to call the television network."

"I'll find him."

Mary seemed indifferent. That indifference terrified Richard. This woman was not one to ever be indifferent, and certainly not to something this important.

They had hardly descended the courthouse steps when, off to their right, an altercation broke out. Turning, he saw the two green-eyed women who had sat behind Mary throughout the hear-

ing. They were now confronting Linus Todd.
They were both beautiful women, one blonde,
the other brunette, and under any other circumstances he would have had a healthy male reaction. Especially to the dark-haired one, who right
now looked like some warrior goddess preparing to do battle.

"You," said the dark-haired one, "are the low-
est kind of slimy life-form, Linus."

"Yeah," said the blonde one. "You're a total
hairball, you jerk. How can you treat your aunt
this way?"

"Who the hell are you?" demanded Linus.
"You can't talk to me that way!"

"I'll talk to you any way I want," the dark-
haired one said. "You're dung on the bootheel of
life."

Linus turned a bright red and opened his
mouth to respond, but his attorney grabbed his
arm and started dragging him away. Linus
didn't follow willingly. He twisted to look over
his shoulder, and he shouted a few epithets,
none of them suited for a public venue.

But the green-eyed Valkyries weren't done
yet. Now they marched toward Rich, battle light-
ing their faces.

"What kind of lawyer are you?" demanded
the elder one, the raven-haired one, when she
reached him. "How could you let them do this to
Mary?"

"I'm not through—"

"Yes, you are through. Because before you can do anything about it, that snake is going to have ruined everything Mary tried to do. And all the money is going to be in his pocket, one way or another. You mark my words."

Rich looked into her blazing eyes and felt a quiver of sexual response that made him ashamed under the circumstances. "I don't believe we've met."

She ignored him and turned to Mary. "Mary, somehow we'll take care of this. Are you going to be okay?"

But Mary didn't answer. Indeed, she hardly seemed aware of the rest of them.

Green eyes looked accusingly at Rich. "This is *your* fault," she said and turned on her heel to walk away. Blondie followed her.

And Rich felt like dung on the bootheel of life himself.

"That lawyer looked good enough to eat," Seana Kelly, the blonde, remarked to her older sister as they drove back to Paradise Beach.

"Anything in an Armani suit looks good to you," Erin, the dark-haired Kelly, replied. She didn't add that she was grateful Seana had never been attracted to motorcycle jackets. Although, to be honest, she'd long since discovered that you could find bums in any kind of male clothing.

"Don't be mean."

"It's okay. Most of us are that way at your age. It's Mary I'm worried about, anyway."

"She didn't look so good, did she?"

"No. And I'm more worried about her state of mind than her money."

"The two are kind of the same thing right now, aren't they?"

"Maybe. Maybe not."

"We need to cheer her up."

"Absolutely."

"So let's throw a party!"

They were stopped at a drawbridge now, waiting for a sailboat to pass beneath the raised spans. Erin looked at her sister. "A party? To celebrate what? That she was declared incompetent?"

"Of course not!"

Erin caught herself and tried to remember that her sister was her sister. Unfortunately, having been responsible for raising Seana for the last ten years, Erin too often treated her like a daughter. But Seana was an adult now, and she needed to remember that.

"I'm sorry," Erin said after a moment. "I'm just upset about Mary."

"It's okay." Seana was a fairly blithe spirit, having been well-sheltered most of her life, first by their parents, then by Erin. Erin, on the other hand, had been thrust into full adult responsibility when their parents had died, and she'd developed a much more serious nature.

"You mark my words," Erin said. "Before this is over, that prig Linus and the lawyers and the judge will all be sorry they ever met me."

The irrepressible Seana couldn't resist. "That's no great accomplishment, sis. Pretty much everyone who knows you feels that way."

Despite herself, Erin smiled. But she certainly didn't feel like laughing. Mary was like a second mother to her, or like a favorite aunt who on the sly had shown her how to get more pizzazz out of life. An aunt who was showing her that it was okay, and even fun and useful, to color outside the lines.

Because of Seana, Erin had never dared do that before, but as she drove homeward, plagued by an aching need to help Mary somehow, she began to remember the lessons Mary had taught her.

Like the sea monster thing just recently. A huge egg had mysteriously appeared on the beach, and just as it had seemed the town was going to tear itself to pieces over whether to protect the egg or destroy it—or in the mayor's case, use it as a circus sideshow for the tourists—Mary had come up with a brilliant plan to draw everyone together. She had simply asked an old friend to take his B-17 bomber up into the air over the beach and pretend to make a bombing run at the egg. In an instant everyone, including the mayor, had drawn together to protect the egg.

And while that same incident was being used

now to prove Mary's legal incompetence, the fact remained that Mary had managed in the blink of an eye to turn Paradise Beach back into a friendly, family-like community. The goodwill from that incident still lingered as people recalled it, laughed about it and smiled with mutual understanding.

So was Mary really crazy? No way. Just unusual. And for a few years now, she'd been encouraging Erin to take steps that were outside the ordinary rules of life, to look at things differently, to believe in the grand gesture . . . or the underhanded maneuver, as long as one intended well.

Of course, Mary had years of practice at it. Erin had none, other than some observation over the last few years.

The idea that she might now need to initiate a Mary-esque plot to save her mentor daunted her. She wasn't sure she could pull it off.

On the other hand, could she afford not to try?

And she wished the memory of that damn lawyer wouldn't keep weaseling its way into her brain, reminding her that he'd looked ready to pull a cutlass in the courtroom. Reminding her that his brilliant blue eyes had actually shown with glee in the midst of battle.

He was just a damn lawyer, after all. And a lousy one, too, if he couldn't even manage his own client.

Not that Mary Todd was manageable. But

Erin wasn't prepared to give him even that bene-fit of the doubt. The simple fact was, the man had gone into the jousting match and had failed to win.

Enough said.

B

The mayor of Paradise Beach, Carl Woods, never liked to be disturbed before his third cup of coffee, which was why his secretary was trained to tell all callers and visitors that he was in a meeting. Every morning. Until at least ten o'clock.

Of course Sheila, his secretary, chosen more for her curvaceous, blonde good looks than for her typing or her intelligence, ignored the order whenever she chose. Or maybe she just couldn't remember it from day to day. All the mayor knew was that he had to remind her on a regular basis that he didn't see anyone—not the governor, the pope, not even the President of These Yewnited States—before ten.

Occasionally the mayor thought of replacing Sheila, but every time he started to get such a thought, it seemed that Sheila read his mind. Right about then she'd come in to work and prance around in some skintight outfit on those impossibly high-heeled shoes, wearing a daringly low-cut or transparent top.

This morning she was teetering on scarlet stiletto pumps that looked as if they'd been designed for a porn movie, a skinny short scarlet skirt, and a scarlet tank top that barely covered her, uh, chest in a decent manner. And when she bent over his desk he got such a look at cleavage that he sputtered powdered sugar from his doughnut all over his desk . . . and her.

Which caused her to straighten and start wiping the sugar off that red top in a way that made the mayor, a poor mortal man, clean forget that he was crazy enough to think about getting rid of her.

She moued at him, an expression that looked like Marilyn Monroe puckering for a kiss. "I'm glad," she said poutily, "that you don't like jelly doughnuts."

At that moment, so was the mayor. Well, except for the powdered sugar that now dotted his chartreuse tie, the one with the Day-Glo orange dolphin on it. The one that matched the orange shirt he was wearing with his favorite green suit.

"There's a man out front," she said, wiping the last of the sugar away. "You need to see him."

The mayor, who was only on his third doughnut with the rest of the dozen awaiting him, shook his head. "It's too early."

She clucked and bent over again, giving him another view of the Grand Canyon. This time he managed not to sputter sugar everywhere. "You need to see him," she insisted.

"Why?"

"He's wearing an Armani suit, a silk shirt, a tasteful tie"—this last was added with a dour look at the mayor's own gorgeous tie—"and gold cuff links. And he blew his nose on a monogrammed handkerchief."

"Probably not gold," the mayor said around a mouthful of chocolate doughnut. "Probably plated."

"I know the real thing when I see it."

The mayor, regarding the two-carat engagement ring she wore on her right hand, memento of some jerk she'd taken for a ride and dumped, allowed as how she might. She'd also fleeced the guy for a Mercedes convertible and his beachfront condo. The odd thing was, the jerk thought *he'd* gotten the better of the deal.

"It's not ten yet," the mayor said.

"It's nine-thirty and that's close enough. Now wipe your mouth, put the doughnuts in your drawer, and I'll bring him in. Unless you don't *want* to get rich."

Getting rich was the only thing that mattered more to the mayor than his morning doughnuts. For all her failings, Sheila *did* understand him.

"All right, all right," he grumped, not wanting her to get the idea that he approved of her behavior. The doughnuts disappeared into the bottom drawer along with the horde of jelly beans, licorice whips, and malted milk balls. The mayor had a sweet tooth. In fact, he had a mouthful of sweet teeth. All of them filled with silver. Of course, he thought, for a man of his stature in life, they ought to be filled with gold.

He wiped his mouth and groaned in response to Sheila's insistence that he let her see his teeth. And he thought his *wife* was a nag?

"Brush your teeth," Sheila said. "They're covered with chocolate doughnuts. I'll give you five minutes."

Huffing, the mayor went into the small private bathroom that had been added by his predecessor, a guy with an incontinence problem. When he finished brushing his teeth, he checked himself in the mirror. No sugar, no stains. Good. But his smile ought to gleam gold, not silver.

On the way back to his desk, he poured himself more coffee. He had just resumed his deep leather chair behind the massive executive desk when Sheila opened the door, announcing, "Mr. Linus Todd, Mr. Mayor."

Linus Todd? The mayor knew that name. He'd never met the guy, but he'd heard enough about him to fill a telephone book, none of it good. Mostly because he'd heard it from Miss Mary Todd, which should have predisposed him to like Linus, given the fact that she'd been a life-long thorn in his side. His reaction was quite the opposite.

Mayor Woods knew a pretentious idiot when

he saw one. Primarily because like recognized like, although the good mayor never realized it. He instead prided himself on having a good nose for jackasses.

Armani suit, gold cuff links and embroidered hankies notwithstanding, Linus Todd was a jackass. In this case, the suit definitely did *not* make the man. Linus had that soft, well-fed look and handsome face of a high school jock going to seed. The look of someone who thought too highly of himself and couldn't imagine that everyone else didn't agree with his opinion. He had, to the mayor's way of thinking, the look of a spoiled brat grown up.

The metaphorical silver spoon was practically hanging out of that well-shaped mouth, and the mayor would have bet this jerk hadn't worked a day in his life. Probably living on the expectations of his aunt's death, and wheeling and dealing himself into enough to get by on. He probably even used designer toilet paper.

Linus's opening did nothing further to endear him to the mayor. "You know who I am."

As if he were God descended from heaven, or at least the governor of Florida. The mayor steepled his fingers and looked at Linus over them. "Uh . . . no."

He was gratified to see Linus's face darken and that self-satisfied smile slip. It also gave the mayor an edge, to his way of thinking. Now Linus would think he was stupid, which would

make Linus careless. Never mind that the mayor
was stupid. He'd never realized it, and nobody
had ever let him in on the secret.

"I'm Mary Todd's nephew," Linus said
grumpily.

"Ahh." Pretending to be much enlightened,
the mayor smiled, offering the perfect insult.
"What can I do for you? Do you need a job?"

Linus's face darkened even more. "No, I don't
need a job!"

"Oh," said the mayor, suddenly wondering if
he was pushing this guy too far. After all, Sheila
had mentioned getting rich. "Then what can I do
for you?"

"It's not what you can do for me. It's what I
can do for you."

At that point a warning bell clanged in the
mayor's brain, a bell so loud it even reached the
dimmest recesses of his minuscule mind. Nobody ever did anything without expecting something in return, and while he might not be the
brightest bulb in the marquee, the mayor had
long ago determined that he wouldn't do anything that might cost him a term in a state correc-
tional facility. Those orange jumpsuits showed
no fashion taste. Which meant he avoided anything that remotely smacked of accepting bribes,
misusing public funds or sexually harassing his
secretary. At least when he was aware of doing
such things. Which, sad to say, wasn't always the
case.

He leaned forward and put his elbows on his desk. "Just what is it you can do for me?"

Linus sighed as if he were the most put-upon man on earth. "I am now the trustee for Mary Todd's estate."

The mayor sorted through that, a ripple of shock and disbelief slowing his already slow mental processes. "*All* of it?"

"All of it."

"How did that happen?"

"The court declared her incompetent."

That astonished the mayor. Mary Todd might be a constant thorn in his side, but she wasn't incompetent. A little crazy, but everyone in Paradise Beach was a little crazy, a fact to which the mayor owed his job. A fact to which he was sensitive. How could he not be? The mayors of neighboring communities had let him know more than once that he ran a lunatic asylum and that he was the chief lunatic. Not that he believed it. It wasn't his fault that all of those stuffy people around him had no sense of style. Would any of them wear an orange shirt with a green suit?

Finally he spoke. "And what does this mean to me?"

"It means," Linus said as if speaking to a dolt, "that I now control all her real estate. And that means that I can help Paradise Beach grow into the great resort community it is meant to be. You, Mr. Mayor, can preside over a thriving town full of tourists, hotels, attractions. And a budget beyond your wildest dreams."

"Hmm." In all honesty, the mayor wasn't all that in love with tourists, even though he made his living off them. They filled the three bars he owned and gave him a comfortable living, but they also clogged the streets, overran the supermarkets, and strained facilities to the point of breaking. On the other hand, he wouldn't mind being the mayor of a more important town, like St. Pete Beach, or Clearwater Beach.

But he also knew something else. "Mary won't like it." And when Mary didn't like something, she made the mayor's life a living hell.

"It doesn't matter," Linus said smugly. "It's all under my control now. She's lucky the judge didn't have her committed."

"Umm," said the mayor, thinking that the judge was the lucky one, because Miss Mary would have made *his* life a living hell if he'd done something so stupid.

"Anyway," Linus said, "what I need is your help in getting some rezoning so we can build hotels, condominiums, and all the rest of it. Now, you ask what's in it for you?"

The mayor hadn't asked that question. He didn't want to ask that question. It sounded too much like getting a bribe. He might have only two brain cells, but they were keenly tuned to anything smacking of bribery and malfeasance . . .

which left him little enough brain for anything else.

"I'll tell you," Linus said, leaning forward eagerly. "When you leave office, I'll have stock options ready to hand to you. A gentleman's agreement, nothing in writing."

First of all, nothing in writing meant nothing at all. But secondly, the mayor knew a bribe when he smelled one. It wouldn't matter if he'd been out of office ten years, the instant this guy handed him stock options, somebody would be investigating Carl Woods's role in the rezoning.

"I don't think so," the mayor said. Much as it hurt to say it, and oh, it hurt. He could feel the pain all the way from his teeth to his toes—or maybe it was just a toothache?

Linus looked stunned. "You don't want all this development?"

At that moment, another circuit flipped in hizzoner's dim brain, and he realized this jackass had seriously insulted him by offering a bribe. The mayor was very touchy about such things. Rising, he went to a corner where he kept a golf bag full of clubs.

The golf bag was decor and nothing more. The mayor had rarely touched it since the day he'd hauled it in here to make a statement, largely because no matter how hard he tried, a par four always turned into a par forty-eight for him, and golf balls were too expensive to feed to the woods and the ponds, not to mention the gators. Mayor Woods didn't like getting within a mile of a gator.

He pulled out a putter he'd seldom used and turned to face Linus. "I said no to the bribe."

"Bribe?" Linus's face paled, then reddened. "I wasn't offering you a bribe. I was offering you a business opportunity."

The mayor took a swing with the putter and approached Linus. "If you want rezoning, you'll have to go to the zoning board."

"Well of course," Linus replied, blustering a little. "I was simply asking for your support."

The mayor hesitated, wondering if he'd misunderstood. But a mental instant replay assured him he hadn't. "You didn't ask for my support. You tried to buy it."

"I did no such thing. I was merely offering you a business opportunity at some date in the future when you were free to consider it."

"Right." The mayor stepped closer to Linus and swung the club again. Near the man's nose. "I'm not stupid." Which was a lie, but the mayor was excused because he didn't know it.

Linus eased out of his chair and began to back toward the door. "Do you know what I could do for this two-bit town?"

"Not a damn thing if you insult me." The mayor swung the club again, this time making it whistle through the air. It felt good to have his putter up. Now that he thought about it, this hadn't happened in a while. "Because the simple fact is, all the property Mary owns is in this 'two-bit town.' No place else for you to go. So . . . you'd better not insult me again."

The club swung one more time, and Linus darted out the door, screeching something about assault. An instant later, the outer door closed behind him.

"Par four," the mayor announced with a great sense of satisfaction.

"Are you crazy?" Sheila asked, coming into the room. "What about being rich?"

The mayor then said the most sensible thing he'd said in his entire life. "Being rich makes no difference in the state pen."

"He'll call the cops."

"No. Because I'll tell them he tried to bribe me." Then, pausing on his way back into his office and his doughnuts, he had a thought. "Sheila, call the commissioners and the zoning board members. Warn them this guy is trying to bribe officials."

Moments later he was diving back into his box of doughnuts. It was a good day indeed.

Linus Todd sat in his car, seething. Wouldn't it figure that Mary Todd had run this town for so long. The place was a nuthouse. His aunt fit right in. In any normal community, like Chicago or New York, or even Tampa, he'd have been able to grease the palms of the right people and been off and running. That was how things were *supposed* to work. You scratch my back, and I'll stab yours. *That* was politics. That was normal.

This was . . .

The thought died in his mind as he stabbed a finger at his personal electronic organizer. He couldn't for the life of him figure out why people used these. His daily appointments were easy to manage: play racquetball in St. Petersburg, buy a new racquet—in Clearwater this time, because every sporting goods store clerk in St. Pete knew him and rolled his eyes when Linus walked in— lunch at a trendy downtown restaurant with lousy food but important people around, home for *Jerry Springer*, which he thought of as research for dealing with the people of Paradise Beach, dinner at another restaurant on the beach where he might draw the attention of the trendsetters, and home for a night with the Entertainment Network, to keep up on the hottest and latest. He had long since vowed that his PalmPilot would contain only the phone numbers of important people—in case anyone should steal it—which meant his phone list was almost empty. One phone number stared back at him, that of Timothy Herschfeld and High Lights Development Company. The guy who had wined and dined him back in January and February, then dropped him like a hot potato when he'd learned that Mary wasn't on her deathbed after all.

Well, it wasn't Linus's fault that the old witch

had recovered from the flu. At her age, that was damn near a miracle.

All in all, life was not treating Linus in the style to which he would like to become accustomed. Aunt Mary's land could change all of that. With a bit of rezoning and his business savvy, Linus would be skiing in Aspen, clubbing in Manhattan, wintering in the Bahamas, and learning polo in Cannes. That was how his life should be. That was the life he deserved.

And in the way, as always, stood that damned dowager. He'd seen the way the mayor's face had screwed up at the merest mention of her name. She had everyone in this town under her thumb one way or another. Her defiant stubbornness was legendary. What Mary wanted, Mary got. What Mary opposed, people too often decided wasn't such a good idea anyway. Especially after she'd connived an angle or three for leverage.

The sad truth was that even though he had control of Mary's estate, he didn't have control of Mary's iron will. The woman defied him still. Well, he could sweet-talk with the best of them, or so he believed. That, like his business savvy, was a figment of his imagination. He would simply have to go talk to her. Now that he had the corner on her land, maybe she'd listen to reason.

Satisfied, he punched another button on his organizer, which set it to beeping, which required him to punch another button, and another, and another, until finally he removed the batteries in disgust. It was time to go see Aunt Mary.

4

Richard Haversham Wesley, III, knocked on Mary Todd's front door. He was concerned because she hadn't returned his calls in several days, and he kept remembering how beaten she had seemed after the court order. He half feared that no one would answer his knock, that Mary had carried out her threat.

Much to his relief, the door opened. Unfortunately, the vision that greeted him was not that of the feisty Miss Mary but one of blazing green eyes and black hair.

"You!" she said.

He'd have given anything at that moment for a snappy comeback, but all he could come up with was a meek, "Me."

"What do you want?" asked the emerald-eyed Valkyrie.

"To see my client," he said, feeling a burst of impatience. "Miss Todd."

"If I have anything to say about it, she's going to find another lawyer."

"You *don't* have anything to say about it. Who are you, anyway?"

"Miss Todd's friend." As if he wasn't. "Erin Kelly."

"Ahh." That explained a lot. With a name like that, she was bound to have a temper. Well, the Wesleys—his branch, at any rate—sprang from the Irish Wesleys who had given rise to the duke of Wellington. The Iron Duke. Rich walked straight past the snapping green eyes into the cool interior of the house.

"Well, Miss Todd's friend Erin Kelly, I'm her friend and attorney, Rich Wesley, and I want to see my client."

"Does she know you were coming?"

"She ought to. Assuming she's been getting her phone messages."

Erin, a spitting image of Queen Maude, bristled. "Are you suggesting I've been interfering with her messages?"

"Are you always so paranoid? I suggested nothing of the sort."

"You said—"

"I *know* what I said," he interrupted bluntly. "I'm a lawyer. The suggestion that she may not be getting her messages is a long way from accusing you of diverting them. If I had wanted to say that, I would have said it."

That seemed to take some of the wind from

her sails, but only a bit. "I'll ask her if she wants to talk to you."

"I don't think so. *I'll* ask her. Where is she?"

For a few seconds, it appeared that Erin was going to tell him where to find a plank to walk off, but she seemed to think better of it. "In the parlor," she said stiffly.

"Thank you," he said with equally stiff formality, and marched that way. He could have been more diplomatic, he supposed, but when faced with a lance-bearing Celtic queen, one generally got further by raising one's own lance. He ought to know. He'd dealt with his aunt Bridget for thirty-six years.

Mary was sitting in her darkened parlor in a rocking chair. Her cane lay abandoned beside her, and she was rocking steadily, staring at nothing at all. Matters clearly hadn't improved at all.

He pulled a Queen Anne chair away from a rolltop desk and drew it close to Mary. Then he sat, taking one of her frail hands in his.

"Mary," he said gently. Queen Maude was hovering somewhere behind him, but he ignored her. The last he had noticed, she wasn't armed with anything except her tongue.

After a moment, Mary sighed and looked at him. But her face showed no animation, and the corners of her mouth drooped as if they were too heavy in her face.

"Mary, you know I'm going to take care of that scurrilous, despicable nephew of yours."

"Too late," she said. "There'll be a condo going up across the street by the end of the month."

"I've asked the appellate court to issue a stay, pending outcome of the appeal. I'm sure they'll agree to it, because if they don't, irreparable harm could occur to your holdings. And I'm trying to put together enough information to get a rehearing from Dipshot."

He thought he saw a flicker in her gaze. It almost looked like devilment, but he decided that must be wrong. She looked too depressed to be up to anything. Whatever it was, it was gone before he could identify it for certain. She sighed heavily. "Linus bought the judge."

Rich was reluctant to respond to that. Freddy Dipshot probably hadn't paid for a single lunch or dinner since he'd been appointed to the bench, but since he was equal-opportunity about the lawyers he allowed to buy his meals, Rich was reluctant to put any illegal cast on it. He was even more reluctant to think Freddy was capable of taking a *real* bribe. Saying things like that about a judge without any proof could get you into real trouble.

Finally he said, "I'll look into it, Mary. I swear I will. If Judge Dipshot took so much as a penny from your nephew or his lawyer, I'll find out about it, okay?"

She nodded, but she didn't brighten a bit.

"In the meantime, I promise you that no matter how Linus wheels and deals, he's not going to turn a single spadeful of earth on your property. I'm going to keep him tied up in appeals until we win."

She looked at him. "The money."

The money was a big problem. It could disappear faster than the appellate court could move even with an emergency order. "If he takes your money, he's going to be in big trouble. Big trouble."

Mary's shoulders trembled. "I want Linus's hands off everything, Richard. Everything. Just the thought pains me. . . ." Her voice trailed off, and she sank once more into her unhappy thoughts.

Richard couldn't stand seeing Mary this way. He'd dealt with unhappy clients before, of course, but none of them had been Mary Todd. Mary was like a grandmother to him. She'd helped pay for his law school, had helped him get started in private practice. He'd had more Sunday dinners at her house than he could recall. For some reason, she had taken him under her wing and kept him firmly there.

He owed her big time. Which meant he was going to use every weapon in his legal arsenal to rescue her. But what he'd really like to do was strangle Linus Todd.

Since it was illegal, he wouldn't do that. Unfortunately. A bit of warrior instinct reared up in him but had to be firmly knocked down. He would, as always, do everything within his power—short of violating his principles and ethics. And he was *sure* there had to be a legal way to handle this.

He gently squeezed Mary's hand. "Mary, I promise. I'm going to make the bad man go away. I don't know what got into Judge Dipshot's head, but he's not the last word, you understand? And I'm going to do whatever it takes to tie Linus up into legal knots so that he can't touch any of your estate, all right?"

She nodded, but she didn't seem hopeful. He sighed and wished he could just vaporize her despicable nephew.

Erin spoke from behind him. "Do you really expect her to believe you? After that court order?"

Prickles of irritation ran along his neck. He turned to face the young woman with the temper. He experienced an absolutely barbaric urge to grab her and silence her with a kiss. Of course, that only worked in the movies. In real life, women charged men with battery for less. "Are you always so pleasant?"

"Only when I see a dear friend hurt."

"Well, she's a dear friend of mine, too."

"Then don't make her promises you can't keep."

Richard rose, drawing himself up to his full

six feet, reminding himself he'd faced greater—and more dangerous—annoyances in the courtroom. Of course, courtroom annoyances rarely oozed so much sexual magnetism, but it made no difference. "There's only one way to go about this," he said flatly. "We take Linus back to court."

"I'm not worried about Linus. I'm not worried about the money and the property. What I *am* worried about is Mary's state of mind."

"So am I. But the only thing to do is to undo the situation that caused this."

"It's *not* the only thing to do," Erin said forcefully. "The most important thing to do is get Mary out of this funk. Once she's herself again, she can handle Linus."

"Are you suggesting we take her to a doctor?"

"When did you and I become we?"

He stifled a sigh and simply shook his head. "Just answer the question, please."

"You're not in a courtroom now, Counselor. And no, I don't think taking Mary to a doctor will make her feel better. It would probably make her feel worse, as if *we* were agreeing she's mentally incompetent. No, the most important thing to do is get her involved again."

Mary sighed, and they both looked at her. "Do you mind not discussing me as if I'm not in the room?" Then she fell once again into her brown study.

Erin took Rich's elbow and pulled him out into the entry hall, closing the parlor door behind them.

"Oh, *this*," said Rich, "is going to make her feel a whole lot better."

"We've got to do something to get her out of this mood," Erin said, ignoring his remark. He had a feeling she was good at ignoring things she didn't want to hear. "She's elderly. Do you know how easily the elderly just fade away when they have a crushing loss? I'm not even sure she's eating."

"What I can't understand," Rich said, "is why she's giving up. I've known Mary for thirty-six years, and I can't remember a time when she didn't relish a battle."

Erin frowned. "Maybe it's different when a judge tells you you're too crazy to handle your own affairs."

"Maybe." Or maybe Mary was just getting old and tired and didn't want to fight this battle yet again. This wasn't the first time Linus had tried to have her declared incompetent. But it *was* the first time he'd succeeded.

Rich shook his head again. "That Flying Fortress bomber is a big thing to get around. If she hadn't done that . . ."

"I might point out, Mr. Lawyer, that she wasn't the only one involved in that little escapade. There was the guy who owned and flew the plane. I don't see *him* being judged incompetent."

"Of course not. He doesn't have any money, or a nephew like Linus. Which I pointed out to the judge, by the way."

Erin's brow furrowed. "You did?"

"Of course I did! I'm not incompetent, whatever *you* might think. In fact, I have a very healthy law practice, and I win most of my cases. I should have won this one." He felt the frown settling onto his face again, as it had countless times a day since Freddy Dipshot's order. He couldn't figure this one at all, Flying Fortress or no.

Just then, crockery rattled. From a door farther down the hall, to one side of the staircase, the younger sister emerged carrying a tea tray. Today the long blonde tresses were caught up in a ponytail that made her look even younger.

She caught sight of Rich and smiled. "Oooh, the chocolate bar."

"What?" he asked blankly.

"Seana!" Erin said sharply. "This is Mary's attorney."

"I know," said Seana, giving him a come-hither look that must have been learned from watching old Mae West movies.

"Richard Haversham Wesley the Third," Richard said, covering his sudden awkwardness. "Everyone calls me Rich."

"Hardly surprising for a lawyer," muttered Erin. "Aren't they all rich?"

"I guess I need to get another cup," Seana said brightly. "I didn't know we were having company for tea. I'm Seana Kelly, Rich."

"Nice to meet you. But don't bother. I really don't care for tea." Not with his stomach in a knot, thanks to Mary's state and Erin's obvious scorn for him, and even thanks to Seana, who was looking at him like she wanted to eat him up. He had another urge then, to flee. But he stood his ground, as his Wesley ancestors would have done, not to mention all the wild Rourkes, Herlihys, Dohertys and O'Bannons they'd married.

Not a Kelly in the lot, though. At least not back to the sixteenth century, which was as far as his aunt had yet been able to trace. Which meant he couldn't plead family ties to save him from these women.

"I can get you something else," Seana offered with a flutter of her long eyelashes.

"No thanks. I had breakfast not too long ago."

"Men," Seana sighed. "So hard to please." With that, she opened the parlor door and carried the tea tray inside. "Tea, Mary," she said brightly. "I even got some of your favorite scones for you."

As far as Rich could tell, Mary didn't answer.

That's when he realized that Erin looked embarrassed. Because of her sister's obvious vamping? Hmm. Well, at least he knew the warrior queen had a chink in her armor. "Your sister seems nice," he said, trying to find a point of common ground on which they could meet.

"She's only twenty-one," Erin said pointedly. "A child."

"I'd already figured that out," he agreed smoothly. "And you're what? Twenty-two?"

She didn't like that at all, and he had the pleasure of seeing her embarrassment give way to another blazing look. Could fire be that green?

"I'm thirty," she said tartly. "You won't pull the wool over *my* eyes."

"I wasn't intending to. I only want—"

He was cut off by a loud knocking at the door. Erin threw up her hands. "Everyone in the world seems to be stopping by today."

She marched past him and opened the door. And there, looking irritated and impatient, was none other than Linus Todd.

Much to Rich's delight, the greeting offered to Linus was far worse than the one he'd received.

"You disgusting slug," Erin said forcefully, and slammed the door on Linus. Loudly.

"How dare he?" she fumed as she turned away and faced Richard again. "The man is a dirtbag. Insensitive!"

Rich had a feeling that being insensitive was a far worse crime in Erin's book than being a dirtbag. The doorbell rang again, more insistently, and Erin turned to face the besieger. But Rich stopped her.

"Is he alone?" he asked.

She looked at him, her eyes shooting fire. "Yes. I'm surprised he has the guts."

"Let him in," Rich said.

"Are you crazy?"

Rich almost laughed. He was getting the feeling that in Erin's world there were only two decent people other than herself: Mary and Seana.

"No, I'm not crazy. Not at all. The thing is, he might say something I can use against him. Especially since he isn't with his lawyer."

Erin's expression changed, growing thoughtful, and for the first time Rich noticed what a lovely mouth she had. And what a cute nose. Irish to the bone, a lovely strawberries-and-cream complexion. He wanted to ravish her on the spot.

"So," she said slowly, "he's a stupid dirtbag?"

"He's been stupid all along. Unfortunately, he met up with an equally stupid judge. But this might be the stupidest thing he's done yet."

"Yes, all right," she said, falling in with the plan. "Shall we give him tea?"

"Anything to make him relax."

"But not in front of Mary."

"We probably don't have a choice. Why else would he come here? Not to see you or me."

"True." Her frown returned. "He'll upset her."

"Right now that might be a good thing. Anything's better than indifference."

The doorbell rang again, this time angrily. "All

right," Erin said. "But he already knows what I think of him."

"That doesn't seem to be a deterrent," he pointed out as the bell rang yet again.

"No. Idiot scumball."

She certainly has quite a list of epithets, he thought as she went back to the door. He looked forward to hearing more of them, as long as they weren't directed at him.

She flung the door wide, and with an exaggerated sweep of her arm, invited the toadstool into the house. Rich was momentarily diverted by the realization that he was falling into Erin's habit of name-calling. Then he realized he wanted to come up with even better epithets than hers. He suddenly wanted to laugh with the love of battle. Hmmm. He'd better watch it. This woman could have a deleterious effect on his carefully controlled lawyer's nature.

"You have some nerve," Erin said to Linus as she slammed the door behind him. "Did you come to gloat?"

Bad way to start an interview, said the lawyer in Rich. Wonderful! said an O'Bannon, Rourke or Herlihy with approval.

Great. Now he was developing a split personality.

Linus looked nonplussed by Erin's greeting. He stood there, a variety of expressions passing over his face, all of them indicating he hadn't an idea in the world how to respond. Rich decided to intervene before Queen Maude routed the intruder and sent him into wild flight.

"Mr. Todd," he said, adopting the formalities of the courtroom, "you understand that I have to protect my client's interests. I can't allow you to see her alone."

Linus drew himself up to his full height, a couple of inches shorter than Rich, and puffed out his chest. "Protecting Aunt Mary's interests is *my* job now."

"Really?" Rich pretended to seem delighted. "This of course means that you'll continue to follow all her wishes with regard to the disposal of her property."

Once again Linus looked uncertain. He made a few noises, sounding like a coffeemaker that couldn't quite come to a boil. "Ah . . . I'm taking care of things for her."

Rich smiled. "Yes, of course. So you won't be building on the property that she's preserving for future generations."

"I didn't say that!"

"No? Then exactly how is it you'll be looking out for her interests?"

"With sound financial management."

"Seems to me she's been doing pretty well all these years."

"Not well enough."

"Ah." Rich pretended to ruminate. Never underestimate the value of silence. It often worked wonders, because most people seemed hell-bent on filling it.

Linus didn't disappoint him. "She's been wasting that property all these years. It's worth millions now."

"Yes, of course it is. Right now, with nothing on it."

"It can be worth more. That's sound financial management."

"Unless," Rich said slowly, "you consider that the land, left as it is, will be worth even more in ten years."

"You don't know that."

"I *do* know that. The amount of undeveloped land in this county is nose-diving to zero. And the amount of undeveloped land on the barrier islands like this, especially beachfront land, is already zip, except for here. Look at it as a long-term investment, Linus. It's like holding growth shares."

"I'm not going to wait that long," Linus said. "Why should I? She's crazy and a judge said so. And Tim Herschfeld and High Lights Development are ready to move *now*."

"But as her trustee, don't you think you're responsible for following the wishes she's been expressing for the last sixty years or more?"

"I'm responsible for making money!"

Rich nodded. "I see."

"No you don't see," Linus said, blustering.

"She's wasting everything, and I'm not going to wait around until I die to get what's rightfully mine!"

Then he turned and stormed out the door. This time it was Linus who slammed it.

"My, my," Erin said. "He's every bit the creep I thought he was."

"Of course he is," Rich replied. "Mary is living too long, according to him."

Erin's green eyes met his. "So, Counselor, did you get what you want?"

"Maybe. He did sort of admit that money is his motive."

"We knew that all along."

"Right, but he never said so. Until now. And you're a witness."

"So you got what you wanted."

"In part." The other part of what he wanted was to lay this woman down on the nearest soft surface and leave her moaning for more.

Ah, such dreams. And dreams they must remain.

5

It had been a long time since a man had looked at Erin Kelly the way Richard Haversham Wesley, III, was looking at her now. As if he wanted to ravish her on the spot.

Or maybe she just hadn't noticed other men looking at her this way. It was possible, because she couldn't remember ever having met a man as attractive as this Richard the Third. In fact, for a lawyer he looked remarkably piratical, even in a three-piece suit. Thick dark hair, astonishingly blue eyes, almost an electric blue. A well-chiseled face with a determined jaw. And a glint in his eye that belied the rest of his careful presentation. He might be a man of substance, but he really did look as if all he had to do was pull off that subdued tie and leap aboard his galleon.

Fearing her cheeks would start flushing and give her away, she averted her gaze. Meeting those blue eyes of his was like agreeing to dance with the devil. Nothing but trouble could come from it.

But even looking away didn't quite ease his spell. As if a demon had taken control of her tongue, she was amazed to hear herself start asking if he'd care to stay for tea. Before more than two words escaped her, she was saved by the bell.

The doorbell, that was.

Richard beat her to the punch, which made her realize just how off-balance she was feeling. He turned from her and went to answer the door.

"I guess," he muttered, "Mr. Toddstool isn't done with us."

"Toddstool?" A hiccup of helpless laughter escaped her. "That's a good one."

"I thought you might like it," he said with exaggerated modesty.

But when he opened the door, Erin saw not Linus but Ted Wannamaker, Mary's lifelong beau.

"Ted," said Rich, apparently acquainted with him. "Come on in. I'm sure Mary will be happy to see you."

But Ted didn't look happy. A distinguished, gray-haired man of about Mary's age, he was looking quite natty in a white shirt, khaki slacks and blue cravat. "What's this I hear?" he demanded without preamble. "I'm gone for two weeks on a jaunt to Spain, and I come home to find out my Mary has been declared incompetent! And that fool nephew of hers has control. What kind of lawyer are you, Wesley?"

"Just what I was wondering," Erin said with satisfaction. Now she wasn't alone in trying to put Richard the Third on the spot. In fact, putting him on the spot seemed to grow more important with each passing moment she spent in his vicinity.

"I'm a good lawyer," Rich said calmly.

"Then what the hell happened?" Ted demanded.

"Well, there was this little matter of a Flying Fortress the judge couldn't seem to get around. And then there was the judge himself."

"What about the judge?"

"I'm not sure," Rich answered. "But something wasn't right."

Erin spoke. "Mary's sure he's on Linus's payroll."

"Hmm." Ted frowned. "It wouldn't be the first time."

"It's also something I wouldn't advise anyone to say in public without proof," Rich continued. "All I can tell you is I've filed for an emergency stay on the order."

"Do you think we'll get it?"

"I'm as sure as I can be, given the way things go."

Ted sighed. "I suppose that's all I can ask for. If you need assistance of any kind, just let me know. I can pay for any additional help you need."

"Thanks, Ted, but I'm not worried about getting paid. I'm worried about Mary. I just wish the two of you had gotten married at some point in the past. Then Linus wouldn't be her trustee."

Ted frowned, hesitated, then blurted, "But we *are* married."

Absolute silence greeted his words. Erin and Rich exchanged looks, and she could see as much surprise and disbelief in his gaze as she was feeling. "Uh. . . ." She hesitated. Some cautious part of her realized she didn't want to do anything to cast doubt on what Ted had just said, even if she suspected he was gallantly lying.

But Richard the Third had no such qualms. Of course not. He was a lawyer.

"Well, Ted," he said, "if you can get me a copy of your marriage certificate, I can probably knock Linus right off his perch."

"Uh, a copy. Well, I don't exactly have one. I mean . . . well, it was a few years ago, and we went to Las Vegas. . . ."

"You can still get a copy. The sooner the better."

Right then, Erin realized that Rich also thought Ted was lying. And he was being a pigheaded lawyer about it. "Why are you being so difficult?" she demanded of him. "Ted's word is good."

Rich looked down at her with those too-bright

eyes. "I'm not questioning his word. But his word won't be good enough in court. They'll want the papers."

"Oh." Fuming, she subsided. Did this guy have all the answers?

"Well," said Ted, looking uneasy, "I'll have to find out where I need to get it."

"Good," said Richard. "The sooner the better. And I hope it was more than five years ago, Ted."

That's when Erin realized the lawyer really was a pirate. Wasn't this what they called leading a witness? It seemed to her he was telling Ted exactly what to come up with.

This of course didn't make Ted look any more comfortable. "Why at least five years?" he asked. It sounded like a complaint.

"Because if it happened long enough ago, then some underhanded judge can't claim Mary was incompetent when she married you."

"Oh." Ted was starting to look flushed.

"It's going to be awkward enough to explain why this didn't come out sooner."

"Oh, that's easy," Erin said, falling in with the scam. "Mary liked to pretend that she would never succumb to marriage. She was upholding her image." She wondered if God was going to strike her dead for conniving this way, then realized she was prepared to connive even worse if necessary, so she might as well resign herself to having to make a daily confession until this issue was settled.

"I see," said Richard the Third. Was that humor glinting in those mesmeric eyes of his? And why was she suddenly feeling hot in unmentionable places? As if he'd touched her.

"Well," said Richard, "as soon as you get me those papers, Ted, I'll put a massive-sized hole in the Toddstool's balloon."

"Toddstool?" Ted looked confused. "Oh, Linus. Well . . . um . . . of course I'll get the papers." Looking desperate, he added, "Reverend Archer married us."

"I thought you went to Vegas," said Richard, ever the laywer.

"Oh! We did. We *did*. We, uh, took Arthur with us."

Erin kept her mouth shut, realizing she was watching a lawyer guiding a witness. Probably as illegal as hell. She wondered what he did by night. Sail up and down moonlit channels in the bay stealing treasure from unsuspecting trawlers? Ravishing mermaids?

Strangely, the thought delighted her.

"Look," said Ted, sounding really desperate, "can I see Mary now? I'm worried about her."

Rich nodded. "Sure. We're worried about her, too. Maybe you can cheer her up a little."

Erin certainly hoped so. "She's in the parlor with Seana," she told Ted. "I'm going to the kitchen to get something cold to drink. Do you want anything, Ted?"

He shook his head. "No, thanks."

After he disappeared into the parlor, Erin looked at Richard reluctantly. "What about you?"

"I'd love a cold drink. I suddenly have a dry mouth."

Considering how he was getting into cahoots with Ted here, she could well imagine. It did, however, raise him in her estimation. Some things were more important than silly laws, things like taking care of your friends and family.

And Ted and Mary had been married in every sense but the law for sixty years anyway.

Rich settled in at the table in Mary's kitchen, while Erin retrieved two cans of cola from the refrigerator. She sat facing him, and they popped their tops.

"What about common-law marriage?" she asked Rich.

"It doesn't exist in Florida," he said. "No papers, no marriage."

"Oh." She met his gaze again and realized that he wanted to move away from this subject. Probably because his ethics were screaming. He could pretend to believe Ted just so far.

"Well," she said, "I'm sure Ted will find the papers."

"I hope so."

Much as she enjoyed seeing him uncomfortable, Erin decided that the wisest thing would be to move to another topic. If she pressed him too far on this one, his ethics might rebel completely.

And, she had to admit, she liked that he so plainly had ethics. The pirate image was appealing, but she wouldn't have liked it at all if he seemed to be perfectly comfortable with collusion.

"What about this High Lights Development thing?" she asked. "What can we do about that?"

"No reason to do anything just yet," Rich said with a shrug. "Deals like that don't get put together overnight."

Erin opened her mouth, ready to argue that it was obvious from his court testimony that Linus had been dealing for a while with Herschfeld's company. But he sideswiped her by totally changing the subject.

"So what do you do?" he asked, having apparently decided that the further they got from the subject of Mary, the better.

She hesitated a moment, annoyed with him. But then she decided it was probably better if she worked on her own to deal with the threat. After all, Richard was a lawyer and might squeal on her. "I own my own pottery shop on the boulevard," she replied. Safe topic. "Mary helped me get started because she liked my work."

"I'm sure she also likes you," he said. "She told me once it was one of her prime indicators in a decision to help someone. She helped me, too, you know."

"Really? How?"

"My folks died in a boating accident when I was nineteen. Mary supplemented my financial aid through college and law school, and then fronted the loan I needed when I started my own practice. I wouldn't be here except for her."

"Me too." Erin smiled. "She's a great old dame."

"Frustrating, too. I sometimes wish she'd talk to me before she got involved in things, but . . ." He trailed off and shrugged. "She wouldn't listen anyway."

Erin laughed. "Absolutely not. Mary can't stand boredom. If nothing's happening, she'll make it happen."

"So it seems."

"But I'm sure she's never done anything criminal."

"I'm not." He suddenly grinned and looked more like a pirate than ever. "So I don't look too closely."

"Probably wise," she agreed, feeling a strange flutter in her heart. A highwayman. Maybe that's what he was. Dashing, daring, romantic. She had the worst urge all of a sudden to just moon over him. Which was ridiculous, she told herself sternly. She was acting as young as Seana, maybe even younger. Women of thirty didn't harbor fancies about pirates and highwaymen. Did they?

Besides, the important thing here was Mary

Todd. "I hope Ted can shake her out of this mood. It frightens me."

"It's certainly unsettling," he agreed. "I can't remember her ever giving up on a fight, and I've known her over thirty years. It's always seemed to me that there was nothing she loved *better* than a good fight."

"That was my impression, too."

He started turning his can of cola in aimless circles, and Erin could hear the hiss of popping carbonated bubbles. "I hope she's not as depressed as she looks. I hope she's sitting in there scheming."

"I hope so, too. But I don't believe it."

He sighed and rose to go empty his cola down the sink. "I don't believe it either. It can't be Linus's betrayal that's bothering her. She's known all along he was out to get control this way." Shaking the last of his drink out of the can into the sink, he turned on the water to wash it down the drain. Then he tossed his can in the wastebasket and faced her, leaning back against the edge of the sink.

"Can you or your sister keep an eye on her? Unfortunately, I've got to get back to my office. I've got appointments and a court appearance tomorrow morning to prepare for."

"I can't keep my business closed either. But . . . I guess Seana and I can take turns checking up on her."

He nodded. "Thanks, Erin. I'd appreciate it."

"Hey, I'm not doing it for you."

A quirky smile curved his well-shaped mouth. "I already knew that."

She flushed, feeling almost naked suddenly. Was she that obvious?

Just then, the doorbell rang once more.

"I'll get it," Rich said.

"I can manage."

"I know you can. But I can manage, too, without slamming doors in people's faces and calling them dirtbags."

She bristled. "I only call people what they deserve to be called."

"I'm sure. But I'm more diplomatic. At this point I'd rather not alienate potential supporters, however annoying they may seem to be."

"What do you take me for? Just because I let you and Linus know what I think of you doesn't mean I'm a brat."

Again that piratical smile lit his blue eyes. "No, you're a wild Irish Valkyrie fighting for someone she loves." Then he left the kitchen.

Erin stood a moment, feeling off center and off guard. Irish Valkyrie? Weren't Valkyries Norse or something? But the inconsistency didn't bother her as much as her reaction to what he had called her. She felt warm and flushed all over. As good as a purring cat.

This could not continue! Gathering her wits,

she went after him, trying to think of something to put him in his place so he would never again say such a disturbing thing to her.

But it was already too late to give him a piece of her mind. The door was open, and walking through it was the mayor of Paradise Beach, looking as garish as a neon sign outside a cheap bar.

"It's terrible," said the mayor, his hands fluttering as he passed Rich, who closed the door behind him. "Terrible! Tell me it isn't true. I had this disgusting man in my office today telling me that he now controls Mary's estate. Now admittedly, Mary and I don't always get along perfectly, but she's infinitely preferable to that slimeball of a nephew of hers!"

Erin met Rich's amused gaze. "We have a majority for slimeball."

"Toddstool is better," Rich demurred. "What can we do for you, Mr. Mayor?"

"I want to see Mary. At once! She can't allow this state of affairs to continue."

"There's not much she can do to stop it just yet."

"Well that's intolerable," the mayor ranted. "Give me the name of the judge. I'll speak to him myself. He can't seriously expect the good citizens of Paradise Beach to endure having their lives upended by that egotistical pretty boy Linus. If anyone's incompetent around here, it's that sniveling, good-for-nothing, conniving toad."

"Toddstool," Richard corrected, looking amused.

"I don't care what you call him. I want him out of my hair and out of this town! Mary's no crazier than anyone else around here."

Erin doubted that was saying very much, coming from a man dressed like an LSD flashback, but she kept the sudden twinge of amusement to herself. Except that she saw it reflected in Rich's gaze. Oh, she didn't want to like that lawyer. Lawyers were awful people. Weren't they?

"Mr. Mayor," Rich said soothingly, "it really won't help if you upset the judge. He doesn't like to be upset."

"Well neither do I! And he's upset me greatly. And I want to see Mary right now. How she can let this happen is beyond me."

"She didn't have much choice," Rich said quietly. "And she's not seeing anyone right now."

"Exactly," said a male voice from behind them. They all turned to see Ted standing in the parlor doorway. "This isn't a good time, Carl," he said to the mayor. "Mary's not feeling well."

"And where the hell were *you*," the mayor demanded, stabbing his finger at Ted. "Why didn't *you* do something?"

"I was in Spain visiting my sister. She's not well." Ted arched an aristocratic brow. "Is that a problem for you?"

The mayor sputtered. "No, no, of course not.

But you should have been here. You probably have a dozen judges in your pocket."

"I don't have anyone in my pocket." Ted was indignant, but also clearly amused. "I wouldn't stoop to put anything so dirty as a judge in my pocket."

For an instant the mayor forgot his ire and chuckled. "Ain't that the truth? Talk about absolute power." But then he turned on Rich again. "It's *your* fault. If you were half a decent lawyer—"

Ted interrupted him. "Don't malign Mr. Wesley. He's a fine lawyer, and he handles all my affairs. The problem here is not Mr. Wesley. The problem is Linus. And Mary's penchant for going over the top sometimes. I'm afraid, Carl, that I have to agree with Rich on one thing. A Flying Fortress is pretty hard to get around."

The mayor snorted, evidently having forgiven Mary for scaring him and quite a few other people nearly to death with a fake bombing run on the beach to protect a giant egg that the mayor had planned to make a mint off of. Of course, the egg had hatched just a little while later, and its unknown occupant had disappeared into the sea before the mayor had even stood to make a dime, so he could perhaps be forgiving now.

"Mary," Ted said, "has always felt the rules apply to everyone except her. One supposes that was bound to get her into trouble sooner or later."

The mayor looked astonished. "I thought you loved her!"

"I do," Ted said simply. "With my whole heart and soul. But that doesn't make me blind to her foibles."

Erin felt her heart squeeze for Ted. How she wished someone would feel that way about *her*.

"Some romantic you are," the mayor muttered to Ted.

"I think he's very romantic," Erin objected, then blushed as she felt Richard the Third look at her with interest. "Love isn't blind. Not true love."

"Maybe not," remarked the mayor with a shake of his head. "But when my wife goes on one of her tantrums, I sometimes wish love was deaf."

His remark was greeted with silence, as if no one was quite certain how to respond tastefully. As if there could be a tasteful response to such a tasteless remark.

"Umm," said Ted finally. "What exactly is it you want, Carl?"

"I want to talk to Mary. We've got to find some way of shutting down her nephew before he destroys our beautiful community."

"I thought you *wanted* development."

"Not if I have to work with that sleaze."

Rich gave another of his piratical grins. "The guy really got you, huh?"

The mayor shuddered expressively. "He won't

show a lick of concern for anyone or anything in this town. All he wants is money."

Erin would have said the same thing about the mayor until this very second. She wondered what Linus had done to get the man's hackles up. She would have expected the mayor to greet Linus with a red carpet and open arms.

"Talking to Mary won't do any good right now," Rich said firmly. "Legally, she can't do anything except feed herself."

"This is an outrage!"

"No kidding," Rich said. "But at the moment it's a legal outrage, which limits our options to legal remedies." He looked sternly at all of them. "No one is to do *anything*. We should get a stay from the District Court of Appeals in a few days. In the meantime, everyone just look after Mary."

"I will," Ted said. "I'm not going to leave her side."

"Good. Now if you'll all excuse me, I'm going to be late for an appointment." The pirate nodded, then walked out of the house.

Erin spoke to no one in particular. "He's entirely too calm about this."

Ted answered. "He gets paid to stay calm when everyone else is in an uproar. Clear heads and all that."

"I still think he's too calm."

Ted shook his head. "Wind yourself down, Erin. Mary has a true champion in that young man."

A knight on a white horse? Erin considered the image, then decided she liked the pirate better.

"All I know," said the mayor, "is that this is a terrible state of affairs. It's time to fill the moat and load the cannons." With this enigmatic statement, he departed.

Erin looked at Ted. "I feel blinded. The colors that man wears! Do you want Seana and me to stay with Mary?"

"Would you please, for just a little while? I'll be back shortly, then the two of you can get back to your lives. I don't intend to leave Mary alone for so much as an instant."

Erin smiled. There ought to be more men in the world like Ted Wannamaker. "Sure," she said. "Where are you going?"

"That's better left between me and the Lord."

Reverend Arthur Archer was having lunch in his office at the church. A peaceful few minutes just to himself between rounds of visiting the sick and meetings with his congregants and committees.

While he dined on a peanut butter and jelly sandwich, the extent of his culinary abilities, he considered what he had heard that morning about Mary Todd. He'd known, of course, that her nephew was once again trying to get her declared incompetent, but like everyone else in Paradise Beach, he'd assumed the outcome would be what it always had been.

What a shock! Poor Mary must be cast down beyond belief. He needed to go visit her this very afternoon.

Not that he had any idea what he was going to say to her. Mary was crazy. He'd always known that. So crazy that she'd had *him* doing crazy things that still made him squirm with guilt and embarrassment. But he couldn't very well tell her that.

Besides, while she might be crazy, she was crazy like a fox. Most definitely *not* incompetent. The two were very different things altogether. That idiot judge apparently couldn't make the distinction.

He took another bite of his sandwich and felt it glue itself firmly to the roof of his mouth. He sighed. There was an art to eating a peanut butter sandwich, one he'd figured out years ago. Apparently he was too distracted.

As he tried to pry away the offending lump with his tongue, his office door opened, and Ted Wannamaker stepped in. This was the downside of allowing his secretary to take lunch at the same time he did. Or, perhaps, the downside of eating in his office.

"I need to talk to you, Arthur," Ted said.

Lord, thought Arthur, Ted sounded just like Mary. Any time she'd said that, Arthur had been in for trouble. But he couldn't talk with food in his mouth, and the sandwich was sticking as firmly as Super Glue. "Mmph," he said.

Ted closed the door and started pacing the small office. Arthur couldn't even suggest he sit, not with his mouth a gluey mess. So he watched, getting a little seasick.

"I need a marriage certificate for Mary and me."

If the peanut butter hadn't been so firmly stuck to the roof of Arthur's mouth, he would have choked on it. Instead all he could do was say, "Mmph?"

"Exactly," Ted said, as if they were in perfect agreement. Panic began to fill Arthur. Maneuvering his tongue wildly, he tried to pry the lump free.

"You see," Ted continued, "if Mary and I are married, if we've been married a while, then the court won't give Linus control of her fortune."

"Mmph!" Oh, God, he could see what was coming, and he didn't have a mouth to defend himself with.

Ted finally slumped into the chair across from Arthur. "I know it's a lot to ask, Arthur."

"Mm-mmph!"

"I'm almost ashamed of myself for lying," Ted went on, apparently oblivious to Arthur's speechlessness. "But it was all I could think to say. I've got to help Mary, and I'm willing to do anything for her. Even lie."

"Mmm." Arthur wasn't so sure *he* was.

"We've been all but married these years anyway. And we *would* have been married all along if Mary weren't so stubborn."

"Mmph."

"I know, I know. She can be *so* stubborn. Sometimes I think the only reason she's refused my proposals all these years is because it gives her a sense of power."

"Mmm." Arthur could easily agree with that. Mary delighted in controlling everyone and everything.

"I suppose I could just wash my hands of this entire mess. After all, it's partly her fault for hiring that idiot to fly that B-17 bomber at the beach."

"Mmph," Arthur agreed, remember that entire fiasco, which had somehow involved him dressing up as an alien and abducting an innocent police officer. He would *never* forgive himself for that.

"If she ever listened to reason . . ." Ted sighed and shook his head. "But I love her, Arthur. Beyond all reason. And I can't leave her in this fix."

Arthur didn't bother to attempt a reply. He thought he was at last working loose the sandwich. There, he'd pried one corner free.

"I've lost count of the times she's done things that frightened me," Ted continued. "And I've resolutely refused to have any part in her hijinks."

Ted clearly had a stronger moral character than he, Arthur thought glumly. Another corner of the sandwich worked loose. His tongue was getting exhausted.

"But this is different," Ted said, leaning forward. "I need to rescue her. As quickly as possible. Do you have any idea how depressed she is? She hardly acknowledged me when I went to see her this morning."

"Mmph!" That was bad indeed. On the good side, the sandwich was almost free.

"So what I need, Arthur, is a marriage certificate from you, saying that you married us five years ago in Reno."

Arthur choked on his sandwich.

"Why won't you tell me what you're up to?" Seana Kelly demanded of her sister Erin a couple of hours later, when they were back at Erin's pottery shop.

"Secrets aren't secrets if they're shared." Although the truth was, she still hadn't come up with a plan worthy of Mary Todd. Not that she was going to admit that to her sister. Everything she'd thought of so far had merely made her laugh at her own silliness.

"But I know you had an idea about how to help Mary! You've been chuckling to yourself ever since the judge ruled."

Erin, who was trying to determine where to place a recently fired turquoise-glazed pitcher in the shop window, merely shook her head. "Seana, trust me. There are things you're better off not knowing."

Seana folded her arms and pouted. "I'm not a child anymore."

"Certainly not," Erin agreed, finally settling on a space a little right of center in the window. "Go out front and see how that looks, will you?"

Seana complied, keeping her arms folded,

looking every inch the thwarted four-year-old. Erin sighed and found herself almost wishing that some dashing young man would come along and sweep Seana off her feet, thus making Seana *his* problem rather than hers.

But not *Richard*, she thought. He'd be too much for Seana to handle.

Then she felt terrible for having such a thought about her sister. It was just that Seana could be difficult at times. But who couldn't? Everyone was difficult at times.

"It looks fine," Seana said grumpily, reentering the shop. "It looks good with those brown and coral coffee mugs beside it."

"Thanks, hon."

Seana flounced across the crowded shop and hopped onto the rattan bar stool beside the beverage bar that Erin kept for her customers, in order to encourage them to linger in the shop.

"You still treat me like a child," she said.

"I'm not treating you like a child. I know you're an adult. But there are some things . . . I just don't want you to get into any trouble." Which was as good an excuse as any for covering the fact that she didn't have a plan.

"Trouble?" Seana's pout gave way to interest. "What kind of trouble?"

"I'm not going to get you into this. And that's final." Mostly because she knew full well that Seana couldn't keep a secret. She was incapable of it. Invariably she would just have to tell *some-*

one, and once she told *someone*, it would be all over Paradise Beach, thus ruining the whole plan.

"I don't think that's fair," Seana argued. "If I'm going to have to bail you out of jail, I should at least know why."

"I'm not going to jail. Nor am I planning anything illegal." Deceptive certainly, underhanded definitely, but not illegal. At least, she hoped it wouldn't be illegal once she fully developed the vague idea that was growing in her mind.

"Then why can't you tell me?"

Erin smothered a sigh and reached for the clay Kokopelli statue to place it beside the pitcher. For some reason, even though this was Florida, the Kokopellis were her top-selling item. She couldn't seem to make enough of them.

She was saved by her phone, which was ringing in the office. "Be right back," she told Seana.

Seana, who was still pouting, suddenly turned into a smiling, beautiful young woman as the front door opened and a customer walked in. At least Seana didn't allow her moods to interfere with her job. Relieved, Erin escaped into her office.

"Hi, Erin," said the familiar voice of an old college friend. "It's Dan O'Doole."

"Dan! It's so good to hear your voice."

"Good to hear yours, too. I got your message. Are you in some kind of trouble?"

"No, but a friend is."

"And you want me to do a freebie?"

"Only if you have time." She had met Dan when he was in theater school and she was following two years behind him. She'd appeared in one of his productions. Dan had graduated and moved on to bigger and better things, but the death of Erin's parents had shifted her priorities from being an actress to being a mother to her younger sister. She'd given up her impractical dreams, dropped out of college and supported the two of them the best she could with the little bit of life insurance and a job as an executive assistant. Since then, she'd thoroughly enjoyed it any time she saw Dan's name on movie credits . . . which wasn't that often. Most of his parts were small.

"I'm between jobs," he told her frankly. "I just closed out an off-Broadway show that isn't going to make it to Broadway, and I've got a job in a touring company, but that doesn't start rehearsals for another couple of weeks."

"Life is hard, huh?"

"It always is in this business." He laughed. "But it's okay. I pay the bills and I have a ball. At least I don't have to wait tables anymore. So what's up?"

"Where are you? Could we meet?"

"Sure. As it turns out, I'm on holiday down here in Orlando. Well, and auditioning for a Disney animation." He paused for a moment. "Very secret, huh? Want to do dinner?"

"I'd love to. But not here. I don't want anyone to know we're connected until it's over."

"Oh, I like this," he said with enthusiasm. "Dinner it is. Want me to come to St. Petersburg?"

"That would be great," she agreed. "That little hole-in-the-wall Spanish restaurant over on Thirty-fourth. You remember the one."

"How could I ever forget?" he asked with a sigh. "Is seven good for you?"

"That's great, Dan. See you then."

She hung up, hoping Dan would still be willing to help her when she explained what she wanted—assuming she figured out exactly what she wanted by then. Her plan was still too vague, but Linus's mention of the developer had planted a seed.

She also had to figure out how to tell Seana that she was going out for dinner, leaving her sister in charge of the shop until ten.

In the end, Seana was miffed enough not to ask questions or give her a hard time. Instead she concentrated on the customers who came through the door. By the end of the afternoon, she'd made quite a few good sales.

Maybe, Erin thought wryly, it would be good if her sister was angry with her more often.

Richard Haversham Wesley, III, had a difficult afternoon. The problem wasn't his clients, many of whom were busy trying to find a way to get money out of someone else, a few of whom were trying to do so illegally, no matter how often he explained that he wouldn't participate in such shenanigans. Nor was the problem the guy who'd created a dangerous nuisance and now refused to hear that he really ought to settle the suit because it was going to get immeasurably more expensive if he didn't. Richard was used to clients who didn't understand the law, didn't want to understand the law, and expected him to be a shyster because he was an attorney.

He was also used to clients who expected him to work miracles when none were available. He even, from time to time, had a client who really was innocent of wrongdoing, whom he wanted to protect with every skill in his arsenal.

No, the clients weren't the problem. They were the same types of people who came through his office daily, people who either wanted a free ride for the rest of their days, or who didn't want to give someone else a free ride, or who were being unjustly sued by someone who wanted a free ride. He was used to it, and he dealt with them as they came in whatever fashion best protected his ethics.

The problem was a certain woman with blazing green eyes. He'd been so involved in those eyes on their two meetings that only now did he find himself remembering the rest of the package.

The day at court she'd been conservatively dressed in a loose denim dress that looked good enough for court but revealed little. But this morning . . . this morning he had discovered she had a rather eclectic sense of color and style. A bright yellow knit tee, with bright green shorts, and a purple belt. It might have been blinding if her eyes hadn't so engaged him.

But today's outfit had also revealed her other assets, and they came back to haunt him that afternoon as he listened to too many familiar tales of woe and tried to prepare for the trial in the morning, when he would attempt to save an elderly widow from paying the last of her savings to a neighbor who claimed the widow's coconut palm had dropped its burden straight on her head, causing a concussion.

In the first place, it wasn't a coconut palm. So whatever had fallen had been considerably smaller and probably less hard. Ah well.

All he could see were those long legs. Shapely legs. The kind of legs he had thought existed only in chorus lines and movies. With the sexiest little dimples just below the knees.

Then there was her waist, wrapped in purple leather and so . . . tiny. Emphasizing perfectly rounded hips. Not boy hips, as so many women sought these days, but a woman's hips. Hips that just begged to cradle a man in their curves. And her breasts. Well. Thinking about them raised his temperature enough that he finally turned on the air-conditioning, which caused his paralegal to pointedly don a sweater.

By seven-thirty, as he finished with the last client, and read the last of the file in preparation for tomorrow morning's trial, and made sure he had the blown-up photos of the widow's palm and a coconut palm, plainly not the same tree, he realized he wasn't going to get Erin out of his mind.

It was time for a little hair of the dog.

Mary sat at her dining room table, enjoying a bowl of creamy clam chowder and a glass of white zinfandel, enjoying more than anything the silence. Oh, it was fun, stirring up everyone and giving the little nudges here and there that put them to work on things they ought to be doing for themselves. But it was also tiring. And pretending to be depressed was . . . well . . . depressing. So, given a few hours to herself, she could review the status of things.

Ted was finally *doing* something about her. After all these years, he was getting off his oh-so-gentlemanly behind and getting his hands dirty. The call from Reverend Archer had come as only a small surprise. She was playing the grieving old lady to Duse-ian proportions, but she hadn't expected Ted to react this quickly. Perhaps decades of hope invested in him weren't entirely wasted. And that alone was worth a smile as she sipped her wine. Ahh, there was little that was more satisfying than putting the wheels in motion and watching the people of her beloved town scurry to catch up.

The doorbell drew a frown and a heavy sigh. Couldn't she at least enjoy a quiet dinner before having to resume her chosen role of gloom and doom? She grasped her ebony cane, made a point of hunching her shoulders a bit, as if the weight of the entire world were resting on her, and let her face fall. She checked the look in the mirror on the way to the door. Yes, she looked every bit like a basset hound that had lost its last bone. Perfect!

"Oh hi, Richard," she sighed quietly.

"Hello, Mary."

He leaned forward to press a kiss to her cheek, and she allowed it as if permitting an executioner to put a noose around her neck.

"You look like you need some company," he said.

Faint, wistful smile. "How thoughtful of you, Richard. Please come in. Is there any news from the appeal yet?"

He shook his head. "Not yet, I'm afraid. But I only filed the petition this morning. It will probably be a day or two, even for an emergency."

She knew this, of course, but managed a crestfallen look nonetheless. "Did you know it takes two hundred years to grow a mature maple tree, and only a few minutes to cut it down?"

He shook his head. "Mary, I know it has to feel

like Judge Dipshot gutted your life's work in that hearing."

She opened a curtain and peered out at the sun setting on the Gulf of Mexico. "Yes," she said wearily. "I guess I should soak up every sunset. I won't see many more."

"Now don't think that way, Mary. We won't let Linus destroy this town. I promise."

"We?" she asked.

"Well, Erin has some ideas, I think. And in fact, I wanted to talk to her about them. Is she here?"

Mary shook her head. "I think she's at her shop." She added, as if pronouncing her own death sentence, "I'm all alone tonight."

He reached out to touch her shoulder, his face creased with concern. "I can stay with you, Mary. I can talk to Erin tomorrow."

"No, it's all right. I'm terrible company anyway. And I need to sleep. I haven't been resting well since this . . . since it happened."

"Are you sure? I can call Ted or someone to come stay with you. You shouldn't be alone at times like this."

She offered her very best frail smile. "No, dear. Really. I'm going straight to bed anyway. But thank you for your kindness. And please do tell Erin not to worry about me. I'll be fine." Long, pregnant pause. "I'm always . . . fine."

He made as if to step by her. "Mary, really. I can't leave you like this."

With surprising strength, she resisted his step and shooed him toward the door. "Go, Richard. Let an old woman rest in peace. I'll see you tomorrow. Maybe there will be . . . good news from the court."

"Okay, Mary. But I feel just awful about all of this."

"You can't prevent every evil in the world, Richard. You can only try to make the good better. Now go."

She almost let out a huge yawn but decided that would be over the top. No reason to arouse suspicions. As she bade him goodnight and closed the door, she was certain that Richard, far from telling Erin not to worry, would worry the two of them into a proper lather. Which suited her purposes quite well. It would give Erin an opportunity to test her mettle, to see if she'd learned anything from Mary's patient tutelage. And, maybe, these two obviously-meant-for-each-other birds would find a tree to share.

So Mary had decided. So it would be.

Erin sat across from Dan at a small table with a plastic tablecloth in the tiny family-owned restaurant. Looks were deceptive, however, because this place made some of the best Spanish food in the world.

"You look really great, Dan," Erin said sincerely. He did, too, with a warm tan, a nicely chiseled face that had aged just enough to make him look mature, and a slender body that suggested muscles without screaming them.

"So do you." He smiled. "My excuse is that I have to be healthy or give up my acting career. What's yours?"

"I work hard and play hard. Or maybe I'm just lucky."

"Whatever you're doing, it agrees with you. The years just make you more beautiful."

She blushed. "Dan . . ."

"I know, I know. You have nothing to fear from me. Attachment is the last thing I need right now. Everything in my life is still too unsettled."

They ordered paella and wine, then sat looking at each other across a flickering candle.

"So what's the gig?" he asked. "You've got me really curious."

Erin bit her lip, hesitating. Since Dan's call her mind had been working overtime, trying to come up with a plan that would be worthy of Mary's heritage. She'd cobbled something together, but at this point she still wasn't sure Mary would approve. On the other hand, she was a neophyte at this. She didn't have Mary's sixty years of experience.

Drawing a deep breath, she spoke. "I want you to play a mob guy."

That caused him to straighten in his chair. "What for?"

"I have this dear friend, a very elderly woman.

And her nephew's just had her declared incompetent, even though she's not. But he wants her money and her property. And she owns most of Paradise Beach."

"So you want me to threaten him?" Dan looked horrified. "Erin, that's illegal. I could get thrown in jail for that."

"No, no. Not that. I swear."

Dan rolled his eyes. "I've heard you say that before. That's how I came to be hanging upside down by my heels from the side of the music building. Then there was that time . . ."

"This is different, I promise."

"You've said that before, too. I distinctly remember. That was the time you got the harebrained notion to glue Farley's bed to his ceiling that night he got so drunk. It wasn't supposed to fall on me, remember? You promised."

"Dan, I'm sorry. But I'm older and wiser now."

"Yeah. Which is why you're talking about me impersonating Carlo Gambino. The mob might not like that."

"I'm not talking about you impersonating anybody. I'm talking about creating an impression. Other people can fill in the blanks however they want."

"That's what scares me."

Erin hesitated, wondering if Dan might be right in his reservations about this. But as she turned it around in her head, she couldn't see any real problems with it. After all, she didn't want him to do anything dangerous or illegal. Not a thing.

The paella arrived and Dan served them both, but she noticed that neither of them seemed in much of a hurry to dig in. Instead he simply looked at her, waiting for her to end the tension between them.

"What exactly is it you want?" he finally asked.

"I want you to act like you're interested in my friend's property. Like you might want to get involved in a deal with her sleazy nephew."

"Nothing illegal so far."

"Exactly. And all I want is for you to do it in such a way that just a few people might think you represent organized crime. Just act a little shady, you know?"

"Why?"

"Because Mary, my friend, is so depressed about what's happened that I'm afraid she'll do something stupid."

"And this is supposed to make her feel better?"

"No. This is supposed to make her mad."

Little by little his expression of puzzlement gave way to a smile. "I gotcha. So this has to be a freebie, all the way?"

Erin cocked an eyebrow. This wasn't like Dan. "Well, I don't have any money, and all of Mary's money is tied up in this lawsuit."

"Hmmmm," he said. That old O'Doole glint was back in his eyes.

"What are you thinking?" she asked.

"Oh . . . maybe they'll do it for the fun."

"They?" she asked again.

He smiled, and she suppressed a shiver. Things had always gotten out of control when he smiled that way. "Well, if I'm going to be a big wheel mobster, I'll need some protection. And I have a couple of friends in mind. I'll need to call them."

For the first time, Erin had serious qualms. She began to backtrack. "Danny, maybe we shouldn't . . ."

But he was already rising from the table and pulling out his wallet. "Where's the pay phone? I need to call some people."

Erin thought she had never heard more unsettling words in her life. But it was too late now. Dan was off and rolling.

And she had no one to blame but herself.

Erin was not in a good mood when she returned to her shop. She should have remembered what always happened when Dan got involved. He blamed her for the excesses, but he was always the biggest instigator. He had the sense of humor of a leprechaun. No offense to leprechauns.

Her mood plummeted even more when she entered the store and found Seana and Richard the Third sitting cozily together at the coffee bar. And unless she was mistaken, Seana had unbuttoned an additional two buttons on her blouse, showing a frightening amount of cleavage as she leaned toward Richard.

Richard was, much to her amusement, looking like a man facing a diamondback rattlesnake. If he leaned back any further, that rattan stool was going to tip. The two of them leaning— Seana forward, Richard back—led Erin to speculate about the architects at Pisa. A ravishing

Italian lass and a befuddled builder would explain a lot.

Richard saw her and leapt off the stool as if he had just seen a choir of saving angels walk through the door. "Erin!" he said with so much relief that Erin almost took pity on him. So much relief that Seana would have been insulted if she hadn't been so busy trying to draw her blouse tighter over her bustline.

"Where have you been?" he asked in exasperation. Then, catching himself, he added, "I got to talk to your sister."

"So I saw," Erin said, enjoying his discomfiture entirely too much and not caring if she did. He certainly didn't look like a pirate now. Well, maybe a pirate who'd just boarded an enemy vessel to find his mother waiting for him. "I've been out. And what are you doing here?"

He seemed to bristle a bit, recovering a bit of his aplomb. "I was thinking I'd stop in and see Mary, to see how she was holding up. She was all alone. So I came over to see why you two had flown the coop."

She sensed in his eyes that wasn't the entire, or even the primary, reason for his visit. That would explain the bristle. That realization sent a delicious tingle through her, and she couldn't resist the urge to play it up. "If you must know, I had dinner with an old college friend."

"You mean the movie star?" Seana asked.

"Yes," Erin said, now thoroughly enjoying the

look on poor Richard the Third's face. "The movie star."

"Movie star?" Richard asked, choking a bit on the words.

"Oh yes," Seana said. "Erin was an actress in college and she and this guy . . . well . . . they're legendary. He's a big-time star now. And drop-dead gorgeous, right, Erin?"

Erin realized that Seana, who had never personally met Dan, was taking this ball and running in a direction she didn't quite want to go. Making Richard uncomfortable was one thing. Scaring the pirate away before she could lower her . . . flag . . . in surrender was entirely another.

"He's just an old friend," she said. And fought an urge to strangle Seana before another word passed the brat's lips. "You may have seen him in the last Bruce Willis movie. He was Thug Number Seven in the opening bar fight."

"Like I said, *big* time," Seana said.

But Erin could see she'd taken the wind out of her sister's sails. Now if she could just put some back into that pirate's spinnaker.

Of course, the man had not yet been made who could both ring Erin's bells and put up with her kid sister, who seemed to have an absolutely evil genius for being intolerable at precisely the wrong time. Or the right time, depending on one's view.

Which was why she said, "Seana, thanks for watching the store for me. You can go home now."

"I have nothing else planned for the evening," Seana said. The girl had gone into brat mode, probably for Erin's benefit, but there were limits. "I'll help you close up."

"Great. I wanted to show Richard my favorite stretch of Mary's beach anyway."

Seana's eyes narrowed. "You mean the place where you and that boy from—"

"Richard, let's take a walk," Erin cut in. "Seana has entirely too many embarrassing stories to tell about me, and the only one I could use in retaliation would be the time she went to Tijuana. . . ."

"I'll close up," Seana said abruptly. But her eyes glinted with amusement.

Great, thought Erin. *My sister the matchmaker.*

"Your sister is . . . overwhelming," Richard said as they stood on the small dune overlooking the site of the famous sea monster fiasco. The moon was high and bright, the sand a ghostly white, the sea sparkling with silver. In the distance over the water, the clouds recalled the sails of galleons and pirate ships.

"At the very least," Erin said.

"I can see she comes by it honestly."

Erin faced him. "What's that supposed to mean?"

"Only that you can be overwhelming, too."

Too smooth by half, Erin thought. Then realized she liked it. "She's still only twenty-one."

"Trust me, I'm not in danger of forgetting that.

On the other hand, you might want to ground her from watching Mae West movies."

Much as she wanted to stay stiff and peeved at the world in general, Erin couldn't. She dissolved into a helpless laugh. "Isn't she a vamp?"

"Practicing, I suppose. Most girls do that, don't they?"

"Oh yes. They like to try their wiles on older men."

"I don't exactly feel like an older man."

Oops. She hadn't meant to insult him. Or maybe she had. She had to admit she'd never in her life felt as confused as she was feeling right now. "How about them seagulls."

"What seagulls? They're sleeping."

"I'm trying to change the subject."

He grinned, looking as if he ought to be brandishing a cutlass and laughing from the rigging. "I know. But I won't let you get away with it. I'm not an older man, at least not compared to you."

"Well, no. I didn't mean that, and you know it."

"Besides, you don't look any older than she does."

"Are you Irish? Because you're sure full of blarney. And what exactly *did* my sister say?" The feeling of panic was real. She knew Seana's penchant for exaggeration. And for making a good story even better.

"Well, actually," he said with exaggerated modesty, "there are a few Herlihys, Dohertys, et cetera hanging from the limbs of the family tree. My aunt Bridget could tell you exactly."

"Oh my God, you have an Aunt *Bridget*?"

"Yes. Why?"

"So do I. Well, I mean I used to. She died years ago."

"Synchronicity." He smiled again, and his teeth seemed to gleam in the moonlight.

What's wrong with this picture? she asked herself. Then as his gaze raked over her from head to foot, she knew what was wrong. *She* was wrong. Because every cell in her body was hot. Hot and quivering with a longing to be swept off her feet.

And that was something she had vowed not to allow until Seana was through with college. She couldn't allow a man into their lives, a man who might not take to Seana, or who might make her life miserable. Caring for her sister was her primary responsibility, and had been for more than ten years.

But she quivered anyway and found it impossible to look away from him. He was wearing slacks and a business shirt with rolled-up sleeves, nothing like a pirate might wear, yet his gaze seemed to plunder her.

Erin knew she was a beautiful woman. She'd learned that by the time she was fourteen. In high school that had seemed important, and her confidence had been firmly shored up. But then her parents had died, and her life had turned on end, and she had been forced to grow up quickly. And in the process of growing up quickly, she had discovered that she didn't want to be wanted for the accident of her genes. She needed to be appreciated for the things inside of her, her heart, her mind, her soul. And so far that had never happened.

And it wasn't happening now. Richard's hungry gaze was based on nothing but her appearance, because he didn't know her at all.

Realizing that allowed her to turn away from him and look out over the sea. And her response to him deflated, leaving her feeling empty and sad.

"Erin? Did I say something wrong?"

His sensitivity surprised her. The men in her life so far had been as sensitive as doorposts. Sometimes even hitting them over the head with a metaphorical two-by-four hadn't gotten their attention. But all she had done was turn away, and Richard had picked up on it.

"No. It's just me."

"You seem sad."

She was. But it wasn't something she could explain to him without embarrassing herself.

"Trust me," he said, "I won't do anything to hurt Seana. No matter how hard she vamps at me."

"Thank you." But she figured he was only a

man like other men, and if Seana went far enough, he was going to be able to resist no more than a beach could resist a hurricane.

"And we *will* solve Mary's problem," he said. "I'm not going to give up. I will do everything within my power legally to see that she gets her life back. I've already filed for an emergency stay with the Second District, and I'm filing a motion for rehearing with Dipshot tomorrow."

Erin felt as if she had been kicked. Here she was mooning over stupid things when her real concern ought to be Mary. Dear, beloved Mary. She turned to Richard. "I'm so worried about her depression. Scared."

"Me, too." He appeared to sigh, but the sound was lost in the pounding of the surf. "Come on. I'll walk you back to the shop before your sister calls out the dogs."

For an instant his hand moved as if he wanted to take hers, but then it fell back to his side. And Erin felt an aching sense of disappointment.

Just as well, she told herself. She didn't need any more complications in her life.

Seana was closing up the shop when they got back. On the beach, Erin had found it to her advantage to open late and stay open until ten o'clock at night.

And, of course, Seana was devilishly curious.

"Did you have a nice walk?" she said with a wink.

"Yes," Erin said simply, not wanting to open the door for more of Seana's machinations.

"Of course," said Richard. "It was nice of you to watch the shop for your sister."

Oh, what a charmer, Erin thought. And exactly the wrong thing to say, because all of a sudden Seana was beaming at him. Round two.

Richard evidently realized it, too, because he was suddenly in a hurry to get away. "Well, ladies," he said, "it's been nice getting to know you better, but I have an early court date in the morning, so I have to be on my way."

He was out the door almost before they could say good-bye. Which left Erin looking into her sister's all-too-curious green eyes.

"Sooooo?" Seana asked.

"I'm not going there with you, sis. You may want to play matchmaker, but I need to focus on Mary." She paused for a moment. "And you really need to think about how you present yourself. You were almost raping him when I came in."

Seana sighed. "You just don't understand, Erin. You've never realized that first you have to get a man's attention."

Erin felt a deep pang. Not because Seana's words hurt, because they didn't. But because of her sister's naivete.

"Hon, you get men's attention by breathing. Just be sure that's the kind of attention you want.

Seana, there is nothing in the world I want more than to see you happily settled with a family of your own."

"You could have fooled me."

"It's a matter of ends and means, sis. If you play the tramp, you're going to find men who are looking for tramps."

Seana hit the button on the register, then printed out the day's receipts. "Come on, let's close up and go home."

The jury agreed that a coconut palm and a Washingtonia palm were not the same tree. Richard could see it in their faces. Well, how could they think otherwise, when faced with the two large photographs. He sensed victory in his hands as the jury went out to deliberate.

He turned the elderly Mrs. Malcolm over to her son and daughter and went out to get an early lunch and call his office. Unless he was sorely mistaken, the jury wouldn't be out long.

Once outside the St. Petersburg courthouse, he turned on his cell phone and called Hester, his secretary.

"Nothing happening, boss," she replied cheerfully. "The Wades called about their lawsuit, and I reminded them these things take months, if not years, and right now everything's been filed and all we can do is to wait for the judge's decision on the filings. They, of course, would like everything to be settled yesterday."

"Of course." The Wades were another of his clients he felt really involved with. Their nine-year-old daughter had died as the result of a misdiagnosis in an emergency room.

"Burgess called. I told him to basically stuff a sock in it and wait for his Friday appointment."

"Good." Burgess was a client he would rather not have. The guy was entitled to a defense under the law, but Rich was beginning to understand why his next-door neighbor had had it in for him. A more unpleasant guy had never walked the face of the earth.

"Anyway," Hester said, "your afternoon's clear except for the five o'clock consultation with the car accident victim."

"Okay. Thanks, Hester." His plate was full enough right now, and he was slowing down on accepting new clients until he'd cleared a case or two off his current list. "Anything from the District Court of Appeals?"

"Of course not. Your emergency and their emergency are not the same things."

"I know, I know. But hope springs eternal."

"In this business it has to."

He said good-bye to her, clipped his phone to his belt and headed a block over to find a place to have lunch. A very fast lunch. He expected that jury to be back *before* one o'clock. Especially if he tried to settle in for a relaxed meal. Juries were like that. Always.

As always, he had his briefcase with him, and

plenty of paperwork to do. Harold Winnegar had, as usual, pummeled him with a seventeen-page motion to dismiss in the Dantzler case, with forty pages of case law attached. Richard couldn't decide which aphorism best described Winnegar's approach to the practice of law: "Briefs are not weighed, but weighted" or "When the law is against you, argue the facts. When the facts are against you, argue the law. When both are against you, argue forever."

Elizabeth Dantzler had been sunning herself in the backyard when her neighbor's lawn mower had hit a plastic coaster that had been left outside after a garden party the night before. The coaster had assumed Frisbee-like flight and struck Elizabeth in the forehead, costing her eleven stitches over her left eyebrow and micro-surgery two months later to repair the scar. Richard's client had done nothing wrong, with the possible exception of occupying herself with the latest Violette Proze novel, which to the best of Richard's knowledge was replete with ripping bodices, surging manhoods, and little else. Although he had to admit that when he had scanned the novel, he'd only answered the intercom after Hester had buzzed him a third time, and he had had to shift in his chair before the next client was shown in. Still, one's choice in reading material did not make a case for comparative negligence, nor did the fact that Elizabeth had been reading in an electric blue bikini that, the neighbor argued, was a deliberate distraction which had caused him to overlook the wayward coaster. He had been operating the lawn mower, clearly dangerous machinery, and thus had had a legal duty to exercise great care. He hadn't, and Elizabeth bore the now-almost-undetectable scar to prove it.

Harold Winnegar's overinflated prose notwithstanding, this was as clear a case as ever walked through a lawyer's office. Winnegar should have accepted Richard's settlement offer, which was limited solely to Elizabeth's medical expenses totalling twenty-one thousand dollars. He hadn't even asked for pain and suffering, despite the time his client had spent wobbling around her house with the aftereffects of the concussion. It had been, he thought, a scrupulously fair offer. Well, yet another case that ought to have been settled reasonably would find itself in court. And if the neighbor continued to insist that Elizabeth had been "asking for it" because of her scanty attire, Richard felt sure he would win a substantial damage settlement.

Still, he had to wade through Winnegar's motion and all of the attached cases, just in case there was some little-known and absolutely absurd legal loophole through which a voyeuristic neighbor who steered a lawn mower with his groin might squeak. He was midway through and thinking up new synonyms for "wordy" and "frivolous" when Seana walked into the restaurant and plopped down at his table.

"Are you busy?" she asked brightly, with neither a greeting nor, apparently, any realization that he hadn't noticed her until the chair had moved, nor that his yellow highlighter had been flying over the sheaf of papers in front of him. Instead, she fingered a pendant that hung between her ample breasts and added, "I saw you and thought I'd say hi."

"And you have," he replied, his courtroom smile hiding his mix of frustration at having been interrupted, relief at the distraction from Winnegar's verbosity, and alarm at the manner of that relief. "How are you, Seana?"

"Hot," she said.

"I'm not sure I want to hear the rest of this," he said cautiously.

"Well, it's ninety-four degrees outside and I walked over here."

Oh. *That* kind of hot he could cope with. "Yes, it's one of those slice-off-a-chunk-of-air-and-chew-it kind of days."

Seana giggled. "I've never heard that before."

The giggle was entirely too playful. And if he were still the twenty-something stud-muffin-wannabe he'd been in law school, he might have been tempted. Now it simply pained him to watch someone so lovely doing something so dangerous. Despite her all-too-obvious beauty and charm, this young woman suddenly seemed very vulnerable.

"Well, consider your horizons broadened," he said. "I'm a virtual font of pithy phrases. Occupational hazard."

"I've always wanted broader horizons," she said.

She is nothing if not persistent, he thought. He was still in the process of formulating a reply when his pager vibrated on the tabletop. He checked the message and tossed a ten-dollar bill on the table. "I'm afraid I have to go. My jury is back with a verdict."

"Did you win?" she asked coyly.

"I should have. Unless the jury got hit by the same phantom coconuts as the plaintiff claims hit him. I'll see you, Seana."

She flashed him a million-watt smile as he left. Someone, he mused as he walked back to the courthouse, needed to talk to that girl before she made a bad mistake.

"Is this Linus Todd?" the unmistakably New York voice rattled into the phone.

"It is," Linus answered. Something in the voice set him on edge. The caller ID on his phone flashed "Private," with not even a phone number. Hmmmm. "And you are?"

"I know a guy who knows a guy," the caller

said. "The guy my guy knows heard that you may have some Florida beachfront property up for development soon."

Linus drew a breath. He'd only begun putting out feelers, in case Tim Herschfeld and High Lights Development weren't offering him the best deal. Already he was attracting New York investors. In the tunnel of his mind, he saw a light appear. He didn't even stop to wonder if it might be an oncoming train.

"Yes, I do. Prime property, in fact. Excellent community, sympathetic zoning." The fact that he didn't like the community at all and suspected zoning might be rough were irrelevant to his desire for a sale and a position on an important board of directors.

"The guy my guy knows knows all that."

"Who is this guy your guy knows?"

"He's a guy who wants to meet you," the caller said. "Are there any good Italian restaurants down there? I heard Prizzionna's was nice."

"I've never eaten there," Linus said. He hated Italian food. Hated it. Ever since he'd tried to make spaghetti and meatballs one night and had learned that boiling pasta for a half-hour left very little except a misshapen lump over which to pour bottled sauce. The mere memory of that futile culinary exercise made his stomach roll.

"Well, another guy my guy knows says it's good, and he's a good guy, so my guy says his guy would like to meet you there tomorrow night. Eight o'clock. Pick a table along the wall and sit with your back to the door."

"Ummm, why with my back to the door?" Linus asked.

"Because the guy my guy knows knows better than to sit with *his* back to the door. Don't be late. This guy hates to wait for people."

"Which guy is that? The guy you know or the guy he knows?"

"You got it," the caller said, and hung up.

Linus knew, just *knew* there was something he should be picking up on. Alas, he couldn't find it amidst the visions of rising line graphs on an online investment portfolio display. In his mind's eye, there were no dips and few wiggles in those lines. They all pointed up, up, up. To Aspen. To Cannes. To an electronic organizer bulging with gilded names and phone numbers. And an assistant who could make it do something besides beep, flash, and vibrate at random moments.

His ascent would begin at eight o'clock tomorrow night, as sure as the countdown to a rocket launch. He was on his way.

Ted Wannamaker felt like he was also on his way, although a bit more circumspectly. Rifling through Mary's diary had been sneaky. Sneakier than anything he'd ever done before. Sneakier, even, than the many things he'd declined to do at her request. But desperate times called for rifled diaries and elliptical conversations with wheezy old men in Las Vegas.

"How *is* Mary?" the man asked between wheezes.

"Not so good, Mr. Lewis."

"Oh, call me Pete, Mr. Wannamaker."

"Then call me Ted."

"Okay, Ted, so what's wrong with Mary?"

"Well, it's her nephew."

The old man let out a wheeze that sounded like a steam whistle giving up to let the train hit the redneck whose pickup truck was stuck on the tracks. "Nephews. I could tell you for nephews. Bane of my existence, nephews."

"Then you know the type, Pete. Miss Mary's nephew is trying to steal her land away."

"*Miss* Mary?" Pete asked. "That little vixen still hasn't settled down?"

Ted found it difficult to think of Mary Todd as a little vixen. She'd been a schemer from the time he'd met her after the war, but a vixen? Her vixen days must have been left behind by then.

"No, she hasn't. And that's the problem. I need to have married her. Five years ago. To save her land from the nephew."

"Now *that's* the Mary I knew," Pete said. "That woman had a mind like a corkscrew. And a will of iron."

The old man seemed to sigh, although it may have been a hurricane sweeping through the other end of the line. Judging that hurricanes were unlikely in Las Vegas, Ted heard it as a sigh.

"Still single," Pete mused wistfully. "The old girl never did recover, I guess."

"From what?" Ted asked.

"It's a very old story, Ted. It wasn't a good time to be a bootlegger, but it was a helluva time to be in love." Pete was silent for a moment, and Ted felt a pang of jealousy when he continued. "My life never had a lot of second chances. I had to make do with the first ones, or not at all."

"Second chances are indeed rare, Pete. But I need to give Mary one. Before this nephew kills her."

"Kills her?" Pete asked. "Hmmph. Nephews are nephews everywhere, I guess. Although mine haven't tried to kill me since . . . ohh . . . I guess it was seventy-four. Good thing that miserable little shit couldn't shoot straight."

"That sounds like a tragic story," Ted said, trying to force the conversation back on track.

"It was, Ted. Just tragic. Sonuvabitch blew a hole in my favorite blender. I never found another blender as good. Damn nephews."

"So what we need," Ted began, still wrestling for control of the runaway train of thought, "is for me to have married her. We'll need papers."

"She definitely should have been married," Pete said. "I can take care of that, no problem. I know a judge here who can't understand that there's no difference between plugging a hundred thousand quarters in a slot machine and dropping twenty-five g's on the Super Bowl, if you never win. I can make her married for you, no problem."

"Is there anything I need to do?" Ted asked. "Any information you need or whatever? We don't have . . . I mean . . . I couldn't . . . er . . . pay much."

"Pfffft. Ted, we take care of our own. Don't worry about a thing. I'll handle it."

"Thank you, Pete. This will mean the world to her. To both of us."

"Second chances, Ted. Here's to second chances."

As he hung up the phone, Ted's heart rose. Then sank. Unlike Linus, he could distinguish the end of a tunnel from an oncoming train. And this train had a wheezy whistle.

Paradise Beach basked in a gorgeous early August day. While most of the rest of the state sweltered, particularly inland, the sea breeze was keeping the temperature a comfortable eighty-nine beneath a cloudless sky.

Or rather, the sky appeared cloudless. In truth a storm was gathering, winging its way east from Nevada, and west from Orlando.

But for now, the main concern seemed to be Miss Mary Todd. Word was spreading about her situation, and longtime residents of the beach were growing concerned and shaking their heads.

Most people knew that development was inevitable, but most people also agreed with Mary that they didn't want development to cut off the beach view from the boulevard more than it already did. And since Mary owned most of that land, none of the locals stood to make much money from the sale of it—something that had a large effect on their view of the situation.

But Mary was also something of a local icon, for better or worse, and people quickly started to grumble that "something had to be done about this."

Before anyone could do more than grumble, however, a stretch limo arrived in town and pulled up in front of the one Italian restaurant.

Linus was sitting inside with his back to the window, but craning his neck like a flamingo trying to preen its back as he attempted to watch the street. The limo didn't unduly impress him: he rode in them from time to time when he could afford it, just to make an impression. Nor was he unduly impressed by the slender guy in the black suit, shirt and tie. What impressed him were the two muscle-bound goons who accompanied him.

Linus had always wanted goons like that at his beck and call. Well, that might happen now, once he sold Mary's property. Unfortunately, the presence of the two goons in gray suits with black T-shirts underneath also suggested that he might be dealing with something here other than a simple real estate deal. Linus began to sweat.

There was easy money and there was easy money. This might be the wrong type of easy money. On the other hand, if he played his cards just right . . .

The tall, slender man with the slicked-back

dark hair entered the restaurant, one goon in front and one behind. The taller of the two muscle-bound guys took a table near the door, facing it. The other followed the boss to Linus's table.

"Are you Todd?" asked the slender guy.

"Yes." Linus's mouth was suddenly dry.

"Good." The man nodded at his bodyguard, who pulled out a chair for him to sit. Then the guard went to join the other one at the table facing the door.

"I'm Floorsheim," said the man who sat facing Linus. "You got some land you want to develop."

Linus wasn't used to working deals so bluntly. He was used to having to wine and dine people at restaurants he really couldn't afford, used to having to woo them for weeks or months just to get the time of day. This approach left him unsettled.

Floorsheim continued speaking. "Could be I know a guy who's interested in investing."

"Who?"

Floorsheim wagged a finger at him. "Not so fast."

Linus gulped and glanced at the goons. He was momentarily saved by the waiter, who brought the menus and asked if they wanted to order. Linus hastily ordered spaghetti and meatballs. Floorsheim, however, took longer, asking all kinds of questions about sauces and things. Finally the waiter and he reached an accommodation and Linus was once again the center of attention. Which didn't exactly thrill him.

And considering how much he wanted investors, he told himself that was crazy. Except he kept looking at the two goons by the door, thinking that anybody who really needed those guys might not be the best business partner.

On the other hand . . . money was money.

In fact, the image of his bank balance rising through the roof stiffened his backbone just a little. He tried to straighten in his chair. "Well, it all depends on arrangements, you understand?"

"Of course I understand." Floorsheim smiled in a way that nearly chilled Linus's blood. "We'll reach an agreement."

"I . . . have other investors interested."

"Sure." Floorsheim apparently wasn't worried about that. "I can deal with High Lights Development."

"Hey, wait a minute!"

Floorsheim stiffened, and the two goons shifted their chairs. All of a sudden, Linus was sweating again. But he still had an ounce of backbone. "I make my own deals."

"Sure you do."

"I do!"

"I just said so."

But Linus had a sneaking suspicion this Floorsheim guy wasn't getting the message. Nor, as Linus measured it, could he see any way to get out the door and leave this guy and his goons behind. At least not without passing the goons, who might take exception to his departure.

Money, Linus reminded himself. All he really wanted to do was get as much money as he could for the property and let someone else have the headaches of actually developing it. Well, the money and a nice title on the Board of Directors to go with it.

"I own a lot of beachfront," he said finally. "I don't have to sell it all to the same person."

"But to the highest bidder, yes?"

Why did Linus suddenly have the feeling there would be no other bidders? This isn't what he had wanted at all.

"Look," said Floorsheim, suddenly all nice, "don't get so nervous. We're just discussing a business deal, right? Lots of things to go over before we get to a meeting of minds."

It was those "lots of things" that concerned Linus.

"I just want to know: are you interested in selling and developing your property?"

"Well, yes."

"Then we have something to talk about further." With that, Floorsheim rose and departed, his goons following him into the limo. Leaving Linus with the bill for two dinners, neither of which he wanted to eat.

"Somebody's got to pay for the limo," Dan told Erin.

"Limo? Why in the world did you get a limo?"

"Impressions, babe. Gotta make a good impression."

They were meeting like guilty truants a mile down the beach in a sporting goods store that Seana would never enter. Hiding among racks of deep-sea fishing poles, they talked in whispers.

"Dan, I can't afford limos!"

"Only this once. I promise. It was a first impression. From now on I can arrive other ways and he'll never notice."

"I hope so. Three hundred dollars sets my teeth on edge."

"Like I said, I won't need to do it again. I don't think. But I had to book a room at the Marriott."

"Oh my God."

"A suite."

Erin groaned. "Why couldn't you pretend to have a house in Tampa?"

"Because he might want to visit me. How am I supposed to explain that tiny condo and my mother? Better yet, how do you expect me to get my mother involved in this deal? I don't want him anywhere near her."

Remembering Dan's mother, Erin had her own concern. The woman had a tendency to babble entirely too much, and her ability to keep a secret was utterly doubtful. "Couldn't you just pretend your mother doesn't know what you're doing?"

"She *doesn't* know, and I want to keep it that way."

Erin couldn't really argue with that, she supposed. She felt a similar protectiveness toward her sister. But a suite at the Marriott? Oh, my word! "I'm going to go broke."

"Nah," Dan said with a grin. "I'll tell him I gotta go back to New York to talk to my guy. I only need to show up once in a while. We just need to do enough to get rumors started, right?"

"That was my plan." But this was going to be one expensive rumor.

She nearly jumped a foot when she heard Seana's voice behind her. "Hi, Erin. I didn't know you were into fishing."

Erin whirled around and realized her sister must have followed her. What now?

But Seana was already looking measuringly at Dan. "Ooh, do I know you?" she cooed.

Dan hesitated. "Ah . . . no. Who are you?"

"I'm Erin's sister. Seana." Seana eased closer, and, much to Erin's amazement, her sister's green eyes reflected genuine interest. And an amazing vulnerability, all of a sudden. Uh-oh. "You look a little familiar."

Dan changed tacks and practically leered at her. "I wouldn't have forgotten *you*."

It was exactly the right thing to say. Seana started preening. She crossed her arms beneath her breasts, lifting them just enough to make her cleavage mound at her neckline, and she flashed Dan a smile that would stop traffic on the Sunshine Skyway Bridge.

"Are you a friend of Erin's?" she asked.

Erin couldn't even think how to answer. She didn't want to lie to her sister, but she sure didn't want to tell the truth.

"A little bit," Dan said, saving Erin from having to answer.

"Oh." Which appeared to be a clear green light to Seana to move in. "Can I buy you a cup of coffee?"

"Sure," said Dan, offering his arm.

"Wait a minute," Erin said. "Seana, you don't know this guy."

"He was good enough for you to talk to," Seana replied pertly, and departed with Dan.

Erin considered wringing both their necks but realized it would do no good. Seana had achieved the coup she needed to make up for being kept out of Erin's secret. And Dan would never hurt her. And then there was that look in Seana's eye, a look she couldn't quite define. As if her sister had become suddenly starstruck. Oh, God!

But all of Paradise Beach was soon going to believe that Seana was hanging out with a mobster.

Erin shuddered. What would Mary Todd do? But she was beginning to get an inkling that, despite all Mary's teaching, she was nowhere near on a par with Mary when it came to scheming.

In fact, she was beginning to think all she had done was roll up a huge bill and risk her sister's reputation.

Richard was strolling down the boulevard in Paradise Beach, telling himself he was thinking about deep-sea fishing tomorrow and that he *was not* considering stopping off by a certain pottery shop. He was wearing a white shirt with rolled-up sleeves, dark blue shorts, and deck shoes, and he was feeling more like a tourist than an inhabitant. It was a good feeling.

And it was only a little after one on a Friday afternoon. In the Tampa Bay area, closing early on Fridays was practically a rule of the legal profession. All the lawyers tried to be out of their offices by noon or one, and even the judges worked hard at getting away no later than three.

And considering that most of his workdays ended at eight or nine in the evening, Rich didn't feel one bit guilty about it.

Deep-sea fishing, he reminded himself. There was a shop up here, he seemed to remember, and he wanted to look at reels. Not that he was going to buy one, but he kept dreaming of the day he could afford a boat and all that went with it. Once he got the damn law school loans fully paid off, which was right around the corner. In the meantime, he dreamed.

He was only a couple of shops down from the sporting goods store when he saw Seana emerge from it. His first thought was to duck into another store before she saw him, but then he realized that the man who came out right after her was with her. And that they were headed the other way.

Relief gave way to consternation. He didn't like the looks of that dude. For heaven's sake, it was the height of summer and the guy was dressed like a crook out of a bad movie. And Seana had been making eyes at *him* only the other day, so what was she doing with . . . He cut the thought off immediately. None of his concern.

Except that he couldn't help wondering if Erin knew about this.

The question was answered immediately as Erin came out of the sporting goods shop and headed in his direction. Again he wanted to duck. Getting close to her was dangerous to his peace of mind. Why else had he set out on a perfectly innocent trip to daydream about fishing, only to find his mind determined to think about pottery . . . and a certain potter.

Man, she looked gorgeous today, and all she was wearing was a simple green cotton shift, something adequate for work, but not overdone. And sandals, of course. Strappy gold sandals that made him wonder why he'd never noticed her feet before. Dainty. Perfect.

Then he found himself wondering how she looked when she was making a pot. Did she get clay all over herself? Was the clay as smooth and wet as it always looked in films? What would it be like to rub it all over her?

Before that thought could get him into an embarrassing condition, she reached him, and he was forced to speak—out of simple courtesy, of course. Even though she was so obviously preoccupied that she never would have noticed him otherwise. And she didn't look very happy, either.

"Hi, Erin."

She started when she saw him. "Oh. Hi."

Not a very enthusiastic greeting, he thought. His pride was wounded. So naturally he did exactly what he should have avoided doing. He spoke again. "You don't look very happy."

"I'm not."

And somehow he was strolling the other way along the boulevard beside her, toward her shop. "Is something wrong?"

"Everything," she said grandly.

It was an Aunt Bridget sort of exaggeration, so he knew how to deal with it. "How awful! Which everything?"

"Everything."

"I'm sorry."

"Don't be. It's my own mess."

"Can I help?"

She finally looked at him then, really seeing him. "Trust me, Richard the Third, you do *not* want to know what my problem is."

It tickled him somehow that she had a nick-name for him. But her answer also piqued his curiosity and concern. "That doesn't sound good."

"It's not, but trust me, I don't need a lawyer."

That was a relief. But it also annoyed him. "I *am* capable of things besides lawyering."

"Did I say you weren't?"

"You implied it."

She stopped walking and put her hands on her hips. "I was merely trying to ease your mind about whether I'm in trouble with the law."

"I beg your pardon."

"And I really don't want a courtroom-style argument with you, Counselor."

She was adorable, truly adorable, when she frowned at him in that defiant way. He couldn't prevent a smile. "Well, there's a problem with that."

"What?"

"I *am* a lawyer. So I tend to interpret language stringently."

"Are you telling me I can't speak English?"

Man, he had a way of putting his foot in it with her. He held up his hands. "No, no. That isn't what I meant. It's like . . . well, when you say something, I look for the possible meanings in it, and if any one of them seems deleterious to my client, in this case *me*, I tend to start with the worst interpretation."

She shook her head and rolled her eyes. "You

must be simply wonderful to have an ordinary conversation with."

He tried to look abashed but wasn't sure he succeeded. "I'm a pain in the neck."

Her look grew speculative. "Why don't I believe you?"

"Because I'm a handsome, sensitive, caring man?"

He saw the laugh start. It began somewhere around the corners of her eyes, trickled to the corners of her mouth, then bubbled out from somewhere deep in her chest. "You are too much."

"So I've been told."

She frowned, but this time it was playful. "Turn off the lawyer brain around me."

"Yes, ma'am," he said too meekly, which drew another laugh from her.

"Lord, I bet you're a handful," she said as they started walking toward her shop once again.

"No more than you are, I imagine," he replied truthfully. "Would you like to join me for a late lunch?"

She looked at him, an uncertain glance from the corner of her eye. "I'm sorry, but I have to open the shop. I'm already late, and Seana's got the day off."

"All right then. How about I bring lunch to the shop? Anything you're in the mood for?"

"Anything fast and greasy. I've been eating salads all week and I'm dying for a burger."

"Fast and greasy coming up. Why have you been eating salads all week?" He hoped she wouldn't say she was dieting. A diet was the last thing she needed.

"Oh, sometimes I go on a rabbit binge, and that's all that sounds good to me. Trust me, I haven't been suffering. I could make you a salad that would knock your socks off."

"I'll bet you could," he said. "And I do love salads, just not as a steady diet."

"Which is why I'm having a hamburger attack."

"Consider it done."

He waited while she unlocked the door of her business, then followed her into the cool interior. Now that he could tear his eyes for a minute from the shop's beautiful owner, he discovered he was surrounded by beautiful things.

"Did you make all this pottery yourself?" he asked.

"No, I wouldn't possibly have time." She went behind the counter, tucked her purse away, and started opening the cash register. "I still make some of it, of course. I have a studio out back, and when Seana's in I often work on things out there. But I also buy things from other local potters."

"What about this?" he asked, pointing to a graceful window-box-style planter that looked like a swimming dolphin. Somehow, there was something erotic about the sinuous lines. Funny, an erotic window box.

"I made that," she acknowledged. "I have whimsical moments at times."

"It's beautiful. I want it." He was reaching for his wallet already.

"You're kidding."

He turned to look at her. "Why would I be kidding?"

"That thing's been sitting right there for two years. Nobody wants it."

"I do." He shrugged. "Can I help it if I'm the only person on earth with taste?"

A smile began to glow on her face. "And just where will you put it, Richard?"

"On the window of my office, where I can see it every morning when I come to work."

Her smile broadened. "Are you sure that's the impression you want to create?"

"Absolutely. Keep people guessing, I say."

"Were you a pirate in a past life?"

"It's possible. I don't remember, I'm afraid." He rocked on his toes and grinned at her. "What about you? A beautiful Irish warrior queen?"

"Oh, absolutely," she said, laughing. "And before that I was Nefertiti."

"I knew it. Okay, I'll go get lunch now, but don't let anyone buy my dolphin before I get back."

* * *

Erin watched him go, wondering how a day that had started to turn so abysmal had transformed into one that seemed to glow.

It was the man's blarney, she decided. Whoever his ancestors were, even with a name like Richard Haversham Wesley, III, the blarney had run true in him.

She sighed, but there was a twinkle in her eye and a sparkle in her heart. The feeling frightened her, because it had been a while since a man had hung around her rather than her sister. And of course, there'd been the men who'd been interested in her only until they'd realized Seana was part of the package. But worst of all, there'd been one creep who, after six months of dating and thinking she'd finally found a real relationship, had turned out to want *both* sisters.

The thought usually made her shudder, but this afternoon the creep and his perversions seemed far away. Richard was blowing into her life like a fresh sea breeze, and he seemed to be sweeping away a lot of old cobwebs.

Her rational mind wanted to put on the brakes. She hardly knew the man, after all. But her heart wanted to sing, and she decided to indulge it, at least for a little while.

Of course, there was the matter of Mary, and of Dan, who was in danger of making her sister look like a gun moll. Or worse yet, diluting his impact by having lunch with Seana.

Gads. She put her head down in her hands and wondered if she'd lost her mind. She'd set this darn ball rolling, and now there was no predicting where it would wind up. And what if it didn't help Mary at all?

Only yesterday it had seemed like such a good, amusing idea, one that was sure to catch Mary's attention. Today it looked like a disaster in the making.

What was it her aunt Bridget had called it? Thinking with her feet. Doing before she'd thought enough about it.

Aagh! Maybe she should stop Dan right now.

But there was Mary to consider. Mary was so old that a depression like this could sicken and kill her in a matter of weeks, regardless of how healthy she had always seemed. And regardless of what the town might think for a brief while, Seana wasn't hanging out with a mobster. She was hanging out with an actor, and Dan wouldn't hurt a hair on Seana's head. He was too nice a guy.

Or at least he had been. There was, she reminded herself, no telling what the last few years and New York City had done to him. Or Hollywood. Eeps.

But the Dan she had known so well in college had been a truly moral and decent guy, if a bit wild at times, and there was no good reason to think his essential nature had changed.

Really there wasn't.

And so much for the sparkle in her heart and the twinkle in her eye. Both were thoroughly banished now.

When Rich returned to the shop, he noticed at once that Erin's mood had changed. He'd managed to get her laughing, and now she was cast down again. Whatever was troubling her must be serious. But he didn't know how to get her to trust him enough to talk about it.

He put a thick, juicy burger in front of her, not the fast-food sort at all, since he'd chosen to go to the bar and grille down the street. He opened one for himself. Two icy bottles of water completed the meal.

"Thank you," she said. "It looks wonderful. Just what I was in the mood for."

"Good." He sat across the counter from her on one of the wicker stools. "You don't seem very busy today." Maybe that was what was concerning her.

"I rarely am at this time of day. Business picks up later when people have had enough of the beach and sun. And of course this is summertime, so there aren't as many out-of-state tourists who are interested in things like this."

"I think it's wonderful you have your own business."

"I wouldn't except for Mary. She kept pushing me to do something with my pottery, and finally she helped me work up a business plan and co-signed the loan with me."

"Hmm. I wonder why she didn't consult me on this." He didn't have an overlarge sense of his self-importance, but he *was* Mary's attorney.

"You know Mary better than that. What did she need a lawyer for? All she was doing was putting her credit on the line. The first few months she paid the note, but I've paid her back for that now."

"Well, then it's obvious she didn't need me. She's a good judge of character, and, as you say, the decision to co-sign a note doesn't need a lawyer." Although in theory Mary should have arranged for some protections for herself by way of a legal agreement with Erin.

A smile turned up the corners of Erin's mouth. A lovely mouth. An eminently kissable mouth. Damn, he didn't want to be thinking along those lines. Not now. Maybe not ever. He didn't want to get into something because of his gonads, and he hardly knew this woman.

"Well," she said looking wry, "it was either that or she was going to buy the shop, buy all my pottery, and have someone else run the store, but she pointed out that I'd make a lot more money if I owned and operated the store. So I started a business plan, and she helped with it. And of course she was right."

"Of course." He smiled. "But she probably neglected to mention how much time you'd have to take away from your potting to run the business."

Erin laughed. "She didn't have to tell me. I knew that was the catch. But I always prefer working with the clay in the mornings anyway. So I just get up early and spin my dreams until it's time to get hardheaded."

"*Spin your dreams.* I like that."

"How do you think about law?"

"Oh." He felt almost abashed.

She eyed him, as if she could read him like a book and was going to wait until the end of time for his answer.

After a moment he sighed. "It's embarrassing. I actually cherished notions of being a Lancelot or Galahad when I entered law school. I was going to fight for right, for truth and justice and the underdog."

"That's a noble dream," she said sincerely.

"Yeah. Also a naive one. Not to mention impractical."

"What do you mean?"

"Well . . . it's not that I don't ever get to fight for the right and all that. Sometimes I do. I've got a couple of cases right now that are going to cost me more to pursue than I could ever hope to make out of my share of the settlement. Cases I really believe in."

"That's a good thing."

He nodded. "It keeps me from becoming a cynic. But in order to fight those battles, I have to fight some battles that shouldn't even be happening."

She swallowed a bite of her hamburger and dabbed at her mouth with a napkin before she asked, "Do you mean you have to take cases you don't think are right?"

"No!" He hastened to say that. He didn't want her to think he was unscrupulous, because he wasn't. That was one vow to himself he'd managed to keep in the day-to-day reality of trying to run a law practice. "Every case I take has merit of some kind. I have to believe the law is on my client's side. But there are too many cases that shouldn't even go to court at all. I mean, neighbors ought to at least be civil to one another, don't you think?"

"You'd think so."

"I just won a case where a neighbor sued my client, claiming a coconut had fallen out of her tree and given him a concussion. The woman doesn't even have a coconut palm on her property."

"Then why was she sued?"

"Because she's a wealthy widow. And this guy

didn't have medical insurance. I don't suppose we'll ever know what beaned him and sent him to the hospital, but it sure wasn't a coconut from my client's property."

Erin shook her head. "I can't believe people sometimes."

"Oh, I can. I've seen it all."

"But the other lawyer should have known better. He shouldn't have taken the case."

He put down his burger and sipped some water. "That's what a lot of people don't understand. The lawyer took the case because it appeared to have merit. The guy got a concussion, was hospitalized for a couple of days, and had some serious stitches. If that happened through someone's negligence, then the responsible party ought to make things right. But you see, lawyers don't sue. Clients sue. And it's just the lawyer's job to represent the client the best way possible."

"But he could have refused to take the case."

"He might have, if he'd thought to go look at the supposedly guilty palm tree. He took his client's word for the situation. It happens. We all have to do that to some degree. My point is, if a person gets cut on broken glass on your property, you ought to pay for the stitches, or have your homeowner's insurance do it. Too many people won't make that neighborly gesture, and consequently, injured parties too often decide to sue."

Erin nodded. "I guess I can see that."

"This is not to say there aren't any nuisance suits, or that there aren't any lawyers ready to sue over anything if some person walks in with a gripe, but by and large . . ." He sighed. "By and large, Erin, despite what the public thinks, taking a case on contingency—which means you only get paid if you win, and then only a percentage of the settlement—means that the lawyer is hanging out on a financial limb. Which makes most lawyers pretty careful about what cases they take."

"Makes sense to me." She took another bite of hamburger, and he thought inanely that he'd never seen anyone chew in such a sexy fashion. Something about the way her lips moved. . . . He yanked his thoughts back from that precipice.

"Anyway," he said, trying to remount one of his favorite hobbyhorses, "the Don Quixote cases are few and far between. But I'm boring you."

"You're not boring me at all. This is something I never really thought about before."

"Well, then, let me add that I do a lot of pro bono work, too." He grinned. "I want you to have the best impression of me."

"Don't disillusion me. I had you down as Captain Kidd or Captain Blood."

He wiggled his eyebrows. "Want to go to Captiva with me?"

The laugh escaped her so abruptly that she nearly choked on her food. Captiva—which meant "female captive" in Spanish—was the island where, according to legend, the pirates of old stashed the women they captured.

"I shouldn't have said that," he announced.

"Why not?"

"Because," he lowered his voice confidentially, "I'm suddenly seeing visions of you and me in a tropical paradise—before they paved it—you all delectably bound and spitting fire at me, the nasty pirate who's carried you off."

All of a sudden, Erin felt flushed. Feverish. Too incredibly warm. She was too young for hot flashes, so she couldn't blame her state on that. Nor could she blame her breathlessness on anything.

Because she was suddenly seeing an image straight off the cover of a historical romance novel. She tried to feel indignation that he'd had the nerve to say such a thing, but she couldn't get the words out.

She suddenly felt like a flustered Southern belle who needed to fan herself and say, "My word, Mr. Wesley! You do take a lady's breath away."

Oh, God. She was in danger of reverting to a less-than-modern-and-liberated state. In danger of becoming a die-away miss, all because he'd had the nerve to say that.

But she liked his nerve. She liked the way he caught her unexpectedly with his boldness. So he was still Captain Kidd, even if he wanted to be Don Quixote.

Hmm. What was the matter with her thinking this afternoon? She didn't like being so internally inconsistent.

He was watching her, too, offering no apology for his boldness, apparently interested in her response to it. And unfortunately, she was sure her face was glowing a bright red. Betraying her.

But then his gaze freed her, and he went back to eating his hamburger. She'd have done the same, except she didn't think she could swallow. Desperately she sought for a way to change the subject without being too obvious, but she could think of nothing to say, except, "When?"

His head jerked up and he stared at her, his finely chiseled mouth slightly open. Then he released a deep laugh that crinkled the corners of his eyes. "Checkmate," he said.

She was relieved that he was treating it as a joke between them, especially since she was appalled to realize that she *hadn't* been joking. Good heavens, she was losing her mind!

Something about the wicked gleam in his blue eyes was overwhelming her with silly notions. Notions of the kind she hadn't had since she was fourteen. Or at least thought she hadn't. In fact, she was feeling downright giddy.

"About that planter," he said, making one of

those humorous, obvious changes of subject, while that devilish crinkle creased his eyes.

"What about it?" she asked blankly, unable to remember.

"I still want to buy it."

"Oh." All of a sudden she found herself embarrassed by the price tag on the thing, never mind the uncounted hours she had spent crafting it perfectly. Never mind that not once in the two years it had sat there had she ever considered lowering the price. Her mind scrambled around wildly, wondering how much she could discount it. But he beat her to the punch.

Leaving his lunch, he rose and went to get it. As he brought it over to the counter, he checked the tag.

He looked up at her in surprise, and she thought he was going to complain about the cost. But he astonished her yet again. "Is that all you're asking? Erin, with all the time and talent you put into this, you ought to be asking a whole lot more."

The warm feeling in her cheeks suddenly moved to her heart, leaving her feeling all aglow. Usually people wanted to pay for her pottery as if it were cheap plastic trinkets shipped in by the boatload. Very few seemed to understand that they were buying a unique labor of love.

"Thank you," she said.

"Don't thank me. Just ask yourself why you undervalue your gifts and labor."

"That's a very nice thing to say," she answered as he slid back into his seat and put the planter on the counter beside them, "but I can't charge so much that no one will buy anything."

"There is that," he agreed, giving a shake of his head. "I suppose if we all earned what we were worth the economy would fall to pieces."

"Or we'd have massive inflation. I was already thinking the planter was overpriced, because it's been sitting there for a couple of years. Nobody thinks it's worth the money."

"No, I do. In fact, I think it's worth more. You just didn't find someone with the right sense of whimsy until me."

Wow, she liked him. She didn't want to like him this much. Liking him spelled disaster, especially since she was virtually certain that he wouldn't like the little scheme she was up to now. She couldn't say for sure why she thought that, but she suspected there was a rigid moral core in this man that might well object to falsehoods.

In fact, now that she thought about it, she wasn't at all sure he'd been leading Ted Wannamaker down a path of deception to convince the court. He had probably just been making it perfectly clear that nobody was going to accept Ted's word for the marriage.

Hmm. Maybe not such a pirate after all.

Just then, much to her dismay, the shop door opened with a ding of the bell over it, and Seana and Dan walked in. She didn't know what concerned her more: the fact that Seana might have discovered the deception and would now let Richard know, or the fact that Richard might think her sister was dating a mobster. Either way, it wouldn't be good.

She had the sudden, wild wish that Richard the Third would toss her over his shoulder and spirit her away to Captiva after all. And hold her prisoner so she didn't have to worry about any of this stuff.

Seana actually giggled when she saw Richard and Erin having their cozy little lunch over the counter. Then her smile faded a bit. "Hi," she said. Richard seemed to blanch at her gaze.

But then, so did Dan. Erin decided that she might as well just settle back and watch events unfold. With her sister involved, there wasn't much she could do to stop them anyway.

"Hi," Richard answered. He rose from his stool like a gentleman and looked inquisitively at Dan.

"Dan Floorsheim," Dan said, extending his hand.

"Rich Wesley."

They shook hands, and Dan nodded. "Seana mentioned you."

"Are you two old friends?" Rich asked.

Seana preened as if she thought the two men were arguing over her. Erin stifled a sigh. She could see the men were measuring each other, but for no reason that involved Seana. They were just doing the man thing.

Dan continued. "She said you were Mary Todd's lawyer."

"That's right."

"So," said Dan, "what's the possibility you'll get that emergency stay?"

Erin saw Rich stiffen. And she felt her own heart plummet. Dan was going to play his role even now. Oh, God.

"Why do you ask?" Richard said.

"Because a guy I know is thinking about buying the property for development."

Richard's face darkened. "I'd wait on that a bit if I were you."

"Oh, I don't know," Dan said casually. "We have our ways."

Seana and Dan left rather quickly, right after Dan made his significant statement and gave Rich a long look. "That man was making a threat," Rich said a minute later.

"Oh," said Erin, tendrils of panic beginning to wrap around her mind. "Do you think so? I didn't get that impression." She didn't want Richard getting upset about Dan. That could be counterproductive, and worse, might cause trouble for Dan and herself. Sheesh, how did Mary pull these things off without having a nervous breakdown?

"That was an unmistakable threat. Who is that guy?"

"Uh . . ." Erin couldn't think of any response that wouldn't be a lie, and she really, really didn't want to lie to Richard.

Richard looked at her, and his face now held none of the charm she had come to expect. He looked hard and dangerous. A delicious little thrill passed through her.

"That man is up to no good," he said flatly. "You'd better tell Seana to stay away from him."

"Oh, right!" she said, her temper flaring and her voice dripping with sarcasm. "*You* try to tell her to stay away from something she wants. You seem to be awfully full of good advice for someone who couldn't even win a simple competency hearing."

He appeared taken aback. "Erin—"

"Do you always go around telling other people how to live?"

"As a rule, no—"

"Good! I'd hate to think you were always this insufferable!"

"Insufferable?"

"Insufferable," she repeated. She knew she was overreacting, carrying on like a shrew, but she couldn't seem to stop herself. It was as if some evil imp had seized her tongue. "You have absolutely no reason to think you were threatened."

Which wasn't exactly true, but she was hoping like mad that Richard might put a different spin on Dan's words if she kept hammering that he'd misunderstood them. Richard was the one person on earth she wanted to keep from believing Dan was a mobster. Exactly why, she couldn't have said.

"Look," he said.

"Look, nothing. Where do you get off telling me how my sister should live her life?"

"I don't want either of you to get hurt."

"Sure. Like you give a damn. I know men like you, Richard Wesley the Third. You just want to keep Seana for yourself!"

Where that had come from, she had no idea, and she wished she could snatch the words back. There had been no inkling that he, like the predator in her past, had been interested in Seana as well. Worse, it revealed that she gave a damn who Richard was interested in. She didn't want him to know that. She didn't want *herself* to know that. And it was so patently unfair to the man, even if he had gotten her goat.

"I'm not interested in your sister. She's just a child as far as I'm concerned. And what the hell's gotten into you?" he demanded. "I'm just concerned that Seana might get hurt by the guy."

"You don't know a damn thing about that guy."

"Neither do you, but I'm certainly going to have him investigated."

Erin's heart stopped. "What do you think

you'll find?" He didn't have Dan's real name, she reminded herself. He couldn't find out anything at all.

"Nothing very savory," Richard said with a frown. "Nothing good at all. Can I use your phone?"

"Why? What difference does it make to you if my sister wants to be a gun moll?"

At once she clapped her hand over her mouth. She couldn't believe she'd said that, confirming every one of Richard's suspicions about Dan. Crawling under a rock and hiding was beginning to look like her best option.

"A gun moll? My God!" He looked thunderstruck. "What do you know about that guy? What aren't you telling me?"

Right now it was a bit too late to claim ignorance. She'd said too much. Desperately she looked around for a way to backpedal without giving away her scheme. Because for some odd reason, she found she really cared what Richard thought about her, and she had a strong feeling that his straightlaced sense of ethics would rebel whether he thought Dan was a gangster or whether he discovered Erin had planned this escapade.

Finally she found her voice enough to say, in a squeak, "Nothing."

Shaking his head, he gave her an odd look and reached past her for the phone. He punched in a number, said hello to someone on the line, then

added, "I want a national wants and warrants
search for a Dan or Daniel Floorsheim. Spelled
either way. Yes. As fast as you can. No, I didn't
bring my cell. I'll call you back later. Thanks."

He hung up and faced Erin. "Now we'll find
out just how squirrelly this guy is."

Oh, Dan was squirrelly all right, full of acorns
even, but not the kind of acorns Richard was an-
ticipating. Nonetheless, Erin felt some of her
anxiety ease. Richard wasn't going to find out
anything about Dan, good or bad. Not that way.

"Now," said Richard, turning his attention to
her. He walked toward her until he had her
backed up against the counter, his hands firmly
planted on either side of her. Imprisoning her.

Their bodies touched, ever so lightly, and Erin
suddenly felt as if she couldn't breathe.

Apparently he recognized her reaction, because he moved a little closer. Just a bit. Just
enough to make every nerve in her body tingle.

"So," he said, looking every inch the pirate,
"what aren't you telling me?"

She had a sudden wild image of herself lashed
to the mast of a boat while the pirate leered over
her. Why in the world was she enjoying this? But
she *was* enjoying it. Dan, Seana, and all her other
problems seemed awfully far away right then.

"Tell me," he said, his voice rough. "I know
damn well you're up to something."

"Who, me?"

The corners of his eyes crinkled with humor.

Humor and heat. "Oh, yes. *You*. Because you'll never get me to believe you're happy with the idea of your sister being a gangster's girlfriend."

She was struggling for breath, acutely aware of the way he seemed to surround her. The way he *did* surround her. She ought to be screaming for help. Instead all she wanted to do was melt . . . right into him.

"I was just popping off at the mouth," she gasped, her breasts heaving.

The sight apparently distracted him for a moment, because he looked down. The touch of his gaze was an almost physical caress. "I don't believe you. You're up to something. I feel it in my bones."

She was feeling something else altogether in her bones, and all she could think was how much she wanted him to kiss her. Now. Wildly. Without quarter or mercy.

But then the pirate let her go, stepping back so suddenly that she felt shocked. He stared at her, his blue gaze at once speculative, hungry and dubious.

She grabbed the counter behind her, steadying herself, trying to calm her racing heart, trying to squash a terrible sense of disappointment. "Nothing's going on," she managed to say. "Nothing."

Little did she know that Linus Todd was already flapping his jaws all over town.

10

Linus wanted the money, but he didn't want the mob. It was as simple as that. He didn't like the idea of anyone muscling into *his* territory.

But he didn't exactly know what to do about it. He didn't want to wind up wearing cement overshoes. Although, when he thought about it, he realized they couldn't afford to kill him. At least not until the deal was done. Without him, there would be no deal.

That made him feel better, but only a little. There were *other* ways they could get him to do what they wanted, ways he most definitely didn't want to think about.

So what could he do to protect himself?

He decided to talk to a couple of friends. At least he thought they were his friends, but then, Linus thought a lot of people liked him. The truth was, all those people were simply too po-

lite or too indifferent to tell him to drop dead.
That included his so-called friends.

How Linus had come to be so universally
loathed was something he could never have explained, because he never suspected it. He had
been raised like most kids, without any serious
problems. But at some point, he'd developed a
rather curious blindness: he was blind to anyone's wishes other than his own. And worse yet,
he believed that his wishes were shared by
everyone.

The mayor, for example, was simply playing
for more money. Linus had no doubt he could
bring the planning board over to his side, because of course they wanted development.

As for that guy Floorsheim . . . well, they all
wanted the same thing, didn't they? He just had
to figure out how to keep himself from becoming
expendable.

The best idea he could come up with was to
get some protection.

Deciding that he was brilliant, Linus went to
look up some of his cronies. While the people
who tolerated him weren't necessarily the mon-
eyed sort, Linus was convinced they were the
créme de la créme. Mostly because they never
told him to drop dead.

Two of them, Budger and Flick, were sitting at
the bar in one of the dives owned by the noble
mayor of Paradise Beach. On a small stage, a

bored girl in a bikini was gyrating to some lackadaisical music. No nudity was allowed in Paradise Beach, by order of the city council—a.k.a. the city commission, depending on who you were talking to. For political reasons, hizzoner the mayor had gone along with the ordinance, hence Cecilia and the bikini.

Neither Budger nor Flick, both of whom looked overnourished and underwashed, displayed the least interest in Cecilia, which was okay, because Cecilia didn't have the least interest in them, either. In fact, it was doubtful Cecilia was interested in anything on the face of the planet except quitting time.

Budger and Flick—Budger being the shorter of the two—were well into their boilermakers, to judge by the empty shot glasses lined up in front of them.

"Hey, Linus," said Budger, who looked as if he hadn't shaved in a couple of days. His suit was rumpled, his tie was undone, and the front of his shirt suggested that he'd dined a few times since last changing it.

Flick didn't look a whole lot better. Linus sometimes wondered why two such successful salesmen weren't more fastidious. But they seemed to be doing all right.

"Hey Budger, hey Flick," Linus responded, sliding onto a stool next to Budger. "How's it going?" He sometimes felt bad that Budger and

Flick hadn't given him a nickname the way they had each other, but he figured they'd give him one eventually. He could be patient.

"Another day another thou," Budger said cheerfully.

Linus couldn't imagine making a thousand a day. Even though he was soon going to be making bazillions off Mary's property. In fact, his inability to make a thousand a day was one of the reasons he didn't hold a regular job. He figured he was better than that. As time had passed, however, living on his expectations had grown more difficult, especially since his aunt Mary had begun to look like one of those octogenarians likely to live to a hundred and ten. Well, he'd showed her. If the old bird wasn't decent enough to kick off at a normal age, he'd get his inheritance another way. And he had.

And things would all smell like roses right now if it weren't for a certain Floorsheim.

He ordered a boilermaker, figuring it was always wisest to drink whatever his companions were drinking, even if he hated beer and preferred his whiskey mixed with something sweet. He took a sip of the beer and managed to hide his grimace of distaste.

"So," he said, "you guys interested in making a little money?"

Budger looked at him. "I got a job. It has to be more than that."

"Well," said Linus, inwardly groaning, "it'll be a lot more than that once I sell my aunt's property." Already the only part of his mind that worked well, his mental calculator, was running sums on how much these guys were going to cost him.

"So we gotta wait to get paid?" Flick asked, entering the conversation for the first time. He didn't look happy about that.

"Afraid so," Linus admitted. Like he had the money to pay these guys now. His credit cards were maxed to the limit, thanks to his damn lawyer, and the trust fund, set up for him thirty years ago by Mary, wouldn't be coughing out any more money for nearly a month.

Budger elbowed Flick. "Hey, the guy owns most of this damn island now. He's good for it."

"He don't exactly *own* it," Flick grumbled.

"Next best thing," Budger argued back. "Let's hear him out."

Flick rolled his eyes.

"Okay," Linus said. "I just need you guys to pretend you're my protection."

"Protection?"

It seemed to Linus that both Budger and Flick straightened on their stools. A good sign, indicating their interest. Or so he thought.

"Yeah," he said, taking a sip of the whiskey and nearly choking. "I need to look like I have some muscle with me."

"Muscle?" This from Flick, whose eyes were getting round as saucers. "I ain't no muscle."

"But nobody has to know that," Linus argued. "You just gotta look like it."

"Sheesh." Flick buried his face in his beer.

"Hey," Budger said, elbowing Flick. "We don't gotta beat anyone up. We just gotta look like we could."

"Yeah?" Flick lifted his head. "And what if they hit first?"

"We run like hell," said Budger with a shrug. "I ain't getting it on with no bad guys."

"Right," said Linus, who wasn't quite sure he understood what Budger had said, but it sounded reasonable to him.

But Flick wasn't so easily persuaded. "So," he said, wiping beer suds from his mouth with the back of his hand, "who are these guys you're worried about?"

Linus, not being the brightest bulb sometimes, let the truth slip. "The mob."

Budger and Flick told Linus to drop dead.

By midnight, it was all over Paradise Beach: The mob was trying to muscle into town.

Erin nearly panicked. She heard the rumor four times before she closed her shop that night, and the next morning five of the neighboring businesspeople had dropped in to tell her the same thing.

Her plan hadn't included getting the whole town in an uproar. All she'd wanted to do was get Mary angry enough to come out of her depression. Instead people were talking about demonstrating at City Hall this afternoon, and would she please come.

All she could think to do was call Dan at the— shudder—Marriott, where his room was running her into financial extinction.

"Time to leave town," she said when she got him at last.

"Huh?" he said, apparently having been dragged out of a sound sleep.

"You've got to leave town, Dan. Everybody's in an uproar about the mob coming."

He didn't reply for a minute. She heard him yawn, and heard sounds that she thought might be him rubbing his eyes.

Finally he said, "Wasn't that the plan?"

"Yes. But it's working better than I hoped. I don't know what set everyone off, but there's going to be a demonstration this afternoon at City Hall."

"Ye gads." Then he laughed.

"This isn't funny!"

"Actually, it is. I never told anybody I was from the mob."

"What exactly *did* you say?"

"Just that I knew a guy who was interested in buying the property."

"And then that threat you made to Richard."

"Hell, that wasn't a threat, Erin. It could have meant anything, including financial leverage."

"That's not how Richard took it."

"So what?" He yawned again. "That's what you wanted. Now you have it."

Which was a very lowering thought. Erin sighed, realizing that her plan was going very much astray because she hadn't counted on the local people getting so stirred up. Nor had she counted on being so attracted to a certain pirate with whom she now had to be dishonest.

"Damn it!" she said in a burst of frustration.

"Besides," said Dan, "I don't want to disappear. I like your sister."

Things just kept getting worse and worse. Closing her eyes, Erin wondered how it was that Mary Todd could pull off these shenanigans and have everything turn out right, when it was obvious that there was just too much chance involved in doing something like this.

And she thought of Richard. There went a beautiful fantasy of being captive on Captiva. In order to avoid lying to him, she was going to have to avoid him. And worse, when the truth came out as it probably would, since Seana had decided to date the "mobster," he was going to lose all respect for her. She wanted to wail.

"Listen," she said finally, "if you think I'm going to support you at the Marriott while you court my sister, you've got another think coming."

"I know. I switched the bill into my name. Hanging around is no longer just about your scheme."

Oh, God! She liked Dan, she really did, and she trusted him, but . . . Oh, Lord, if Seana fell for him, and found out he was playing a role, there was going to be hell to pay. But why was she assuming that Seana would fall for Dan anyway? She was leaping too many fences too fast. But that's exactly what her mind seemed determined to do. It was hopping all over the place, bouncing between fear that she was messing things up, and fear that she wouldn't mess them up the right way. She wished she could run to Mary right now and ask for advice. But Mary was in no state to help anyone. At this moment, she didn't even seem able to help herself.

"I have a headache," Erin announced.

"Me, too. I'm a night owl, and right now I've only had about five hours of sleep. And do you have any idea how hard it's going to be to stay in character if you keep reminding me I'm acting? Call me back and yell at me later. Cripes, Erin, I only did what you asked!" With that he slammed down the phone.

Erin sat staring at the phone for a long time, wondering how she was going to navigate this mess without losing everyone's respect. Why had she ever thought she could pull a Mary Todd?

Right then, adding to her emotional turmoil, Richard walked into her shop. He smiled at her, that warm smile that always made her heart skip a beat. She wished she could crawl behind the counter and pretend nobody was at home.

"Good morning," he said. His voice was as smooth as honey, the kind of voice she could have listened to for hours. "How are you this morning?"

The truth would never do. All she could do was stare at him mutely. How was it possible he could swashbuckle in khaki chinos and a red polo shirt?

"Erin? What's wrong?"

"My life is going to hell." The words burst out of her before she could stop them, and as soon as they came out, she clapped her hand over her mouth.

"What's wrong? Do you want to talk about it?"

His concern seemed sincere, but she told herself that it was just his natural suavity, the practiced manner of a courtroom lawyer. Not that she believed that for one instant.

"Erin?"

She shook her head. "It's not important."

He took the wicker stool again, entirely too close for comfort. "It's important enough to have you moping around like Rover does whenever I forget to put my trash cans out the night before the truck comes."

Rover, as every Paradise Beach resident knew, was a crossbreed of a gray Airedale and one of Dante's lesser demons. His mischievous wanderings had once prompted the mayor to push for strict leash laws, a proposal that, when all was said and done, served only to teach the mayor his proper place in the town's pecking order.

"I'm not moping," Erin said. "And even if I were, I wouldn't want to pick through your garbage."

"I don't know. They say you can learn a lot about a person by picking through their garbage. Maybe that's why Rover is so smart."

"And what does Rover know about you that I don't?" she asked. Anything to keep the conversation about him and away from Dan and the mess that was threatening to subsume her existence. "Has he found your collection of pirate porn magazines?"

"Hardly," Richard replied. "I never throw away an issue of *Cutlass Babes* or *Very Jolly Rogers*."

Erin burst into a helpless laugh. "Darn, you're quick, Richard the Third."

He winked. "I have to be to keep up with my Irish Valkyrie."

His Irish Valkyrie, Erin thought, trying to catch

a breath and restart her heart without him noticing. This was going *way* too fast. And yet, the thought of being his Cutlass Babe and making him a Very Jolly Roger was more than a bit appealing. It was downright entrancing. Until he found out what a mess she'd created with Dan, of course. Pirates were known to make mutineers walk the plank. And while he wasn't exactly the sole captain of the SS *Mary Todd*, she had made a radical course change without so much as letting Mary's lawyer know. Yes, he would definitely make her walk the plank.

"You're getting that crestfallen look again," he said. "Are you going to tell me what's going on, or do I have to lash you to the yardarm and torture it out of you?"

Damn him with his attractive images! And why was there never a yardarm around when you needed one? Still, it was obvious he wasn't going to give up. Not that she had expected otherwise. "Quit talking dirty," she said desperately.

His eyes crinkled. "Why? You like it."

Right then she wanted to kill him for the simple crime of seeing right through her. At least about that. She shuddered to think what his reaction would be if he found out about her schemes.

Richard, she was realizing, might be a lawyer, but he was also one of the most ethical men she had ever met. Somehow she figured that he would loathe subterfuge, no matter the reason for it. Of course, he'd been Mary's lawyer lo these many years. Maybe he wasn't quite the prig she was painting him.

She looked at him, perplexed by her own confused thoughts, wondering why she kept seeing him as a buccaneer when he was so obviously an escapee from the ministry. Of course, Reverend Arthur Archer wasn't exactly saintly, either. No one who hung around with Mary for long could be a perfect saint.

"What thoughts are going on behind those beautiful green eyes of yours?"

She almost blushed. No, darn it, she *did* blush. "Mind your own business."

He eased closer, leaning across the counter until their faces were only inches apart. "I'm going to find out all your secrets," he promised in a husky voice that sent both thrills and chills racing along her spine. It would have been so easy, right then, to lower her flag and surrender.

"Maybe not right away," he continued, sounding like a big cat purring. "But eventually."

"You don't want to know my secrets." Her voice quavered.

"Yes, I do. All of them. More than I've wanted anything for a long, long time."

Another shiver passed through her, this one decidedly delicious. She felt herself teetering on the brink of confessing all . . . and that would *not* do. Suddenly her backbone snapped stiff, and she lifted her head, increasing the distance between them.

"I need to go out," she announced. "Mind the store for me, will you?"

He was clearly startled. "What?"

"I need to go to church. Just stay here and mind the store. If anyone wants to buy anything, tell them I'll be back shortly."

She headed for the door, trying desperately not to look back.

"Why do you need to go to church?" he asked.

"I need to make a confession."

"Ahh." His voice suddenly took on a warmly humorous tone. "Too many lustful thoughts?"

She slammed the door on him, wishing that he couldn't read her mind.

She found Father Dave Penwick playing checkers with the Reverend Arthur Archer. Apparently it was a slow day for religion in Paradise Beach. The two men had set up a card table in the rectory garden, and each had a tall glass of iced tea at his elbow.

Father Dave looked up at her. "Again?" he said.

"Please."

"You just confessed two days ago."

"I seem to be living a life of constant sin these days."

Reverend Arthur nodded. "Anyone who associates with Mary Todd has the same complaint. Remarkable woman. She can lead the flock astray faster than I can say lickety-split. I've often wondered whether she's a gift from God or a curse."

Father Dave raised his eyebrows at his old friend. "Now don't be so harsh, Arthur. Mary has a good soul."

"Her soul may be good, but it's her brain I worry about. Why don't you convert her to *your* church?"

Father Dave laughed. "Sorry. She's *your* hair shirt."

"An apt description. Well, go do your duty for this poor young lamb, who undoubtedly has Miss Mary at the root of all her problems. I'll reset the board for another game."

Father Dave took Erin into his office. They never used the confessional anymore, although there was one available. Erin had the suddenly cowardly wish that she could hide behind a screen and pretend to be someone else.

"What's up, Erin?" Father Dave asked after they were seated.

"I'm going to burn in hell."

"I seriously doubt that. What's going on?"

"Well, I brought the mob to town, and I'm lusting after a pirate."

"Hmmm." His eyebrows didn't even raise.

"You know, it's very unsatisfying to confess to someone you can't even shock."

He chuckled. "My dear woman, you wouldn't believe the things I've heard over the course of twenty-five years. A little lust and perfidy seem like child's play."

"Don't you even want to know what's going on?"

"Probably not." He smiled and reached out to pat her hand. "So which mob did you bring to town?"

"None really. I hired an actor to pretend to be the mob. Well, actually, I asked a friend who's an actor to do it."

"To what end?"

"To try to stop the real estate deal that Linus Todd is working with High Lights Development."

"And why do you want to do that?"

"Because he has no right to Mary's property. Because he'll ruin our town."

"I see." He nodded and stroked his chin. "Is this friend of yours threatening anyone?"

"No. He's just pretending he knows someone who is interested in buying the property."

"Then I don't see what the problem is."

"You don't?" Erin nearly gaped.

"Well, what Linus Todd has done is a crime, actually. There was no motive in his heart other than greed. What you're doing is an attempt to protect a friend, and all the people of town. As long as your actor friend isn't hurting anyone, I don't see a problem."

"Oh." She felt momentarily deflated. "What about the rest of it? What about the pirate?"

"Is your pirate married?"

"No."

He laughed. "Then falling in love isn't a sin."

She rose and frowned at him. "You know, you're very unhelpful."

"Sorry. If I could, I'd help in your little scheme to save Miss Mary from her nephew. And you have my blessing to fall in love." He was laughing as she left.

That was exactly what she didn't want to hear. The whole world was going crazy. Absolutely crazy!

Falling in love? Indeed she was not. And no blue-eyed pirate was going to change her mind.

Unfortunately, Richard hadn't abandoned ship by the time she returned to the shop. Indeed, he was standing behind the cash register, holding forth about what great pottery the shop held, and saying he was sure that everything signed by Erin was going to become a collectible in the future.

She'd have blushed if she hadn't already been so disturbed. Instead, all she could do was boil over internally with things she wanted to say but couldn't in front of two giggling old ladies who were succumbing to Richard the Third's Irish blarney. Well, boil over internally and ring up nearly a thousand dollars in sales between the two women.

They left the shop, still giggling, promising to return before they went back to Germany, and Erin found herself alone with her nemesis.

"So," he said, that devilish smile crinkling the corners of his incredible eyes, "do you feel better now?"

"Why should I feel better?"

"Well, I assumed confession does that for most people. It certainly does for me."

Oh, heavens, he was a Catholic, too. She couldn't even reject him on those grounds. Not that she'd ever been one to choose a suitor by his religion, but still, it would have been nice to have an excuse. Any excuse.

"Erin, what are you afraid of?"

She bristled. "Nothing."

"Really." The word was full of doubt.

"I might better ask you if you're afraid of *anything*."

He rubbed his chin, studying her thoughtfully. "I'm afraid of lots of things," he said after a moment. "Do you want the laundry list?"

"Try me."

"Well, I'm afraid of losing cases for clients who have just causes."

She waved her hand impatiently. "I'm not talking about things like that."

"No, I know you aren't. I'm just wondering how far I can trust you. You want to get inside my most private places, but you've got a moat full of alligators around yours."

"Typical lawyer, looking for quid pro quo."

"No, just a man who doesn't want an Irish warrior queen's lance through his heart."

All her irritation and annoyance seeped out of her as if a balloon had been punctured. That was such a vulnerable statement, and she didn't want him to be vulnerable. She wanted him to be the brave, dashing pirate who grinned into the teeth of danger. She wanted him to be invincible.

Why? So she could dismiss him out of hand? So she could convince herself he was beneath contempt? Or so she could have a reason not to trust him.

She looked deep into his eyes then and saw nothing but honesty. She frightened him. She didn't know whether to be exhilarated or disturbed by that fact.

"I don't want to hurt anyone," she said finally.

"I know. I don't either. So what say we go to the rally?"

"Rally?"

"Haven't you heard? The town is holding a meeting to protest the mob presence."

Oh, Lord, this was getting out of hand. Mary might be able to cackle with glee in these circumstances, but Erin couldn't. She hadn't wanted to upset the entire town, just save it.

How could Father Dave say she wasn't doing anything wrong at all? She had a conscience and knew better.

And she had to admit, much to her dismay, that she wasn't made of the same stuff as Mary Todd.

Not at all, at all.

11

That afternoon, a considerable crowd gathered in front of city hall, even though it was Saturday and no one was inside. Which was not to say that the city commissioners hadn't heard about it. They, like everyone else in Paradise Beach, heard about it on the grapevine.

The commissioners held a clandestine meeting in the living room of chairman Julius Swank, seven men, all of them looking extremely unhappy. Swank was a retired navy man, and his entire house was decorated in nautical themes, with seascapes cluttering every wall. Unfortunately, Mrs. Swank was in Michigan for the summer visiting relatives. That meant that every painting hung at a slightly different angle—the preference of Mr. Swank, which he was free to indulge in the absence of Mrs. Swank—but which left the other commissioners feeling slightly seasick. It also meant that the only refreshments served at the meal were Julius's favorites: chili cheese dogs slathered with onions, and copious quantities of his home-brewed beer. If the skewed seascapes weren't enough to make one nauseous, the noises from the rest room would.

"Captain on the bridge!" Julius announced as he returned. His voice, irritatingly gravely when he was sober, now boomed with the lowered inhibitions born of alcohol. "I have returned from the poop deck."

"Evidently so," said Kyle Lonagan, one of the few who could get away with challenging Julius in his lair. The photos he'd taken of Julius bellowing sea chanties while dancing *in flagrante delicto* on a table during a private party at the mayor's nightclub had protected him for several years. "By the way, Julius, I sent this beer of yours off to a chemist friend of mine for analysis. He wrote back: 'I'm sorry to inform you that your horse has diabetes.'"

"That's what I'll call it!" Julius said, ignoring the ancient joke. "Thoroughbred Beer. I'll make a million!"

Kyle nodded. "Yeah, I guess Glue Factory Beer probably wouldn't have the same market appeal."

"Gentlemen, please," Len Tremaine cut in. "None of this is getting us any closer to keeping the mayor's mobsters out of our fair city. If all we're going to do is belch Julius's hot dogs and insult his beer"—he actually said that with a straight face—"I suggest we skip this meeting and go back to my place for poker and porn videos."

"*My* mobsters?" a voice boomed from the door. They turned to see the mayor standing there in relaxed weekend wear: a pair of bright red swim trunks with giant ducks on them, a neon green flower-printed Hawaiian shirt, lemon yellow socks, and sky blue tennis shoes. "They're not *my* mobsters!"

"Then whose mobsters are they?" Julius thundered, sounding like gravel rolling around in an oil drum.

"I don't know whose mobsters they are," the mayor retorted.

"Ah, but," said Kyle, who was equally unafraid of the mayor, since he had a photo of hizzoner dancing too close to a bored Cecilia, "he was first seen at *your* office."

"Uh-uh, uh-uh," said the mayor, wagging his head vigorously. "That was Linus Todd, Mary Todd's nephew."

"But," said Kyle, "Mrs. Rorschach says Linus met with the mob at the Italian restaurant. Which means Linus is with the mob."

"What mob are we talking about?" demanded Malcolm Cornish, one of the newest electees. He paused to scoop chili off the front of his shirt. "There are all kinds of mobs."

Len looked down his nose at Malcolm. "So you're an authority on the mob? Care to enlighten us?"

"Hold it, hold it," squawked the mayor. "Linus is in the *mob*?"

"Well," Malcolm said, "you got your good old Sicilian mobs, like the Vermicellis in New York. Then you got your Chinese Tong mobs, like the Moo Goo Gaipans in San Francisco. Your Columbian drug cartels, like the Arabicas in Miami. There's the new Russian mobs, the Borscht family in Los Angeles. There's all kinds of mobs."

"This beer really is awful, Julius," Kyle said after taking another sip. "What's this sludge at the bottom?"

"Vermicelli is made by mobsters?" the mayor asked.

"I can't stand that moo goo gaipan stuff," Len said. "Give me Cantonese any time."

"I think it gives the beer body," Julius boomed. "Like one of those rich English ales."

"Nah, the Vermicellis have gone legit," Malcolm declared. "The Linguinis took over their rackets."

"My wife cooks Cantonese," offered Neil Rogers, who looked up from the Rubik's cube he'd been trying to solve for eleven years. "That's what she calls it anyway. I call it compost."

"Got any more beer?" Kyle asked, having drained his glass, including the sludge.

The mayor stamped his foot. *"But what about my mobsters?"*

Richard and Erin stood at the edge of the gathered crowd, taking in the variety of faces, modes of dress, and methods of protest. Richard figured there was probably a crowd of six hundred or so, a not insignificant gathering in a town where most people preferred to go their own way undisturbed. The last time they'd gotten this many people together over something, it had involved wearing dog collars in defense of Rover, the hound from hell that belonged to Cal Lepkin. Not even the sea monster egg had brought a turnout this big . . . probably because most people had been terrified of what might have been inside that egg.

The event started off very slowly. Even in Paradise Beach, people were reluctant to be the first to take the dance floor. A few signs were being waved, hand-lettered posters telling the mob to leave town, but most of the people were milling around as if uncertain exactly what they were supposed to be enraged about.

"I figured," Richard said to Erin, whom he'd managed to spirit away from her store under duress—namely that he wouldn't buy her dinner if she didn't come with him—"that everyone would already be pretty wound up."

"Well, you know this town. It's pretty much a case of the blind leading the blind."

"I wonder where the mayor is. I can't imagine him missing this opportunity."

"He's probably hiding in a bomb shelter somewhere."

"The way he dresses, he'd be visible from a satellite in space. You're probably right." He scanned the crowd again, feeling an itch to take charge but reminding himself he didn't want to get involved in any civil disturbances. Being an officer of the court sometimes hung heavy on his shoulders.

"Are you going to do anything, Bluebeard?" Erin asked.

"Me? Why should I do anything? And I'm not Bluebeard. I haven't even had one wife."

"That's reassuring, I suppose. I just meant, you're the one with the silver tongue."

Looking deep into those enchanting green eyes of hers, he was conscious of a strong desire not to disappoint her, to somehow leap to the head of this disorganized demonstration and unite the milling crowd into a force for right.

The only problem was . . . something in the way she was looking hinted that she'd rather be anywhere else on earth. That the presence of these people preparing to demonstrate disturbed her somehow.

Hmmm. His legally trained mind, which was always looking at every possibility, and always ready to connect seemingly disparate things into a picture of possible truth, suddenly made a connection: her sister was dating some guy who had, however subtly, threatened him.

Could Erin be involved with the mob?

The thought felt like a kick in the heart, stunning him so that he didn't even notice the joker who climbed atop a planter, pushed the branches of a shrub out of the way, and tried to call the gathering to order.

Surely those shimmering green eyes couldn't conceal anything so appalling?

But tumblers were clicking into place, tumblers that made an ugly *snick* in his mind. She'd protested that that Dan Floorsheim guy hadn't made a threat. She'd come out of the sporting goods store right after Seana and Floorsheim had headed up the street. And now, when he would have expected her to be the most indignant person in Paradise Beach—primarily because indignation seemed to be part of her nature—she was merely looking . . . uncomfortable.

Hmmm.

With difficulty, he tore his attention from Erin to listen to the jerk who was peering through the shrubbery and shouting at the crowd.

"We aren't gonna let the mob into our town!" the guy shouted.

"No!" the crowd shouted back, apparently having at last found one voice.

"We don't want that racketeering!"

"No!"

"We don't want those guys in their ugly black suits and shirts filling our streets!"

"No!"

Erin muttered, "He should run for mayor. The two of them share the same twisted logic."

He might have laughed at her sarcasm another time, but right now, he was feeling as if his heart had been pierced by a lance.

A voice from the crowd shouted, "Tell 'em to get a fashion consultant!"

"Yeah!" yelled the crowd.

"It'll be war, I tell ya," the guy on the planter shouted. "All-out war! We'll fight 'em in the streets, in the alleys, on the beach!"

"Yeah!"

Richard shook his head. What were these yahoos proposing to do? Patrol the streets with tommy guns? In this town, people were more apt to fight with mud pies and peashooters. Maybe he should speak out for some rationality here.

But suddenly Erin was tugging his arm. "I've got to get out of here," she said. "Please. Now. Or I'll leave by myself."

And once again, ugly suspicions reared their heads.

The noise from the demonstration had, by that time, penetrated into Julius Swank's den.

"Looks like the natives are getting restless," he said. "It's time we exercised some leadership."

He paused for a moment, screwing up his face. "I'll be right back."

"Some leadership," Kyle said as Julius left the room. "With leaders like that, no wonder this town is going into the sewer."

The mayor, however, was not amused. "He's right. It's time for us to lead. Gentlemen, let's go address our constituency."

At that point, anything seemed preferable to listening to Julius's growling bowels, so they rose and followed him to the door. When Carl opened it, however, Dan Floorsheim was standing on the stoop, flanked by two burly bodyguards.

"Did I miss anything?" Dan asked with a bright smile.

"Where are we going?" Erin asked. Rich had been driving for the last forty minutes, and beach communities and islands were slipping away one after another.

"I said I was taking you to dinner. I just didn't say where."

She looked at him. "Are you kidnapping me?"

"The thought has crossed my mind more than once." He looked at her, but the usual smile in his eyes was utterly missing. "However, I forgot my cutlass, so I suppose I'll have to make do with dinner as far away from that madhouse as we can get. Somewhere nobody knows either of us."

"You're thinking about Seattle?"

Again his smile was conspicuously absent.

"No, but there's a really nice waterfront restaurant in Tarpon Springs that I love."

"So long as it's not greasy," she said.

"Nope. It's Greeky."

She turned to him, wondering why she sensed such tension in him. Such . . . anger. "Greeky? Is that a word?"

"I just invented it."

She subsided, for some reason feeling as if she were locked up in a tiger's cage . . . with the tiger.

An hour later they were dining on souvlaki, while looking out at the sun glistening on the gulf. Fishing boats were moored at nearby docks, and sponge divers were sorting and weighing their day's catch.

"I sometimes wonder if Paradise Beach is on the same planet as the rest of the world," Erin said. "This place seems so . . . normal."

"Until the local boys go diving for the cross on the bottom of the bay on Epiphany Sunday. I understand it's a madhouse then."

"Not like Paradise Beach," she said.

"I think every town is like Paradise Beach once you really get to know it. Oh, our denizens may be a bit ditzier than average, but every town has its absurdities. At least ours are harmless."

"I hope you can still say that when this is all over," she said, biting her lip.

He put his fork down and caught her eye. "What aren't you telling me, Erin?"

She wanted to run then, run as far away as she

could get. But at the same time she just wanted to dump all her problems on those broad shoulders of his. At some level she was absolutely certain he wouldn't treat all of this as lightly as Father Dave had. Father Dave might be right that she was doing nothing wrong, but she feared Richard might not see it that way. Nor did she right now, largely because she feared what might happen to Seana.

That much, she decided, she could tell him. "I'm worried about Seana. Ever since I heard that guy at the rally talking about black suits and shirts."

He nodded slowly. His dinner apparently forgotten, he propped his elbows on the table and folded his hands beneath his chin. "You think someone might try to hurt her?"

"I don't know. Richard, they were talking about *war*."

"I know. But I also know it's Paradise Beach. I've lived there most of my life, Erin. My neighbors aren't about to turn into vigilantes."

"I wish I could be as sure of that." And wished she could somehow yank her sister safely away until all this settled down. She was going to have to call Dan and warn him. Maybe this time he'd listen to her.

Richard pushed his plate aside and touched the back of her hand lightly. The light caress made shivers run through her. "How about I try to talk to Seana."

Erin sighed. "Sure. Why not? Maybe she'll listen to you. She sure never listens to me."

But then he leaned forward and shattered the rest of her evening. "I don't know what you're not telling me, Erin, but I know you're not telling me all of it. Maybe when you get around to it, we'll have something else to discuss."

Her heart plummeted then, like a stone sinking to the bottom of the ocean. There was not a smidgeon of doubt left in her that she had created the biggest mess of her life.

12

"What was *that*?" Julius asked after Dan and his henchmen left.

"I don't know," Len said, looking confused. "He didn't exactly say anything, did he? Or did he?"

"He didn't *have* to say anything," Malcolm pointed out. "All he had to do was show up with those goons."

"Yeah," said Len, looking glum. "It was an implied threat."

"I didn't hear any threats," Julius *harrumphed*. "That's what I mean, what was that all about?"

"What I'd like to know," Malcolm said heavily, "is how the hell he knew we were having a meeting. Nobody knew we were having a meeting."

"The mayor didn't know either," Len said. "*He* showed up."

"Hey," said the mayor. "I'm supposed to be here. Were you trying to cut me out?"

"Always," said Julius, with a roll of his eyes. "So why did this guy show up? He didn't say anything. He just said he wanted to meet us."

"He wanted," Len said heavily, "to show off his goons."

Silence fell over the room for a bit, except for a belch from Julius.

"Well, it's obvious," said the mayor, breaking the silence. "We need to get our *own* goons."

Most of the beaches closed at sunset, but Rich found one that didn't close until later, so he parked there, fed quarters into the meter, and together they crossed the dunes and headed down to the water's edge. People were scattered here and there, but as far as the eye could see, there was no crowding, not even by the high-rise hotels.

It was after eight now, and the sun was hanging heavy over the water, glowing orange and turning the waves into a rainbow of hues from slate blue to purple and red. The waves were large tonight, suggesting that somewhere out on the Gulf of Mexico there was a storm. But here the sky was nearly cloudless, and the breeze was soft and kind.

A sensual breeze. At first they walked side by side, leaving prints in the wet sand behind them, prints that were washed away by the next wave. Occasionally they had to dart up a little higher to keep from getting their shoes wet.

But then Richard reached out and took her hand, and the evening became magic. Each star that emerged from the dusky sky seemed to emerge just for her.

His palm was warm, Erin noticed, and his touch was unexpectedly comforting, as if it were a touch she'd been yearning for forever. And her mind started to wander down forbidden pathways, pathways involving a pirate and a captive lady.

The breeze over her bare skin felt like gentle caresses, and the way it tossed her hair made her feel strangely wanton and free. Something elemental was awakening in her, something she had never really felt before. And along with it came exhilaration.

"Where are *we* going to find goons?" Kyle demanded of the mayor. "You can barely find topless dancers with tops. How are you going to find goons?"

"What kind of goons do you want?" Malcolm asked.

"I've always liked the big, heavyset goons," Len said, shifting to make room for his own ample belly. "They have a certain *je ne sais quoi*."

"French goons?" Kyle asked. "You want *French* goons?"

"He just wants heavyset goons," the mayor said. "He didn't say they have to be French."

"No," Malcolm agreed. "Just heavyset."

"Good," Kyle *harrumphed*. "We have enough problems without bringing Frenchmen to town."

"You just don't want anyone in town who's more arrogant than you are," Julius suggested.

"Damn right!" Kyle agreed.

The mayor put up a hand. "So, does anyone know some heavyset goons who aren't French but still have that jenny-whatcha-callit?"

"Actually," Malcolm said, "I think I do. But they're . . . kinda . . . experienced in life."

"No," Julius said, as if reading his mind.

Malcolm bristled. "Why not? They were good enough to chase off a building full of ghosts!"

"And they'd be cheap," the mayor said. "This isn't such a bad idea."

The sun was sinking into the water now, and the beach was suddenly empty. Rich paused and turned so that they were both staring out over the water to watch the sunset's last glorious moments. Behind them were the blank eyes of the hotels and condos, reflecting the sunset. Anyone could have been watching, but Erin didn't care. It was as if she had moved far away from reality and all its problems, to a place where nothing could touch her . . . except Richard.

Hand in hand they watched the sun sink lower, a visible movement now that it was so close to the horizon.

"Right now," Rich said, "I fancy I can feel the earth moving beneath my feet."

That struck Erin as a poetic statement, and she suddenly felt very close to him emotionally, despite knowing her secret would probably appall him. But in these moments, not even that could touch her. It was as if some part of her had decided to seize the moment and refuse to worry about anything. As if she were lifted out of herself.

The colors of the fading day were changing rapidly, reminding her somehow of how truly brief life really was. Reminding her that for all it seemed to go on forever, time was really passing very swiftly.

The sun disappeared behind the water. For an instant there was a bright green flare, then it was gone. Erin turned her face up to watch the stars emerge one by one as the light steadily faded.

And then Richard kissed her. The caress came without warning, yet it seemed to have been coming forever. As if this moment in time had been plotted at the very beginning of the universe.

Helplessly, she turned into him and felt his arms close around her. Strong arms. Arms that knew just how to cradle her. A mouth that knew just how to touch hers, as if tasting, testing, asking. Not at all demanding.

But when their bodies came together, pressing

breast to chest and belly to belly, it was as if a flare rose between them, like the last green flare of the dying sun. Heat raced through Erin, filling her every cell with a longing so intense it defied words.

And with the longing came fear. Terrible fear.

"What the hell is Albermarle's number?" the mayor asked, picking up the phone.

Julius flipped through the phone book and called out the digits one by one as the mayor stabbed the phone with stubby fingers. This, Julius thought, would even the score. The men of Colonel Albermarle's Dustbuster Brigade were all experienced combat veterans. They'd be more than enough for some muscle-bound mobsters from New York. Even if their combat experience did date back to World War II.

"Albermarle," the mayor said into the phone. "Did I wake you? Oh sure, I can wait." The mayor put his palm over the mouthpiece and turned to the council members. "He has to turn down Lawrence Welk."

On second thought ..., Julius amended silently.

"Yes, how are you, Colonel?" the mayor said. "Great, fine here. Yes, she's fine too."

The mayor seemed to wince at what had to be an inquiry about his wife. Having met the mayor's wife, Julius understood entirely. Julius referred to her as "Madame Medusa." Never to her face, of course. Not even a lifetime facing the ravages of the sea had instilled that kind of courage in him.

"Listen, Colonel," the mayor continued, "I have a mission for you and your men. Think of it as a security mission. Good versus evil. Honor among thieves. All of that." The mayor paused a moment, listening. "Well, I was wondering if your men would be up to the challenge of serving as the House Guards for myself and the members of the city council. Well, sure, I think we could come up with uniforms. Of course you'll need to ask them. How about if I stop by the shuffleboard courts tomorrow morning around eight-ish? Great, see you then."

The mayor hung up the phone. "We have goons now," he said proudly.

Just please don't let the mayor design these uniforms, Julius thought. Anything but that.

With her whole body awash in hungers she hadn't allowed herself to feel in years, Erin was almost unable to respond to the stab of fear that pierced her. But the fear won. She couldn't allow herself to get close to a man again. She couldn't survive that pain again. And the promise of the pain was written in the plan she had set afoot, in the secret she was keeping.

With a mighty push, she shoved herself backward until nearly a yard separated her and Rich. "You shouldn't have done that," she said, suddenly shaking from head to foot.

"Why not?" His piratical smile gleamed in the deepening twilight.

"Because . . . because."

"Because. That's always a good reason."

In that instant, Erin felt so stupid that she was sure, absolutely sure, she was never going to speak to this man again.

"Please take me home," she said stiffly. "Now."

Mary Todd sat by her window, rocking slowly, looking out at the view she had treasured for years. The last of the day was fading away over a gulf that was dappled with color, across a beach that was nearly as white as snow, and palm trees that clattered gently in the breeze.

This was her world, all of it from one end of the barrier island to the other, and if Linus thought he had taken it over, he was sadly mistaken. Mary knew better; Linus was nothing but a pawn on her inscrutable chessboard.

The fact that the unfolding events were going to remove him as a problem in her life for a long, long time to come was only a side issue as far as she was concerned. There were other people she was more interested in managing at the moment, among them Richard, Erin, and her suitor of fifty years, Ted Wannamaker.

Linus's move to have her declared incompetent

had at first irritated her. Whether that nephew of hers knew it or not, she could have him by the short hairs with a mere flick of her wrist.

But it suited her now to have everyone worrying over her. It suited her to have Erin scheming—though after watching the young woman's attempts, Mary realized a great deal of instruction was yet required there. Erin was simply too simplistic. To truly be Machiavellian, one needed to be far more inscrutable and complex. Layers upon layers, and actions that couldn't be directly linked to one's goal. That was the trick.

Who, for example, would ever guess that Mary had put herself in this position to achieve certain ends involving her friends?

No one. And since she was alone, she allowed herself a brief, gleeful laugh. A word whispered here, a glance there, a pathetic-sounding sigh . . . just a little nudge . . . was all it took. No one, but no one, would ever guess what she was causing here.

Linus's thoughts were not nearly so gleeful. In fact, they weren't even remotely happy. The mob. What should have been a simple, straightforward, and profitable business transaction had become a mess. The mob.

The news was, of course, all over Paradise Beach. And if even half of what he'd heard about that little burg was true, that meant the natives would get restless very soon, and very loudly.

The campaign to save that stupid dog had made the news all over the state, and the protests and hullabaloo about the sea monster egg had made the national and international news. How long before the citizens of Paradise Beach came up with a protest symbol and mocked him? How long before he had FBI agents knocking on his door about inviting the mob to that stupid town?

He shook his head and took another sip of his Irish cappuccino. The bar was almost empty, and there was no one left who was worth impressing, so he ought to ditch his drink and order something real, like a banana daiquiri with an umbrella. But on the off chance that someone important might walk in, he went on sipping Irish cappuccino and trying to hide his disgust while he thought things through.

He hadn't the resources to stop the mob. That Dan guy had goons. And more goons available at the touch of a cell phone, no doubt. Linus was goonless, and trying to recruit help from his friends had left him friendless as well. He didn't have the money to hire any goons. Nor even to hire any friends. Which pretty much left him all alone.

He ordered another Irish cappuccino and thumped his chin onto his hand, staring glumly at the mirrored liquor shelves behind the bar. *Think*, he told himself, noting that the third glass of this swill didn't taste all that bad. He could get used to it if he had to. What would Donald

Trump do here? Nah, he couldn't get out of this by writing a book and making a board game. So okay, what would Bill Gates do? Nope, that wouldn't work either. That's what the mob was doing, after all. What would Malcolm Forbes do? No, he couldn't afford tickets for a cruise, and it wasn't even his birthday. He considered Ivan Boesky and Michael Milkin and quickly nixed that idea. Hostile takeovers, it seemed, usually landed people in prison, and while people there would want to know him, he didn't want to be known *that* way. And that was if he got lucky. Hostile takeovers of the mob usually led to cement overshoes and a short swimming lesson.

With no one else left to emulate, he finally asked the one question that seemed to have an answer.

What would Aunt Mary do?

As the idea began to form in his mind, he decided that he liked Irish cappuccino after all.

13

Erin tried to find it within her to laugh as she walked past city hall toward her shop. Colonel Albermarle, Welsh Fusiliers, retired, and his newly appointed, elderly Paradise Beach House Guards—a.k.a. the Dustbuster Brigade—were absurd by any standard. Black Bermuda shorts, black shirts, black ties, black lightweight suit jackets, black socks, black shoes, black pith helmets. It was, she thought, what a sartorially challenged mobster might have worn in India back in the forties. If the mobster were British and watched too many American movies.

She ought to be laughing, she realized. And yet all she could feel was glum. That kiss on the beach had put everything in sharp focus. She knew two things to be certain. She wanted more of those kisses from Richard. And she would never let herself kiss him again. She had too much else on her plate, what with Seana falling head over heels for Dan, and the mess she'd created in trying to help Mary. Richard the Third might be well-intentioned, but in the end he was a distraction from the larger concern of how to rescue Mary. But even more than that, she didn't want to get burned again. Never again.

She opened the door of her shop to find Seana gabbing away on the phone. It didn't take an NSA computer to figure out who was on the other end of the line. Seana was dressed to the nines and beyond again today, with the glitter of a rhinestone choker around her neck. She was dressing the role of gangster's moll.

"If it's not too much trouble, Seana, I was thinking that maybe I'd save the business phone for *business* today?"

Seana scowled at Erin. "I gotta go, sweets," she said into the phone. "Goneril is here. You know, from *King Lear*? Wow, a man of culture! See you tonight? Oh, okay. Business. Well, take care of business, and I'll see you after, then."

She hung up the phone and turned on Erin. "Why is it you're constantly interfering in my love life? Don't blame me if your Chicken Little routine has frightened away Richard the Third. I'm not letting go of my man."

"Of course not. He'd have you whacked if you did."

"You don't know *anything* about him!" Seana said. "He's not like other gangsters."

The shame of it is that I know more than you, Erin

thought. *And you're right. He's not like other gangsters.* But if she told Seana, Seana would tell everyone, and the whole plan would come unglued. So there was no way to unravel this mess. Frustration overcame her. "You know, Seana, sometimes you have the maturity of a toddler."

With that she stormed into the back of the shop, plopped herself at her wheel, and began slamming clay onto it. Clay, at least, didn't throw surprises at her. It simply was. And that's what she needed right now. A heavy dose of is-ness.

She was halfway through drawing a pot when she noticed Seana at the door. One look at her sister's face told her she'd gone way too far.

"I love him, Erin. I know it's stupid and he's a bad man. Or maybe he's a good man in a bad business, or whatever. But I love him. So color me immature."

And that cut worse than anything. Truth was, Dan was a good man in a perfectly legitimate business. And Erin's web of lies—told in a worthy cause—meant she couldn't offer her sister that simple comfort now.

"And maybe you're right and I am immature," Seana said. "But I'm going to try to make this work anyway. Because no one's ever made me feel like Dan does. When he smiles, the sun shines brighter. When he hugs me, the ocean sparkles in the moonlight. When he kisses me, dolphins leap in play. So I'm going to try to make it work and if that's immature then I'll just be immature."

Seana's words were like a knife turning in Erin's heart. Erin could have easily said those same words about Richard. She could be saying them to him right now. Perhaps the only difference between her and her sister was the fact that when it came to matters of the heart, Seana knew no fear, and Erin knew nothing else. And much as she might try to cloak that fear in the mantle of mature, responsible thinking, the fact was that she was just plain scared.

"I'm sorry," she said. Then, before Seana could poke into any more of her weaknesses, she added, "And if it's okay, could you mind the front today? I need to work with my hands and not say anything to anyone for awhile."

Seana's face softened. "Sure, sis. I'll cover for you. You have a lot on your mind."

The kindness made Erin feel even worse. The whole world, it seemed, was determined to remind her of her every failing.

Richard shot to his feet. The courtroom around him was suddenly silent. "With all due respect to my learned opposing counsel, Your Honor, that's just absurd. To suggest that *Willingham* implies that a defendant who has made a potentially incriminating statement in a police interrogation room has waived his rights in the same way he would if he pled guilty in a courtroom is . . . well . . . it's just plain wrong. That interpretation would gut the Fifth and Sixth Amendments. And while that may be more convenient for the police and the state attorneys, when the government starts spitting on the Constitution we're all in trouble."

"Your Honor!" the state attorney shouted, but the judge was already banging his gavel.

"Mr. Wesley, that was dangerously close to contempt of court. I've known you to be a better lawyer than that, so I'm going to suggest that counsel for the state accept the apology you're about to offer and not file disciplinary charges with the bar. Have I made myself clear, Counsel?"

Richard took a deep breath and let it out slowly. "Yes, Your Honor." He turned to the cocky young lawyer at the prosecutor's table. "And I do apologize for my comments. Sometimes we say things we shouldn't in the heat of battle. I'm sure the learned prosecutor respects and protects our constitutional system."

The judge turned to the state attorney. "Well, Ms. Bennigan?"

"I accept Mr. Wesley's apology, Your Honor. As he said, heat of battle."

"Do either of you have any other *legal* arguments to make?" the judge asked. Both lawyers demurred. "In that case, I'll take the defendant's motion under consideration and have a ruling by the end of the week. Next case."

Richard walked out of the courtroom, fuming at himself. His mood got no better when Jared Holmes pulled at his sleeve.

"What the hell was *that*?" Holmes asked. "I have enough trouble without my lawyer pissing off the judge!"

"And if you'd learn to call a cab instead of driving home after a night on the town, you wouldn't be in this trouble," Richard said. "Now if you'll excuse me, I have another hearing in another courtroom."

"And maybe I'll find another lawyer," Holmes said.

"And maybe you should."

As he walked to the elevator, Richard silently kicked himself. Dumb. He'd heard in law school that it took seven positive impressions to overcome a single negative impression. If that was true, he'd just buried himself in Judge Paddington's court for a long, long time.

The fact was, he hadn't been thinking in there. He'd been reacting emotionally. And his clients didn't pay him to be emotional. *They* were emotional. They paid him to be calm and reasonable. Which he normally was . . . and would be now but for Erin.

He wanted to kick his own butt for his stupidity last night. Here he was, harboring suspicions that Erin had mob ties, yet he'd taken her to the beach for a romantic stroll and *kissed* her. Now didn't that take the cake for idiocy? And when he had kissed her, worse yet, he'd realized that he'd move heaven and earth to untangle her from her unsavory acquaintances. If they were her acquaintances.

And that was the other thing. The woman was bound and determined to let him know absolutely nothing about her, other than that she had a hot temper and a sister who was a gangster's girlfriend. How could he possibly be getting so tangled up emotionally. He wasn't supposed to be emotional. He was supposed to be a lawyer.

If he didn't watch it, he was going to wreck both his career and his life.

But then he thought of Erin's bright green eyes, and that absolutely wonderful sort-of-impish, sort-of-imperious smile of hers, and he knew he was a goner.

Well, he would have been if she hadn't made it so clear that *she* wasn't in any danger of becoming a goner. She'd pushed him away, saving him from himself, it seemed.

And never, ever in his life had he felt so damn confused.

He went through the next hearing on automatic pilot and called his office to say he was on his way to lunch. He wasn't hungry, but eating was better than thinking. Especially when all he could think about was an Irish Valkyrie who had him tied up in knots.

He was turning those thoughts over in his

mind when Dan Floorsheim walked into the restaurant.

"You don't mind if I join you," Dan said, in a tone that left no doubt as to what answer he expected.

Oh great, Richard thought. He couldn't escape this mess even in an out-of-the-way restaurant.

"I don't think I have a choice. So sure, I don't mind at all."

Dan sat, his two bodyguards taking the adjacent table and doing their very best version of a menacing hover.

"You don't think much of me, do you?" Dan asked.

Get it in gear, Richard thought. This might be his best opportunity to rescue Erin and Seana from this guy. "I respect the rule of law, not the rule of brute force," Richard said. "You act like you have power, but all you really have going for you is fear. A pretty sad way to make one's way through the world, if you ask me."

"I don't remember asking you," Dan said.

"Actually, what you said was, 'You don't think much of me, do you?'" Richard was suddenly in his element. He'd nailed more than one witness to the wall with his ability to remember conversations verbatim. "So you did ask, and I answered. Was there anything else, or may I finish my lunch now?"

"You're cocky," Dan said.

"It's easy to be cocky. I'm right."

"Well, right or not, this guy I know is still going to do some business here in town. If you get in the way of that, you could get hurt."

"I'll take my chances," Richard said coolly, wondering why the hell this guy felt a need to threaten him. "So what exactly did you want to accomplish with this little visit, other than a dose of intimidation?"

Dan scowled. Then sighed. Then folded a napkin into a bunch of squares, and unfolded it again.

Around bites of his sandwich, which was settling like lead in Richard's stomach, he watched the process. It didn't look very moblike.

"Well," Dan said. "Well. We got a little conflict of interest, Counselor."

"We do?"

"We do. We're dating sisters. That makes us practically family."

"Hmm." Now the sandwich felt like a ten-kiloton bomb in his stomach. "Uh . . . family's a little extreme, don't you think?"

"No, we're real big on family."

Oh, God, thought Rich as the bomb in his stomach exploded. Next thing he knew this crook was going to be asking for some blood ritual, then bruiting it all over Paradise Beach that the two of them were brothers. His legal career was going to sink. It was going to wash out on the next tide.

"Don't push it," he said. "We're nothing yet."

Dan smiled. "I heard otherwise."

"Well, you didn't hear the *rest* of it."

"So what *is* the rest of it?"

Like Rich was crazy enough to tell this guy that Erin had run from him in apparent fear? Or that he was racking his brain trying to find a way to disentangle the sisters from this turkey? Not likely. "Let's just say we're a *long* way from family."

Dan scowled. "I don't want you messing with my relationship with Seana."

"I wouldn't dream of it."

"And I don't want you telling Erin to mess with it."

"I would never do such a thing."

"How can I believe you?"

Not a blood oath, Richard thought. *No way!* "You'll just have to take my word."

"Not good enough. We need to share a bond."

"I don't want any bond with you!"

"Hey, a little prick with a needle. No big deal."

"Right. No big deal in a restaurant across from the courthouse, a restaurant that's full of lawyers who are already looking at me cockeyed because you're here with your goons, not to mention a couple of judges in the corner over there, and you want to make a blood oath?"

"It wouldn't bother them any," Dan said calmly. "From what I've heard, lawyers are a bloodsucking lot anyway."

"We suck green blood, not red. Forget it."

"Hmm. Maybe if I give you some money?"

Rich was beginning to feel his eyes bug out of his own head. He couldn't believe this two-bit friend of Erin's was putting him in this position. Just wait until he got his hands on that woman. He was going to rattle some sense into her if he had to tie her to the yardarm, threaten her with walking the plank, and hold her captive in Captiva for the next twenty years. "No!"

The word came out so loudly that at that point everyone in the restaurant turned to look.

"Well, if that's your final word on it, we'll just have to see how the dust settles," Dan said. He turned to his goons. "Let's go, boys. We have business to do."

Richard fumed as he tried to make a thorough study of the knickknacks on the wall after Dan left. The mob! He was in bed with the *mob*. Could things get any *worse*?

And at that moment, who else but Elise Bennigan, the state attorney he'd insulted in court not an hour ago, walked up to him.

"Who was that?" she asked.

"Just some guy I don't want to know," Richard said.

Gawd, he thought, *now I'm talking like a bad movie mobster!*

"Should I be interested?" Elise asked.

Rich could see the prosecutorial wheels turning in her head. The last thing on earth he wanted to do was turn Elise Bennigan and her wolves loose on Erin or her sister . . . and if the woman went after Dan, the sisters were bound to become involved. "Uh . . . no. I can handle him myself."

"Well, how about I check into his background?" Elise suggested. "Maybe he's got some wants and warrants."

"Don't bother. I already checked. He doesn't exist."

And that, thought Rich a moment later, was surely the biggest instance of foot-in-mouth he'd ever had. He'd asked himself if things could get any worse. They had.

"Erin, you have to see me."

The voice on the phone was remotely identifiable as Richard the Third. But only remotely. Part of her wanted to slam down the receiver in fright and keep him out of her life for good. The other part felt an instant concern for him. "What's wrong?"

"I've got to see you *now*."

"Well, the shop . . ."

"To hell with the shop. I've been stuck in court all afternoon, and all I can think of is how to keep your friend Dan out of jail."

"What?" Erin exclaimed the word in horrified disbelief. "Don't joke with me."

"I'm not joking. A certain state attorney picked up a folded napkin this afternoon and took it in for fingerprints. Dan folded the napkin. *You've got to see me now.*"

"I'm sure he's never been fingerprinted."

"I wouldn't bet on it. Cripes, these days you can't cash a check or get a job without being fingerprinted. I can already hear the warning sirens going off at the FBI. Now will you let me see you?"

"Ah, sure. Come on over." She wanted to see him. She didn't want to see him. She wanted to, she didn't want to, and why the hell didn't she just buy a bunch of daisies and sit around plucking the petals. *I want to, I don't want to. I want to, I don't want to.* A daisy might give her a better answer than her own brain would.

He arrived so soon that she figured he must have been calling from his cell phone practically in front of her store.

"We gotta get out of here," he said without preamble. "I don't want anybody walking in and overhearing this."

Erin stared at him in amazement. He was still in his perfectly tailored suit, obviously straight from court, but none of the polish was evident now. He looked rumpled, and his tie was loose and askew, and his eyes held the look of a man who'd just walked into a tiger's maw.

"Richard, I'm open until ten."

"Not tonight you're not." He flipped the sign on her door and pulled the plug on the neon Open sign. "This is more important than business."

"I don't see . . ."

"You will when I tell you what happened. Now get your handbag and come with me."

"Richard—"

"That does it." Without a word, he picked her up, slung her over his shoulder and carried her out of the shop. A moment later she was sitting in his BMW.

"Give me the keys so I can lock up for you," he said.

Bemused, she did so. Was it so wrong to like the masterful way he'd swept her up?

The feminist in her said it was terrible. The woman in her loved it. The feminist said she ought to roll down the window and scream that she was being kidnapped. The woman in her said to shut up and enjoy it. Of one thing, she was sure, however: no man had ever cared enough about her to toss her over his shoulder. Whether that was bad or good she couldn't begin to decide.

Moments later he jumped into the car beside her, tossing her both her keys and her handbag. "We're outta here," he said and hit the gas. Tires squealed on pavement.

"Am I being kidnapped? Where are you taking me?"

"I'm figuring this out as I go," he said.

"Okay, so *why* are you kidnapping me?"

He turned to her with a look of pure bafflement. "Because if I don't get out of this town for awhile, I'm going to go crazy. And if I don't take you with me, I'm going to go crazier. So . . . I'm kidnapping you."

"Should I be scared?"

Then, as if he'd undergone a complete personality change, a laugh escaped him. "Only if it turns you on."

14

Seana looked at Dan as if he'd lost his mind. "Why did you go to see Richard the Third? He's a lawyer! Are you *completely* crazy?"

"I didn't want him twisting Erin's arm to mess up our . . . what we're . . . this, uh, relationship."

"Oh." Seana's heart melted. All she could do was smile. A smile that would warm all of Alaska and Siberia besides.

Dan beamed, proud of himself.

"But you still don't want to mess around with the law," Seana added, shaking her finger at him. "You could get yourself arrested."

"I haven't done a thing to get arrested for."

Seana didn't believe that. She thought he was just trying to protect her, and again her heart melted. Dan was such a sweetie for a big-time crook.

Dan, sitting on the couch in his suite at the

Marriott, looked at his Lady Love and thought she was surely the sweetest person to ever walk the face of the earth. He loved the way she worried about him.

And he hated the way he was deceiving her. His secret was weighing on his heart like lead. He wondered if she'd ever be able to forgive him when he was able to tell her the truth. He wondered if she would find him less attractive when she found out he was only an actor. Which to a lot of people seemed like a wimpy profession, even if he was making a pilot for his own TV series as a detective. Which in turn reminded him that he still hadn't heard back from his agent on whether the network had bought the series, which meant it probably hadn't. Yet. He had to remain optimistic, however difficult it was at times. He'd waited more tables than he ever wanted to count.

"What?" Seana asked, a look of concern on her face.

"Oh, it's nothing. Just waiting to hear back from a guy about a business deal."

"I hope no one will get hurt," Seana said.

"Oh, I doubt that. Disappointed, maybe. But not hurt. It's a cutthroat business, but in the end everyone can go home."

"It doesn't look like that in the newspapers."

Oh, just tell *her*, Dan thought. *And end this charade.* But then what would she think of him? Was she attracted to Dan O'Doole the man, or Dan

Floorsheim the mobster? Was it the danger she craved?

"Well, newspapers don't get everything right." He paused. "Life happens and then people write about it. And what was real? What happened, or what was written?"

"I guess maybe they're both real in a way," Seana said. "It's just . . ."

He took her hands in his. "What?"

She studied his eyes for a moment, then withdrew her hands and looked away. "Do you have anything to drink?"

The withdrawal left him feeling wounded. "Sure. What would you like?"

She looked up into his eyes. "No, Dan. What would *you* like?"

Right now he didn't feel safe interpreting that question in its broadest sense. Even though he desperately wanted to. "A glass of ice water would be fine. But I have soda and tea in the fridge, and I can open a bottle of wine."

"Water is perfect," she said, rising and walking into the kitchenette.

He studied every move, every curve of her form, as she took down two glasses and set them on a tray, then added ice cubes from the freezer. She took two bottles of water from the fridge, poured each into a glass, and set the bottles on the tray, then turned. Her smile was . . . his heart caught in his throat. Dreamy. Beautiful. Open. This wasn't about glasses of water. This was about . . . what? What was that glow on her face? Was it echoed in his own smile? Was this moment beyond perfection real?

Seana picked up the tray and walked back into the room. Slowly, gracefully. Sinuously. Elegantly. With pride, but something more. As if their souls were drawing nearer with each step she took. She reached him and set the tray on a side table, picked up one of the glasses, and kissed the rim. She held out the glass to him and whispered.

"Thank you, Dan. For . . . being you."

For a man who made his living responding to the every flicker of feeling that passed between actors onstage, he suddenly found himself wondering what to feel. How to respond to so simple, yet so beautiful, an offering? For every fiber within him hummed with the certainty that if he accepted this glass of water, he would be accepting something far more.

The phone rang.

Jarred, he couldn't even move. Then with heavy reluctance, as if he were turning his back on some great miracle he might never see again, he picked up the receiver.

"Daniel?"

Oh gad. His *mother*!

"Yes?"

"Are you in some kind of trouble?"

More than you know, Mom. "No, everything's fine. Why do you ask?"

"Because one of your college friends just

called to ask me why a prosecutor was calling him. Asking about you. What have you gotten yourself into now, Daniel?"

Oh gad no!

It was Richard. He knew it. That little weasel had sicced the government on him!

"What's wrong?" Seana asked.

"Daniel?" his mother demanded.

"It's nothing," he said first to Seana, and then into the phone. "Look, I need to go."

"Who was that girl, Daniel?"

"I have to go now," he said firmly and hung up the phone. He turned to Seana, who was still standing there, holding out the glass of water. "I need to make some phone calls, Seana. I'm sorry, but I'll need privacy for this."

Her face fell. "I understand."

His heart felt like lead, every beat a struggle against the hole that was swallowing it. "Seana, I'm sorry. Can I call you tomorrow?"

"Yes. Tomorrow is fine." Her voice was wooden. She set the glass down on the tray and turned for the door. "Tomorrow is fine."

When the door closed, he dropped his head into his hands. What had Erin gotten him into? He picked up the phone and dialed her number. It was time to get out of this role before his life blew apart.

If this is kidnapping, Erin thought, *sign me up*. She sat on the veranda watching the seagulls and terns flock to the sugar sand beach to pick over the night's leavings.

"I ordered breakfast," Richard said, stepping out to join her. "Room service."

Yes, she thought. If this was kidnapping, sign her up. Richard had been a perfect gentleman after abducting her. They'd driven to Captiva, arriving in the late evening, and he'd swept her into a resort, ignoring her embarrassment as he checked them into a cottage with two bedrooms. Then, surprising her no end, he'd departed for his own room, leaving her to toss the night away in a king-size bed that felt huge and empty for some reason she told herself she couldn't understand. After all, hadn't he said that he would go crazy if she didn't come along? Only to put her up in her own room? Still, she was here, and he was here, and even if she absolutely, positively *was not* going to get involved with him, it was at least a nice break from the stress of the past few days.

She told herself she believed that, and smiled. "Sounds lovely. Truly lovely."

"As lovely as befits my Irish Valkyrie." He winked.

It's amazing how much he can say in a smile and a wink, Erin thought. Everything that words would have cluttered up. Everything her heart wanted to hear but her mind rebelled at. If life were reduced to that smile of his, that twinkle in his eyes as he winked, that gentle seduction of a single look, love would be so easy.

Love? Whoa. That was a word she wasn't ready to go anywhere near. Attraction, yes. Arousal, definitely. Captivity, for certain. But love? That was a noose over a bottomless pit.

But even as he winked and smiled, she had another sense, one that made sure she wouldn't give in to the romantic feelings this abduction was inspiring in her. She'd caught him giving her speculative looks as they'd driven down here last night, looks that seemed almost suspicious. And the more she thought about that, the more she wondered just what in the world Richard the Third was up to. Because it didn't quite seem like he was up to an ordinary abduction.

"Look at the birds gather," she said. Anything to change the subject. Any excuse to look away from that smile of his. "They come to pick over the shells that wash ashore with the morning tide."

He came to stand beside her and looked. "And every morning brings new hope. A fresh promise."

Damn him and his lawyer's gift for words! And if that weren't bad enough, he was so obviously reading her mind. One person in her head was enough. And damn him for looking so incredibly fetching in that white cotton shirt and black tennis shorts. She could see every ripple of muscle in his firm thighs as he sat. His hair, wet from the shower, glistened in the morning light. And those eyes. Eyes she could fall into forever.

"You look nice," she managed.

"Looks can be deceiving. Consider Albermarle's House Guards."

"They're not deceptive," Erin said with a smile. "They look absurd, and they are absurd."

He shook his head. "I don't know. I'll concede that they look absurd. But somehow when they put their minds to something, it seems to happen. Even if they have nothing to do with it."

"Isn't that always the way with life?" she asked. "We do our very best to make something happen, and screw it up royally. And if we're lucky it happens anyway."

He paused for a moment, considering. "Lucky? I don't know. I think we nudge the river and the river nudges us. And when it seems to work, it's usually because we've accepted where the river is taking us anyway."

Erin sighed. "That's awfully deep for seven in the morning on three hours' sleep."

He chuckled. "In my experience, deep conversations are best held on three hours' sleep. They sound so silly when you're fully functional."

"Maybe that's why there are so many barroom philosophers."

"Probably so."

Something had definitely happened within

him, she realized. He'd pulled back. Had she said something wrong? Done something wrong? Not said or done enough?

She reached over to gently touch his hand. "Richard?"

"Yes?"

"What are we doing here?"

"Well, lass," he said, trying to affect a piratical brogue, "I've taken you away. And we're waiting for the galley crew to serve us breakfast, before we hoist the main and set out for treasure."

"Mm. Sounds nice. And what is the galley bringing for breakfast? Gruel? Limes and salt fish?"

"I think this galley can do a bit better than that," he said. And, as if he had summoned the universe, there was a knock at the door. "That would be breakfast."

Breakfast was more than "a bit better than that."

Erin's eyes widened as the server lifted gleaming silver tops from the serving dishes. "Fresh strawberries and cream? Champagne? My my, Captain, but you do run a classy pirate ship."

He offered another of his patented winks. "If you can't pillage and ravish in style, why pillage and ravish at all?"

Her hunger was not the only appetite this performance had aroused. She felt a softening deep within her. "Shall we eat on the veranda?"

"It would be a shame to waste the cool of the morning inside. But when things get hotter . . ."

Yes. When things got hotter. Except she saw that shadow in his gaze again, and now she was absolutely certain that Richard had some ulterior motive in bringing her here. And the motive wasn't sex.

The mayor looked out his office window and smiled. This was how things ought to be. A personal house guard. No more Philistines at the gate. No. This was how things ought to have always been.

He was pondering whether he could slip a small stipend for Albermarle and his men into the city budget—nothing too pricey, of course, maybe enough to buy them coffee and doughnuts occasionally—when his secretary rang him. "Ted Wannamaker's here to see you."

Ted Wannamaker. The mayor hadn't talked to him in weeks. Not since Mary Todd's fiasco at the beach. If ever there was a man who was whipped, Ted was that man. If Mary said "Jump," Ted started changing shoes and gobbling vitamins.

"What does he want?" the mayor asked.

Ted spared her the problem of searching for an answer by opening the mayor's door and walking on in. "The mob is coming to town."

"They're already here," the mayor said. "And how was your vacation?"

"It wasn't a vacation. My sister was ill. And no," Ted said, "another mobster is flying in today. I'm picking him up at the airport in an hour."

"*More* mobsters?" hizzoner asked, feeling the world reel around him.

"Isn't that what I just said?"

The mayor spewed jelly donut–laden spittle. "But why are you telling me this?"

Ted shrugged. "You're the mayor. I thought you might want to know."

"And why are you picking him up?"

Ted suddenly grinned. "I invited him. We wouldn't want to make it easy for Linus to sell out the town, now would we?" With a nod of his head, he strode out.

Leaving the mayor to wipe jelly off his tie and reflect on the awful possibility that Paradise Beach might become the battleground for a mob war.

And all because some stupid judge thought Miss Mary was incompetent.

Troublesome, aggravating, a major public nuisance, yes. But incompetent?

He buzzed his secretary. "Sheila, get me the judge who is handling Mary Todd's competency case."

"Do you know how many judges there are in the courts around here?"

"I don't give a damn, Sheila. Find out and call him. I want to talk to him *today*."

She sniffed, a sound that was loud over the intercom. "See if I bring you doughnuts in the morning."

"I'll get them my damn self."

A click told him she'd gone away. Troublesome woman. His wife was right. He really should replace her.

15

"Let's go swimming," Richard said. Anything to get them out of this cottage before he fell over the edge and did something decidedly piratical, and decidedly unsafe, with a woman he wasn't sure he could trust. Watching her nibble strawberries had been a severe test of his self-control. "We both need some sun." And he needed an opportunity to seriously talk with her about Dan Floorsheim before he could go any further on this insane emotional tumble he was taking.

Disappointment flickered across her face, then gave way to concern. "Seana must be scared to death. She doesn't know where I am."

"Actually, I left a note in the shop for her." He wasn't totally inconsiderate. Even if he *was* wondering what kind of women he was hanging out with.

"Oh." She hesitated. "But . . . I have other things I need to keep an eye on."

"Somehow I think that will handle itself for a day or two." He wasn't sure he believed that, given the fact that he wasn't sure just what she was referring to. He was certainly beginning to feel that everything had gotten way, *way* out of hand. But "one catastrophe at a time" was his motto in lawyering and in life. Erin was the catastrophe he wanted to deal with at the moment.

A faint blush came to her cheeks. "Well, I can't go swimming without a bathing suit, and I really could use a change of clothes."

He waved a hand. "Mere trivialities, me fine Irish wench." Yeah, try to sound upbeat, as if everything were okay and they were just here for some fun in the sun.

"But dear sir, whatever am I to do?"

She was playing the captive for all it was worth, and he dearly would have loved to be able to join in with a free spirit. Instead, he felt a pang and gently took her hair in his hand to give it a soft tug. "Up with you, fair Irish Valkyrie. We're off to buy you a bathing suit which befits your personality."

Which was how they came to be safely out of the hotel room. Both of them, Richard realized, were feeling a little relieved at the postponement of certain, er, possibilities. He knew better than to rush his fences, and when he thought about it, dragging this lass off to Captiva last night had been rushing a bit. Hell, it had been more than rushing a bit, qualms or no qualms. It was a good time to pull back a bit on the reins and settle into an easier pace. At least for now.

The hotel shop proved to be so expensive that Erin blanched. Too bad, thought Richard. He could afford it, and that bright green thong bikini would have looked marvelous on her. Or maybe it was the thong that made her blanch. Pity.

So they wandered out to check out the shops in the area. Like most resort areas, you could spend a fortune on schlock or spend a fortune on good stuff, or get cheap schlock if you found a place far enough out of the way. On Captiva, there was no place out of the way. Anyway, he had his limits. The village was quaint in a lot of ways and had an ample number of places to buy swimsuits.

"Oh. My. Goodness." Richard looked at the shimmery gold bikini in the shop window. It wasn't so small as to be obscene, but it would definitely display her curves to maximum advantage. And, he thought, she deserved gold.

The thought gave him pause. Erin deserved gold, no doubt about it. The woman was magic on two legs. If she had been around, Paris would never have set sail for Troy, Homer would have had to make up another story, and no one would wonder about wooden horses in their parking lots. Okay, he thought, maybe that was a bit over the top. But damn, that woman was something. And everything in him yelled out, *Stop now, you fool!* He couldn't allow himself to forget his doubts in the romance of sea, sand and sun. Instead, he blurted, "That's the bathing suit for you. Fine as gold, you are."

To his amazement, she agreed. "At least it would cover me more than the others you've pointed at. And . . . it's cute."

"It's more than cute. It's golden magic. Like you."

Oops. He'd said too much. There were some thoughts that were better kept to one's self. Once they saw the light of day, even if only in an ephemeral word or two, there was a commitment.

Worse, Erin's smile left no doubt that she'd heard every word. *You're digging fast*, he thought. Instead, his mouth tumbled on. "Pure gold. For pure gold."

Oh gawd. And wasn't she blushing like a rose of Shannon? He needed to get his foot out of his mouth right now. Or find the brake.

But the brake wasn't working, and the downhill was getting steeper by the minute.

"Mr. Mayor," said a no-nonsense voice on the phone, "please hold for Judge Dipshot."

"Sure," he said. Although in hizzoner's world, people held for him, not the other way around. But right now he was on a mission, and he wasn't going to let that damn judge get away.

"Your Honor," the judge said.

"Your Honor," hizzoner replied.

"Okay, now we've dispensed with the hon-orifics. What do you want?"

The mayor had heard that judges were abrupt. This wasn't abrupt. This was a piano falling on you while you were strolling down a sidewalk. Kerplunk, kerplang, change of plans. "Well, Judge, we have a mess here in Paradise Beach. And I was wondering if—"

"I made my ruling on Miss Todd. What the hell kind of town do you run, that people are running bombers at the beaches?"

"That was only Mary. No one else has done it." No sooner were the words out of his mouth than the mayor realized how utterly lame that sounded. He stumbled on. "But Judge, we have bigger problems here. The kind of problems that fit people for cement overshoes."

There was a sputter at the other end of the line. "What are you talking about, Mayor?"

"We have an outbreak of mobsters in Paradise Beach."

"An outbreak of mobsters? What the hell? Is that some new kind of virus, like that Ebola thing?"

"I mean *mobster* mobsters! They're popping up everywhere, Judge. Guys with goons, and I have my own goons but—"

"Goons?"

"And there's more coming!"

"Mr. Mayor, may I ask you a question?"

Hizzoner thought about it for a moment. "Sure."

"What have you been drinking? And have you thought about rehab?"

The bathing suit was even more stunning on Erin than it had been on the mannequin. With every breath she drew, every step, every reach, every move, he had the image of liquid sunshine pouring through him. And another kind of liquid building.

The suit he'd bought for himself was more modest. He'd demurred when she had suggested a Speedo, and instead had settled on loose-fitting white trunks with navy blue stripes down the sides. Loose-fitting was a necessity at the moment. And damn that Irish wench if she didn't realize it.

"I need to get wet," she said with a deliciously wicked grin that left little doubt how many entendres she'd managed to squeeze into five words. And yet, at the same time, he saw a terrible vulnerability in her eyes behind that game, teasing grin. He felt as if he was being pulled in different directions all at once. Part of him wanted to protect her, part of him wanted to ravish her, and part of him wanted to head for the hills before the hurt came.

She rose and strode down to the surf, only a flash of a wink over her shoulder and the shimmy of her hips beckoning him to follow. She may as well have been dragging him by a chain. The thought flashed across his mind: who was kidnapping whom here? Still, he got up from the blanket and followed her down to the water, theorizing that it would be cold and thus . . . settling.

He had almost caught up to her when she put her arms over her head and plunged into the gentle surf. With long, easy strokes, she remained out of reach, laughing back at him. Trust him, a jogger, to have hooked up with a silkie. The woman swam as if she'd been born in the water, and his merely average crawl looked like flailing by comparison.

She finally turned and trod water with languid ease, the golden suit now glistening in the sunlight. Laughter rolled up from her belly. "Why Richard, how ever are you going to capture me if I can outswim you?"

Evidently she had forgotten all about her worries. And he was certainly willing to join her for this little while. Serious conversation could wait. He caught her leg as he drew close and pulled. "Brute force, my dear. Brute force."

She winked. "Promise?"

In a moment she was into his arms, their legs tangling as they cycled to stay afloat. He was captivated by the feel of her skin against his, the water letting them glide against each other. How had he forgotten how sensual it was, how erotic, to feel skin slip against skin in the water, or how erotic it was to feel the currents wafting around them?

She smiled, then, as she glanced over his shoulder, a look of concern passed over her face. "Richard, we're too far from shore. The tide."

He turned and looked at the distant beach. They were much farther from the beach than they should have been, for the little swimming they had done. Other beachgoers looked tiny on the snow white sand, and the hotel seemed awfully far away.

"Riptide," she said. "It's carrying us out." He automatically turned and started for shore, but she called out, "No, don't fight it. Follow me."

She began to swim, an easy, energy-saving sidestroke, parallel to the beach. He followed as best he could, finally finding a rhythm that kept pace with her. "It's still pushing us out," he said between breaths.

"Yes, it will, until we get out of the riptide. They're not usually very wide. We'll catch the incoming tide soon."

And as if by magic, her golden magic, he felt the change in the water around him. The beach no longer receded. Instead, it seemed to beckon. They turned toward shore, swimming lazily now, letting the ocean carry them home.

"Whew!" Erin said as she stepped up on the beach. "I haven't done that since . . ."

He watched the thought play over her face. Her eyes grew distant and soft. "What, Erin?"

"My dad taught me to swim," she said simply. "I don't even remember when. It seems like I could always go out into the ocean with him. We played tag with a dolphin once." She picked up a towel, scrubbing herself dry as if to scrub away the memories, and sat on the blanket.

This was a different side of her than he'd ever seen.

Something closed off in her face as she took a drink from a bottle of water. He searched for words. "Is he . . . did he?"

"On my nineteenth birthday. Him and mom. Car accident. I went from schoolgirl to responsible big sister in as long as it took for a drunk to swerve across the road."

"I'm sorry, Erin."

She looked at him. "Why? You didn't do it."

He nodded. "No, but I probably defended him in court. If not him in particular, someone like him."

"Did you ever get them off?" she asked.

Richard looked down at the sand on the blanket and brushed some away. "Yeah. Some of them. When the cops had messed up."

"Well, thank God you didn't have his case," she said simply. "I don't have to hate you for it."

"Did he get off?"

She picked up her towel. "I need to go shower off this salt."

He climbed off the blanket and folded it absently, watching her walk up the beach. The mood of earlier was lost as surely as if it had been punctured.

Damned riptide.

Ted stood in the airport, watching the people file off the incoming flight from Las Vegas. While he had no idea what Pete Lewis looked like, he recognized the wheeze. Lewis still stood ramrod straight, though probably not as tall as he had as a younger man. Penetrating blue eyes gleamed from beneath shaggy white brows.

Ted felt truly awkward for one of the few times in his life. At eighty he should have been past such things, especially with a man who had to be somewhere in his late nineties. But all he could feel was an angry stab of jealousy that this man had been Mary's beau first.

The man extended a hand. "Are you Ted?"

"And you must be Pete," Ted said, shaking the hand. Firm handshake still, too. "Welcome to Florida."

"Glad to be here."

"Did you . . . were you able to . . . take care of things?" Ted asked.

Pete nodded and patted his breast pocket. "Piece of cake. She won't have to worry about that nephew anymore. Always knew she belonged married. Now she is."

"I can't tell you how much this means to me," Ted said cautiously. "To us."

"No problem," Pete said. "I should've married her long ago."

Richard turned off the water and stepped out of the shower, toweling dry. Erin had hardly spoken a word since the beach, and that concerned him. In the first place, he didn't want her to sink into some hole of despair. But he also needed to get her to talk about the issue of Dan Floorsheim and her relationship with the mob. At this rate, he wasn't going to succeed.

Although he felt icky for even thinking about that right now. The sadness on her face when she'd spoken about her father had made him ache for her. He wanted to forget that he was a suspicious attorney, and just be a man for a while. But just being a man had gotten him into this fix, and he needed to remember that associating with known associates of the mob could kill his career and reputation.

But all of that seemed so unimportant beside the fact that Erin was hurting.

He dressed swiftly, then went to knock on the door of her room. A minute passed before she peeked out at him and let him in, and he felt his heart squeeze. She looked drawn, and old pain seemed to darken her eyes.

"Let's go play tourist," he said, as if he didn't

notice her mood. "Paint the town red and all that. The only thing I can promise is I won't get you arrested."

After a moment, her face lightened a little with something like gratitude. "Great," she said gamely. "You can show me all your pirate lairs."

His heart seemed to open up then, and he felt a wave of protectiveness that nearly deprived him of breath. Protectiveness and admiration for her spirit.

She was one hell of a Valkyrie.

16

Mary Todd was rarely fit to be tied. But rarely was not never, and this morning was an exception. Ted, almost always suave and debonair, felt as if he had stepped on a land mine.

"What were you *thinking*, Ted?" she said, rapping at the legs of his chair with her cane and forcing him to shift his own legs out of the way. "I can deal with Judge Dipshot and his finding of incompetence. That, at least, is temporary. But you went and got me *married*! Marriage is a life sentence!"

"You were supposed to be marrying *me*," Ted said. His voice quivered a bit. While this development had apparently left Mary feeling annoyed, it had left *him* feeling brokenhearted. For fifty years he'd been trying to persuade Mary to be his wife, and now that he'd stooped to getting her by hook or by crook, in order to protect her, the *crook* had gotten her.

Mary took another swipe at the legs of his chair. "Balderdash. Pete Lewis never did an honest thing in his life unless he could find a devious reason for it." She paused to smile. "Damn man taught me everything I know."

The smile at least lightened Ted's heart. He hadn't seen her smile in weeks. She had ignored all of the maneuvering and scheming that had been going on in town lately. But this, *this* had finally pushed her out of her bubble.

And down his throat. Her smile turned positively lethal, the smile he'd seen too many times. The kind of smile that launched bombers at the beach.

But then she rapped at the legs of his chair again, causing him to jump. "And *where*," she demanded, "do you get the lunatic notion that I'd be any happier being married to *you*?"

"Well," he said, clearing his throat, "we *have* dated these past fifty years."

"Apparently that was one of the biggest mistakes of my life! If I hadn't dated you, I wouldn't now be married to the biggest failure of a mobster ever to grace the criminal hall of fame!"

Ted was momentarily arrested. He blinked at Mary, wondering if his hearing was at last failing. "Failure of a mobster?" he repeated blankly.

"Oh, yes," Mary said tartly. "He made money on bootlegging primarily by looking the other way, although to hear him tell it, he was the mastermind. In his entire career, he never hurt so much as a fly. Basically, he was somebody's mascot."

"Oh." Ted was relieved, actually, although he would never admit it, because Mary would be displeased with him if she realized he was thankful she hadn't been hanging around with a *real* bad guy. He also felt a little more kindly toward Pete Lewis. "So he's all talk and no action?"

"Which," Mary said severely, "is at least fifty percent better than *you*. You have neither talk nor action!"

Ted put his hand to his heart. "Mary, I'm wounded." Although he wasn't, really. In truth, he was rather proud of the strict set of standards by which he lived, even if Mary scorned them. Although this latest little bit of bother he'd gotten himself into—namely, getting Pete Lewis to get a forged marriage certificate—had stretched his ethics to the breaking point and maybe even snapped a few of them.

"Okay, Mr. Wannabematchmaker. You started this mess. You figure out how to solve it."

"Mary—"

"Ted, it's time to prove yourself. You've avoided my schemes all these years, what with one excuse and another. But you kicked this little adventure into gear. So you'll have to deal with it." She put a hand over her chest. "I'm depressed, after all."

Ted was beginning to wonder whether she'd ever been depressed at all. This, he thought, could get interesting. Mary had snapped out of her funk, at least temporarily. And he had no illusions about her sitting around idly while he came to her rescue. No, the sensible course here was to *appear* to be trying to resolve things while staying out of her way as she *did* resolve them. It would help, of course, if he could keep her from getting herself committed in the process. Or, come to think of it, keep *himself* out of jail. Funny how that concern popped up so often when he was around Mary.

"Oh, and Ted? Not a word about this to anyone. The good folk of Paradise Beach are entangling themselves quite nicely in my absence. I'd hate to spoil their fun."

Or her own amusement, Ted thought. Yes, this could definitely get interesting. Especially since he was furious that Mary was now married to Pete Lewis. For once, the thought of things getting interesting didn't make him want to remove himself from the vicinity.

Dan O'Doole, a.k.a. Dan Floorsheim the mobster, was dining in solitary magnificence in the dining room at the Marriott. Seana wasn't speaking to him, primarily because she had found a note from Richard Haversham Wesley, III, a.k.a. Richard the Third, announcing that he had carried Erin off to Captiva for a few days.

Now it was Dan's humble opinion that escape in the company of a man she was so plainly attracted to, namely Richard the Third, would do Erin a world of good. His big mistake had been saying so.

Seana had erupted, putting Mt. Etna to shame. "Do her good? To be carried off by a *lawyer*?"

Dan, forgetting for the instant that he was supposed to be living on the wrong side of the law, had further compounded his error. "What's wrong with a lawyer?"

Seana had looked at him as if he'd lost his mind. "What *isn't* wrong with lawyers? Jeez, Dan, don't you read?"

In fact he'd played a lawyer—third Assistant District Attorney—in a movie once. Admittedly, he'd only had two lines. The first was asking if his boss, the star of the film, wanted coffee. The second was slapping a hand on the table and saying "Yes!" when the verdict came in. But he'd done a lot of research for the role regardless, and he'd liked the few lawyers he'd met. Of course, he couldn't tell her that.

"My *consigliere* is a good guy," Dan said lamely, belatedly remembering who she thought he was.

"So *call* him!" Seana said. "Right now. Get your soldiers or triggermen or goons or whatever you call them to *go down there and get my sister back*!"

"That wouldn't be prudent," Dan said. That statement didn't sound very mobbish. It sounded more lawyerish, truth be told.

"Prudent? My sister's being ravished by Richard the Third, and you're worried about prudence?"

My, how her eyes did sparkle when she was enraged. A man could fall in love with those eyes. He might not live to regret it, but he could definitely fall in love with them anyway. But right now he had to scramble for a way to convince her that his mighty minions—of which he had none—couldn't go racing to Erin's rescue because it would be stupid. Because if he couldn't convince her of that, she was either going to be very angry with him, or she was going to head off and try to do it on her own.

"You know, Seana, we didn't get as big as we are by using power on a whim. We have to be careful."

"Oh horse patootie!" Seana spat. "You guys got as big as you are during Prohibition, and the government supported and protected you until the early 1960s. I may be only twenty-one, but I have seen *The Valachi Papers*. You have to be careful because the FBI and everyone else is looking for you now."

It was sad, he thought, that his girlfriend knew more about the mob than he did. If Erin hadn't made it sound like such a lark of a role, he'd have done more research. He made a note to never again make that mistake.

"I don't know what my grandfathers and their

fathers did. All I know is that *now* we can't just charge off and kidnap your sister on a whim."

She put her hands on her hips and glared. "*Richard* kidnapped her on a whim!"

"Yes, but if we kidnap her back, it could get messy."

"Dueling Kidnappings" did not sound like a tune he wanted to play. Especially when he was just an actor pretending to be a tough guy.

"So you're a wimp after all!" Seana said. "A man with power who's afraid to use it for what he knows is right."

With that, she spun on her heel and stormed out, leaving him to wonder how he could ever explain. And wondering how he had ever got himself into such a lose-lose situation. Oh yeah, Erin.

And thus he found himself eating alone when a tall, older gentleman caught his eye across the dining room, then wheezed.

Dan froze, fork halfway to his mouth—not that he was tasting a thing. Something about the guy seemed familiar. Something . . .

Then Dan realized that they were dressed exactly the same, in dark suits, black shirts, gold cuff links. The only difference was that while Dan wore a black necktie, the other guy wore a white one. And since Dan knew there was only one actor in the room, his stomach lurched.

Oh, cripes, Dan thought, and he began to won-

der how fast he could exit the room. He tried to
catch the waiter's eye so he could sign the bill,
but of course the waiter decided at that moment
to drool over a blonde customer in a low-cut
dress.

And the wheezy guy's eyes never left him.
The hackles on the back of Dan's neck began to
rise. This was not good. Playing a mobster was
one thing. Actually running into one was another thing altogether.

Then the wheezy guy wiggled a finger at him,
a finger that said, "Come here."

Dan wondered if that was an offer he could refuse. Or if he dared to. Which would be worse,
running as if he had something to hide? Which he
did. Or getting within two feet of a trigger man?

Then it occurred to him that if *he* had bodyguards, so would the wheezy guy, and they'd
only catch him and staple him to the wall if he
tried to leave. Dan swallowed hard and wished
Erin to the devil, and Seana and her temper
along with her. Damn Irish vixens. His legs feeling leaden, he rose and walked over.

"Pete Lewis," the other man wheezed. "And
you must be Dan Floorsheim."

Oh God! The man knew him already! Closing
his eyes, Dan reached for his best Brando, figuring that letting the wheezer know he was scared
would be a big mistake.

"Yes. From New York."

"Ha!" the man wheezed. "An actor working

in New York, that's what you are. But not to worry, son. Your secret is safe with me."

Shock rolled through Dan in hot and cold waves. Now he was as vulnerable as an ice cream cone lying on a Phoenix sidewalk. Now he didn't have even the implied threat of his pretend goons to shelter him. "How did you . . ." His throat clamped shut before he finished the sentence.

Pete smiled. It was a surprisingly kindly smile. "Dan, would you like to know what you had for breakfast yesterday? There isn't much we can't find out when we want to. And I wanted to."

"I'm at a disadvantage," Dan said, feeling a bit more secure, for reasons he couldn't possibly explain. Time to turn on the O'Doole charm. "And you are?"

"I'm a guy who *really* knows some guys," Pete said. "Isn't that how you put it?"

Dan could feel an unwelcome flush climbing his cheeks. "Umm, yes."

Pete shook his head, a slight laugh coming out like a cat coughing up a hair ball. "We haven't talked that way in years, Dan. If we ever did. But it sounds good. I might use it sometime."

Dan realized he had been stripped naked. Of course, as an actor, he sometimes had to get naked in front of hundreds of people. This guy was saying he would only be naked in front of *him*. Which might be a small blessing. On the other hand, it could be used for blackmail. It was *definitely* time for the big O'Doole charm.

"So how can I help you?" Dan said, turning on his best, warmest, most open smile.

"Just keep doing exactly what you're doing," Pete said. "Only do it more. Do you need more help? Money? Extras?"

"I have a couple of guys who stepped in once," Dan said. "But this is a low-budget production."

Pete smiled again. "Not anymore, it isn't. Call them back. And a couple more besides. Don't quibble too much about money with them. But quibble a little. I have money, but I do have limits." The old man rubbed his hands together. "We're going to have some fun, Danny O'Doole."

"Uh . . ." Dan paused a moment. Helping Erin help Mary was one thing, but this was the *real* mob. "What is it we're doing here, exactly?"

"You're going to act," Pete said. "And I'm going to win back an old love. Simple as that. No one gets hurt. Nothing illegal. No felonies, anyway. And what's a misdemeanor between friends?"

"Oh, about six months in jail," Dan answered.

Pete coughed up another hair ball. "I like you, son. I think we're going to get along just fine. Of course, you don't know me, you've never met me, we didn't have this conversation, and so on."

Dan looked around at the half-full dining room. "This is kind of a public place, Mr. Lewis."

"Just Pete is fine. And I wouldn't worry about

any of these old stiffs." Pete winked. "They won't talk. They won't have seen a thing."

As he rode up in the elevator, Dan considered how many ways there were of making Erin pay. That woman was definitely going to owe him. Huge. Next time he was between jobs he'd just take the Disney World gig. Playing a storybook character sounded like a dream after this.

"That mobster who's in town?" Sheila said to her boss. Evidently she'd picked up on his disgust over the call to the judge, because today she was wearing a teal top so tight she practically burst out of it, and a pair of stiletto heels better suited for a dark room in a dark club. Also, she bent over his desk as she spoke, giving him a view of cleavage as deep as the Grand Canyon.

"What about him?" the mayor asked irritably. He had promised himself he wouldn't give in to this again.

"Well, he met with another mobster at the Marriott dining room."

The mayor, who had decided he needed to diet and thus had bypassed the doughnuts this morning for a dozen low-fat cinnamon buns, almost choked. When did they start putting corners on buns? "How do you know that?" he asked, his voice smothered by the recalcitrant hunk of bun, caught somewhere halfway down.

"I saw them."

"And when did you become a judge of who's a mobster and who's not?"

"Who else wears black suits and black shirts in *this* climate?"

The mayor, who was sporting a bird of paradise shirt and olive chinos, with orange flip-flops, had to admit she might be right. But he didn't want to tell her that. He still hadn't forgiven her for her insurrection the other day.

"And what were you doing in the Marriott dining room?"

Sheila tossed her hair over one shoulder with a flick of her head. "I had a date."

"Who's the lucky guy?" hizzoner asked. What he really meant was, *Who do I need to run out of town,* but of course he couldn't say that.

"No one you know," she answered. "He doesn't have frosting on his tie, though."

The mayor *harrumphed*. He was definitely going to have to fire this girl. Or dump his wife and marry her. One or the other. This . . . this would not do.

"So what did this other mobster look like?" the mayor asked. "In case I want to invite him over for coffee or some such."

The look on her face told him she thought that possibility to be unlikely in the extreme. Still, she made a point of leaning forward as she answered. "He was old. Wheezed a lot. Seemed nice. Kinda cute, too."

Cute? *Cute?* This was insufferable.

"That would be Ted Wannamaker's friend."

"You know about him?" Sheila asked, as if genuinely astonished that he knew anything except where his candy stash was hidden in his desk.

Ah, to be one up on her, just this once. Never mind that it left him a few hundred points down. It was a start.

"Sheila, I'm the mayor of Paradise Beach. It's my job to know."

"Well congratulations, Mr. Mayor," she said, turning to walk to the door. She paused in the doorway, turned her face back to him, and smiled. "You finally figured that part out, anyway."

Insufferable. He'd have to marry her. It was as simple as that.

Well, it would have been simple except for his wife. The mayor sighed and gave up on the dream. He rather liked his face arranged the way it was now.

17

Night was falling over Captiva. Streamers of red cloud streaked the west against a darkening sky. The beach was quiet, deserted, the only sound the steady lapping of the waves off the Gulf of Mexico. Magic was settling over the world, the magic of night and water, and emerging stars.

Richard and Erin sat on a blanket and watched night fall. They were sitting so close that their shoulders brushed, but all day, as they'd wandered around Captiva, they'd carefully avoided getting too close.

Romantic without romance, Erin found herself thinking almost sadly. She'd wanted to be abducted by a pirate and found herself instead with a gentleman. Too bad. It would have been fun to be with a pirate, and pirates weren't anywhere near as dangerous to her heart as a gentleman might be.

A gentleman who could hint at dangerous

things, yet dangle himself just ever so slightly out of reach, so that she felt a building impatience in herself. An impatience she couldn't remember ever having felt except on her first date wondering if the boy was ever going to kiss her.

But Richard made her feel those dangerous things, and the more so for having been so perfectly perfect all day. If he had come on to her at all, she would have locked down immediately. She would have done so out of self-defense.

But he hadn't. So instead she was sitting here feeling like a girl on her first date, wondering if the boy would even touch her hand.

And willing herself to forget, for now, that she had a secret that was apt to blow up in her face as soon as Richard learned about it. For all he reminded her of a pirate, she'd already figured out that he wasn't keen on deception. In fact, she'd found he was the most honest person she'd ever known.

But it had been such a relaxing day otherwise. They'd talked and laughed, but only about inconsequential things. Paradise Beach and all the problems there seemed so far away now. Relaxation was filling her heart, even if every cell in her body seemed poised with anticipation.

"I wish sunsets lasted longer," Richard said.

"Me, too." The previously bright red streamers of cloud were becoming a darker, duller red now. The water, too, was darkening, the last of the blue turning to black, except for a few sparkles of red from the clouds above.

"Have you ever listened to *Bolero*?" Richard asked.

"Yes, of course. Why?"

"Well . . ." he hesitated. "The view reminds me of it."

"How so? I always thought of it as a driving, pushing piece, not quiet like this."

"It's the colors that remind me of it."

Curious, she turned to look at him. She could still read his face, but not for much longer.

He shrugged one shoulder. "I have this thing . . . I think maybe it's called synesthesia, but I'm not sure. Anyway, I don't just hear music and feel it emotionally. I see it as colors. And *Bolero* is all blacks and shades of red. With maybe a bit of deep purple in it. So . . . this reminds me of it."

"I can't imagine what that must be like."

He laughed. "All I can say is, if the music gets too complicated, the colors can wear me out. Or make me feel jarred. I don't know how to explain it. Well, maybe I do. You know how dissonant sounds can wear on you?"

Erin nodded.

"Well, dissonant colors wear on me in the same way. So I can't really say it's complicated music I have trouble with as much as it's music that makes dissonant colors for me."

"Wow, that must be something else."

"I don't know. I've lived with it all my life. It was weird for me when I discovered that everybody doesn't do that. But anyway, that's why the sunset tonight reminded me of *Bolero*. It was so much like the colors I see when I hear that music."

"I find *Bolero* to be sexy."

A leprechaun must have seized her mouth, because surely, *surely* she had never meant to say that. Why, those words hadn't even so much as crossed her mind!

Thank goodness there was almost no light left, because he couldn't see her fiery blush. Or if he did, it could be blamed on the dying ruddiness of the sunset.

But suddenly her gentleman friend turned back into the pirate. She could see that wicked grin even in the night.

"Really?" he asked.

She couldn't answer. Something had stopped up her throat, clogging it completely.

That grin was coming closer ... closer. ... Then she nearly jumped when she felt his hand cup the back of her neck, sliding so smoothly beneath her hair. The brush of his warm fingertips sent chills of sheer pleasure running down her back. Her heart almost seemed to stop.

Caught between his hand and his mouth, with his mouth coming closer, Erin felt as if she ought to panic. But panic refused to rise in her, refused to even make a prickle in her psyche. All she could feel was the touch of Richard's hand, and the sizzling hunger that leapt through her mind, body and soul.

Then his lips touched hers. A gentle, warm touch, almost comforting, and even distant thoughts of resistance evaporated into the night. Here and now were the only moments that mattered. The only time that existed.

His breath was warm, still faintly scented with the wine they had had at dinner. In and of itself, his breath was a caress, the merest brush over her cheeks as his mouth opened a little and tenderly brushed against her lips.

Never had the touch of a man's mouth promised so much and offered so little. It was a teasing touch, and she barely realized that she leaned into it, wanting more.

Then he took her. In an instant he went from suggesting to taking. His hand tightened on her neck, pulling her toward him, holding her prisoner. His mouth took hers, demanding and claiming. His tongue penetrated her, searching out her secrets, promising delights even as he seemed to take what he wanted.

Erin was lost, awhirl on a tornado of newly awakened needs. Not even his hand holding her to him was enough. She wanted him to take all of her, to claim her every secret, to give her no chance to think or object, or be rational. She wanted to be swept away by his mastery.

And he was doing just that. His mouth left hers, trailing over her cheek as if he wanted to devour her, his breath in her ear making her shiver with pleasure. Past her ear, down to her neck, he began to nip her, little bites of pain/pleasure that made her gasp for air and try to let her head sag back so he could have more of her.

But his hand never released her head, and somehow, someway, she was lying on the blanket on her back. His body half covered hers, letting her know there was no escape. Nor did she want any. All she wanted was for him to abduct her, taking her away from all thought and reason.

And it seemed he was going to do just that.

His hand slipped up beneath her shirt, finding her breast and squeezing as if he owned it. Nothing timorous, no touch that asked permission, just complete possession.

Thrills danced along her nerve endings as he kneaded her flesh through the thin fabric of her bra. Her body was heavy with the weight of longing, and desire made her throb deeply between her legs. She felt owned and she wanted to be owned.

Just, please, don't . . . let . . . him . . . stop!

And then it happened. All of a sudden he was gone, rolling away, lying beside her. Stunned, she couldn't move as she tried to reclaim her sense of place and time.

"Damn" he said, panting. "Damn."

She felt almost physically wounded by his absence. Her mind teetered, trying to grasp onto even one ephemeral straw of control and clear thought. But she ached. She hurt. She felt as if some part of her had been ripped out.

And she still throbbed for him.

"Damn," he said again.

Suddenly he was on his feet. Bending over, he tugged her up and grabbed the blanket, barely pausing to shake the sand out of it before he tossed it over his shoulder. Still holding her hand in a viselike grip, he urged her back along the beach toward the hotel.

She managed to walk, although she had no idea how. Deep inside her, shock was starting to give way to something equally strong, something very much like fury.

"Dammit!" she burst out.

"Yeah," he said. "I'm sorry."

"Sorry? *Sorry?*" She yanked her hand out of his and felt the worst urge to slap his face. "Do you think *sorry* even begins to cover it?"

He stopped and faced her. "What the hell is eating *you*?"

"I might ask you the same question!"

"For Pete's sake, Erin, we can't do that on the beach! Do you want to get arrested? Or maybe become a sideshow for a bunch of teenagers?"

Her jaw dropped. She hadn't even thought of that. Horror filled her as she realized how much she had revealed to him through that. And feeling totally exposed and vulnerable emotionally did nothing to ease her temper. *Stupid, stupid, stupid*, she thought as she turned on her heel and stormed toward the hotel.

"Erin?"

She didn't want to look back at him. She didn't want to see the light of knowledge in his eyes, knowledge that he'd been able to make her forget everything except him. It was too humiliating. Never in her life had anyone done that before, and now that someone had, she realized that she really didn't like it. She didn't *want* to be out of control. Ever.

She could hear him right behind her, pacing her step for step, which meant she wasn't going to be able to escape him. She didn't trust him enough to believe he wouldn't use what he now knew to hurt her.

Part of her realized she was being unfair to him, but men had been nothing but a source of pain in her life, and she wasn't prepared to believe that Richard was any different from the rest of the testosterone-based life-forms that wandered the planet wreaking havoc on the lives of women. If they weren't slaughtering deer or some other helpless animal, they were slaughtering women's hearts.

"Erin?"

He was now beside her. She wished a huge wave would come out of the Gulf of Mexico and sweep him away.

"Erin, what is your problem? I was just trying to protect you. Well, both of us."

At the end of this touching statement, his voice took on the hint of a laugh, and she could imagine that piratical smile of his without even looking. "Drop dead."

"Not today, thanks." Again he sounded amused. "Look, I just wanted us to go back to the hotel where we'd be private."

"Huh."

"Hmm." He was silent for a minute, while their rapid steps brought them closer to the hotel. "You wouldn't want sand in all your delicate parts, either."

She couldn't believe he had mentioned *that*. Her hands clenched into fists, but she controlled the impulse to give it to him.

"I mean . . ." he hesitated. "Well, you know, it's supposed to be romantic to make love on a beach, but there's all that sand, and people could come by, and the cops might take an interest. It's worse even than making love in a hayloft. Do you have any idea how that stuff prickles?"

"When in your life have you ever been in a hayloft?" she snapped.

"Trust me, I have been. I was sixteen and Gretel was—"

"Gretel? You're kidding." She did not want to be amused, but she couldn't help herself.

"Honest, that was her name. I was visiting my

grandfather up in Pennsylvania, and Gretel lived on the next farm over, and . . . well, suffice it to say, we didn't get very far. Hay is awful on bare skin."

"Hmph."

"Regardless, I was trying to protect you."

"Some pirate."

"Oh." He was silent for another hundred paces or so, until the hotel lights were beginning to illuminate the beach. "Trust me, the cabin on my ship would be better. So would the cottage."

"As if."

"You know, my fiery wench, you're a pain in the butt."

"Good."

And none of this did anything to ease her humiliation because it was so patently obvious that he knew, absolutely *knew*, that he could have had her on the beach, in the hayloft or in the middle of Gulf Boulevard at noon. God, this was so awful.

It was one thing to envision being swept away by a pirate; it was another thing for the pirate to know that was what she wanted. It was like putting a weapon in his hands.

She wouldn't even turn to look at him as they entered their cottage. She was afraid she'd notice again just how handsome he was. And that she'd feel the desire all over again, and lose her head, and invite him into her room.

No way. She was going to bid him a civil goodnight at the door, then get him to take her home tomorrow and forget that she ever knew him.

It was the only wise thing to do. But how the thought hurt!

Of course, it didn't work. Before she could do a thing, Richard took the key card from her and inserted it in the slot. Next thing she knew, he followed her right into her bedroom and closed the door behind them.

"Okay," he said, putting his hands on his devastatingly narrow hips, "what the hell bug bit you?"

As if she was going to tell him. Threats of torture wouldn't drag the truth out of her. She tightened her lips.

"Hmm," he said. "You're never this quiet."

She wanted to argue with him, but she refused to give him any opening at all. Folding her arms stubbornly, she simply looked at him.

"Okay," he said, "time to walk the plank."

Plank? What plank? What in the world was he talking about? He took a step toward her, and she instinctively took one back.

All of a sudden he threw up his hands, and any humor was gone from his face. "I'm not going to hurt you, you know. I don't do that. I was joking. And I wish you'd tell me what lit your fuse. I can't undo something I did unless I know what's wrong."

Her anger was beginning to seep away, mainly because her mind was starting to function more coolly now, and she realized, with a sharp twinge of embarrassment, how unfair she was being to him.

Her anger, after all, came not from anything *he'd* done but from her own fear. A fear that went back to boyfriends in the past. And she was mature enough to admit that Richard didn't deserve to be judged by what others had done.

But she still felt afraid of her own vulnerability. Terrified of it, were she to be honest with herself.

"I'm sorry," she said. "I'm sorry." She turned her back to him, hoping he would just accept the apology and go away.

An instant later, she felt his warm hands on her shoulders, gentle in the way they touched her.

"I scared you, didn't I?" he said.

Oh, God, he *knew*. She felt naked all over again.

"Well, I scared *myself*, too."

His words arrested her. Everything within her seemed to grow quiet and still. Could they both have as much at risk? It seemed that's exactly what he was saying. Even though it didn't seem possible.

Slowly, she turned and faced him, then felt his arms wrap around her, holding her tightly.

"It's okay," she heard him say. "It's okay, Erin."

She felt safe all of a sudden. Safer than she had felt in years. As if she was no longer alone in the big, bad world.

She sighed, wanting to lean into him even more and luxuriate in the feeling of being cared for.

But then he said something that destroyed the illusion completely.

"We need to talk," he said. "About your friend Dan."

And then the phone rang.

18

"*Dan* called? Did I hear that right?"

Rich glanced over as he made the exit for I-275, heading for the Sunshine Skyway Bridge. He was still speaking in single syllables.

Erin sighed beside him. "For the hundredth or two hundredth time, yes. Dan called."

Enough is enough, he thought as he plunked the quarters into the toll basket and headed up onto the bridge. Whatever this woman's secrets were, he intended to know them *before* they got back into the mess. She was up to something; that much was obvious. And it had to do with his client Mary Todd. And damn all his feelings and his hormones, he was tired of practicing law in a vacuum. Erin was going to talk. Now.

"Okay . . . spill it," he finally said. "What the hell is going on? I have to protect Mary, and I can't do it if the people on *my* side—*her* side—are hiding things."

Erin blanched and stared out the window, down at the bay beneath them. Rich reached over and touched the back of her hand, not recoiling as she flinched. He hadn't meant to come on *that* strong. He looked for another line of approach, but the only other line he could find went into dangerous waters. *Well*, he thought, *she's worth the risk.*

"Erin, if we're going to . . . if this is a . . . look, what we did and what we're doing and . . . you have to be honest with me. Please?"

Erin turned to face him. "You can't say it, can you?"

And that was the simple truth. He tried to escape into logical, legal mode. "Honesty is essential to any working relationship."

She smiled. It wasn't one of her million-watt smiles that made his heart skip. Instead, it was a sad, wistful smile. She looked out the windshield and mouthed, almost silently, "Working relationship."

"At the very least, Erin. So what's going on? Are you . . . look, I'm a lawyer and if you need to talk about an issue . . . it's confidential. If I'm representing you. Which I would. No matter what."

The words had tumbled out without his meaning to say them. But there it was. If she was involved with the mob, he'd stick by her. It had probably happened when she was too young to know or decide any better, regardless. Maybe she'd had to find a way to make a living to support her sister. Whatever . . . it didn't matter. He would stand by her. And having finally admitted that to himself, a calm swept over him.

"No matter what, Erin. Even if you're . . . connected . . . to . . . you know."

She turned to face him and laughed. Laughed, damnit!

"My God, Richard the Third, what are you imagining about me?"

He stammered. They were nearing the end of the bridge, and rather than continue to the barrier islands and toward home, he selected a turnoff and headed back over the Skyway. Up here it was as if they were suspended between heaven and earth, almost flying. The water, and the world with it, were far below and far away. It was the perfect place, the only place, to broach the truth.

"It's just that, well, you knowing Dan and . . . what he does . . . and you being so secretive . . . I don't know."

Her laughter spilled out like a spring rain. "Ohhhhh, my dear. I do know Dan. But not the way you think. Not at all the way you think."

"So what's going on, then?"

Erin mused. *He thought she was in the mob!* That would explain a whole lot about how he'd been acting. But, a working relationship? Would that do? Was that all there was. No, she thought, looking at his bewildered eyes. He was . . . she was . . . smitten. But would he still be smitten when he knew how conniving she'd been? Aye, there was the rub. She glanced down at the dashboard, then out the window, then back at him. She drew a deep breath and looked for words.

"I know Dan from college, Rich. We went to theater school together. He's an actor."

His jaw nearly landed in his lap. "What?"

"He's an actor, Rich. The one Seana told you about. Thug Number Seven?" She waited for a nod of recognition, then continued. "I asked him to play the role of a mobster. To stir things up. Get Mary's blood pumping again. I never imagined it'd go this far. Or that Seana would fall for him. I've made a mess. I don't know how Mary does these things. I tried to . . . it sounds so *simple* when she talks about it, y'know? But actually doing it . . ."

She fell silent, looking at him. The moment stretched on agonizingly. Finally she could bear no more. "Say *something!*"

Now it was Richard who laughed. He shook his head and fell silent for a moment. She followed his eyes, watching the yellow cables that rose like an inverted fan in the center of the bridge, holding them aloft.

"You are some piece of work, Erin."

She studied his face in profile. Was that a scowl? No. It was something else. She waited for him to continue. Finally, he turned to her, a devilish glint in his eyes. She could fall into those eyes forever.

"You tried to pull off a Mary Todd, huh?"

She nodded. "I'm not up to the task, though."

He chuckled. "Quite the contrary. I suspect Mary would be proud." He paused for a moment, taking the turnoff at the south end of the bridge this time, circling back toward home. "So Dan's an actor, huh?"

"Yes."

"And his bodyguards?"

"They're actors too."

"Interestinger and interestinger," he said.

He's not mad, at least, she thought. But what was turning in his mind? That was the question. Of course, there was the other shoe to drop. It wasn't *her* mess, not that one, but he'd have to do something about it regardless.

"There's more," she said cautiously. "Mary is married."

Rich chuckled. "Ted pulled it off. Son of a gun."

"Not exactly."

He turned. "What does 'not exactly' mean?"

No, that wasn't the look she wanted. Damn. "Umm . . . Mary's married to a mobster from Las Vegas. Apparently she has been for . . . well . . . a long, *long* time."

"Hmmm," Rich said, his face darkening.

"And he's here in town."

"Well, shit."

She nodded. "Exactly."

"And Dan told you all of this. Which means he heard it from—"

"Seana," she said.

"And Seana heard it from Mary?"

Erin nodded, a feeling of foreboding sinking her further into the car seat. "And if Seana knows, you can bet that everyone in Paradise Beach will know by the time we get there. If they don't already. So you can't tell Seana about Dan."

Richard smiled wickedly. "Oh, I wouldn't dream of it." He paused for a moment. "Oh yes. This has . . . possibilities."

Married! Linus thought. That was simply impossible. And to a mobster, no less. It was only a matter of time before her lawyer found out and went to court to transfer Mary's property to her . . . husband. Mobster husband. It was no longer a matter of ducking out of a deal he didn't want. He was stuck.

Or was he?

Mary was conniving. In his situation, Mary would connive. So . . . the real question was . . . how to get Mary unmarried.

How would Mary do that? Ideas swirled in his head. Hire a WWII bomber to attack this Pete Lewis guy she was married to? Have him abducted by aliens? None of those ideas seemed practical. Mary had connections all over Paradise Beach, and they could do her dirty work. He, on the other hand, had already tried to recruit his friends to make a run on Dan Floorsheim's mob and had struck out. Was it any more likely that they'd do anything to a Las Vegas mobster?

No, he'd have to handle this all on his own.

Or would he? Perhaps he could recruit some Paradise Beach helpers without them knowing they'd been recruited. Now *that* was Mary Todd-esque! A rumor. Yes, that was it. Gossip was practically an art form in Paradise Beach. A rumor would be just the ticket.

But what rumor?

This Pete Lewis guy had supposedly married Mary decades ago. Then they'd separated, obviously. And he was back, obviously, to steal her land from Linus. So what would it take to send him scurrying to divorce court, leaving Mary alone and leaving Linus with the property?

Mary's land was worth tens of millions. What kind of rumor would be a stronger motivation than that? It would have to be one hell of a whopper.

Linus sipped a cherry cappuccino, wrinkling his face in disgust at what was trendy today but drinking it anyway, as he ignored the swirling yuppie-wannabes at the bar. This would take some serious mulling over. But he knew, albeit mistakenly, that he was smart enough to find the best answer. Persistence, he told himself. That's the key to the whole ball game. And he would persist.

At least until a curvaceous blonde, who had cleavage enough to build a home in, sat down next to him.

"You're Linus Todd, aren't you?" she asked, batting her eyelashes.

Not that Linus noticed her eyelashes. He was too occupied with her bosom. "That's me," he said to her breasts. He'd seen those breasts before. "Have we met? You look familiar."

The woman extended her index finger and hooked it under his chin, lifting his face until their eyes met. "Yes, we have. I'm Sheila. Executive assistant to the Honorable Carl Woods, mayor of Paradise Beach. I showed you into his office."

"Ahh, yes," he said, his eyes slipping down to the creamy mounds below. "I remember."

She dug a lacquered, acrylic nail into the tender skin beneath his chin and tipped his head up again. "We need to talk, Linus."

"Ted. Ted, Ted, Ted, Ted, Ted."

Ted tried not to roll his eyes as he looked across Mary's dining room table at Pete Lewis. "Yes, Pete?"

"It's the garlic, Ted."

"Yes, Pete?"

"You have to crush it twice, Ted. Otherwise

you don't get enough garlic juice to give the dressing that pop you're looking for."

That pop you're *looking for*, Ted thought but did not say. Instead, he said "Pete. Pete, Pete, Pete, Pete, Pete. Thank you for that advice. I'll remember that next time I make salad, Pete."

"That's great, Ted."

Either Pete couldn't take a hint, or he enjoyed getting on Ted's nerves by using his name at the end of every sentence. On the whole, it didn't much matter. Either way, the situation was intolerable. Pete had not stopped at redecorating Mary's living room. Now he was changing her diet, nudging her toward an earlier bedtime, and generally redecorating her life.

Which rankled Ted for a couple of reasons. First, Mary had gone a lot of years making her own decisions, living by her own rules. And on the whole, she'd been a happy woman living that way. So Ted couldn't imagine that Pete's changes were helping her spirits any. And second, Ted was jealous. Quite simply, if anyone was going to rearrange Mary's life, it ought to be him. Not Pete Lewis, whom she had jettisoned years ago, and for good reason, Ted thought.

Still, the man was too damn genial to fight with. And there was the rub. How do you work yourself into a thoroughgoing jealous lather when you're dealing with a man whose courtesy and charm would melt snowballs at the North Pole?

Answer: you couldn't.

And dammit, Pete knew it. And played it for all it was worth. Which was a lot, to judge by his tastes in food, wine, and furniture.

To make matters worse, Mary sat there watching the two of them, her dark eyes darting back and forth, but saying not one word one way or the other. It was as if she were enjoying the game, which in fact she probably was. That would be her style, Ted thought. To throw a live mouse into a room full of cats, then stand back to see which cat got dinner. In this case, she was the mouse, and he and Pete were the cats. And there she sat, quiet as . . . well . . . as a mouse. Dammit again.

So the question was simple—the question males of his species had been asking themselves for eons when in the presence of other males of his species. How to get one up on the other guy?

"Pete. Pete, Pete, Pete, Pete, Pete."

"Ted. Ted, Ted, Ted, Ted . . . what?"

There was a time to be a wealthy retiree and the erstwhile-and-soon-to-be-again beau of Miss Mary Todd. And there was a time to once again be the Most Honorable Theodore Julian Wannamaker, onetime speaker of the Florida House of Representatives, then junior senator from the State of Florida, then senior senator from the State of Florida, Minority Whip during the brief interlude when the other party held sway, and finally three-term chairman of the Senate Intelligence Oversight Committee. He had overseen more dirty tricks than Pete Lewis had ever thought of. It was time to put some of them to use.

"So Pete, how is it, exactly, that you became the nation's oldest living mobster who's not in jail or in the Witness Protection Program?"

Pete made a show of stabbing a cherry tomato with his fork, then eating it, before replying. "Ted, it comes down to careful business practice."

Ted nodded. "You must be very careful, Pete. I mean, Pete, you've never even shown up on the FBI's Most Wanted List. That's in, what . . . sixty years?"

Pete went to stab another tomato, but it did a passing imitation of a politician being grilled about his affair with an intern, first ducking beneath the lettuce, then hiding amongst the olives, before finally being surrounded by a ring of onion and run to ground. By then Pete looked as if he didn't want it anymore. He looked up. "I flew below their radar."

Ted knew better. He'd contacted an old friend for whom "scruples" were not an issue, who had procured copies of Pete's FBI file. He knew the truth according to J. Edgar Hoover, the last FBI director to take even a passing interest in Peter Allen Lewis. And while that might not be the whole truth, it was at least a better starting point than Pete's own tacit claims to ill fame.

"You must have lived a very circumspect life, Pete. Why, even I have an FBI file."

That drew a look of intrigue from Mary, which suited Ted just fine. Never mind that Hoover and Co. had built and maintained dossiers on every elected official during the Cold War years. Never mind that his file contained nothing more than his family finances and a handful of entertaining but fictitious rumors that had arisen back when he'd refused to turn a blind eye to a scheme to sell arms in the Middle East to raise secret funds for a war in Central America. He suspected Mary would have a hearty laugh if she read the rumors. But he'd let those secrets hang for awhile.

"Ted, I learned early that the secret to maintaining power was not to be the king, but to be the man who could whisper in the king's ear. Kings come and go, Ted. But a trusted advisor can move from one king to another, without ever attracting attention."

"So you were the Clifford Clarke of la Cosa Nostra?"

Ted suppressed a chuckle at the momentary pause. Pete had never heard of Clifford Clarke, who had been a private advisor to Washington power players for four decades yet was little known outside the Beltway. Or, if he had heard the name, he didn't remember. Which was hardly surprising. Ted only knew Clarke because they'd been golfing buddies during the Nixon administration.

Pete recovered with aplomb. "Ted, you could say I was the E. F. Hutton. It wasn't my money, but when I talked . . . people listened."

"Or laughed," Ted said. The truer comparison, Ted knew, would be to the famed Philly Phanatic. Pete had never been part of the game, but he'd been an amusing mascot on the sidelines. Or so said J. Edgar.

Pete was starting to rile, but he covered it well. "Now Ted. Ted, Ted, Ted, Ted, Ted. That's not the most polite thing to say."

Ted smiled. "I'm sorry, Pete. I meant no offense." *But the truth hurts, doesn't it?* he thought. "I'm just trying to get to know you. And I thought you might want to catch Mary up on what you've been doing these past few decades. The story about your nephew and the blender was especially amusing."

Pete leveled his salad knife and his gaze. "If I didn't know better, Ted, I'd think you were trying to make a fool of me. Maybe even . . . interfere with my marriage to Mary here. But I know you wouldn't do something like that, would you, Ted?"

"Oh, of course not, Pete. I wouldn't dream of such a thing. You're too nice a guy to treat that way, Pete." Which might have been a compli-

ment to someone else, but Ted knew it was a
stinging rebuke to a wannabe-but-never-was
mobster.

Pete was about to answer when the doorbell
rang.

19

This is not good, Erin thought as she thought of the icy glares being fired across Mary's kitchen table. She could feel the tension even in the next room. Pete and Ted were not getting along. That couldn't be good for Mary, although somehow she looked cool, calm and collected amidst the urbane combat. As if she were in her element.

"You have to do something," she whispered to Rich. She had dragged him off into Mary's kitchen, on the pretense of making more coffee. Her face fell. "What a mess I've made. As if things weren't bad enough already."

"Why do you think you've made a mess?" Rich asked.

Erin stared at him wide-eyed. "Just look at them! They're like two bulls in a pasture, except that they're too old to do more than paw the ground and snort."

"And this is a problem, why?"

Damn him, she thought. Wasn't it obvious? "Because all this fighting can't be good for Mary."

Richard snickered. "If Paradise Beach were at peace, Mary would go around poking hornets' nests just for the entertainment value. Somehow, I think that old woman is enjoying this no end. In fact"—he paused a moment to scratch at his chin—"I'm beginning to wonder if maybe her whole depression isn't a put-on. But we'll reserve judgment on that for the time being."

He looked at her. "But rest assured you haven't made a mess. Just an . . . interesting situation."

"So what are you going to do about it?" she asked. For a moment, the thought gave her pause. Why should she expect him to solve it? Well, why not? He was the one who found it all so amusing, after all. "Do you have any ideas?"

"Oh, I think I could come up with something," Richard said. "In fact. . . ."

"Yes?"

He seemed far away for a moment, within his own thoughts. Then his eyes fixed on hers, and she saw that piratical glint emerge. "Oh yes. This could tie together quite nicely, I think."

"And none too soon," Erin said. "The coffee's done."

They returned to find Ted and Pete bristling over the historical character of Robert Kennedy.

"He was a mentor of mine, Pete, the driving

force behind the resolution of the Cuban missile crisis, and a damn fine poker player. Sirhan Sirhan denied this country a bright star."

"Ted, all I can say is this: you were never dragged before his committee and accused of Communist ties. The way he persecuted Jimmy was shameful. Shameful, Ted."

"Hoffa broke the law, Pete. Bobby was trying to root out organized crime."

"Ted, dear boy, organized crime is what made the Kennedys rich!"

Richard chuckled. "Isn't this the place where one of you is supposed to look condescendingly at the other and say 'I knew Bobby Kennedy, and you're no Bobby Kennedy'?"

Pete cast him a disparaging look. "And what would you know about the Kennedys, son? You were barely alive then."

Richard flashed his best courtroom smile. "I don't know much about the Kennedys, but I do know a spitting match when I see one. And as Mary's attorney, with a case pending which involves her state of mind, I do have a certain responsibility here."

Erin caught the flicker of a smile on Mary's face, offered when none of the men were looking. She too began to wonder if Richard was right. Wouldn't it be just like Mary to set this whole town a-tither just so she could watch the sparks fly? Had Mary manipulated *her*? More than once, probably. But what was Mary maneuvering Richard into? And whatever it was, was he up to the role?

"Ted and I are simply discussing history," Pete said. "Old men don't have much else to discuss."

"That's right," Ted agreed. "Pete has one way of seeing things, and I'm trying to expand his horizons. Never too old to learn, I say."

"When a man's through changing, he's through," Pete offered with a nod.

"And you can lead an old dog to water, but you can't trick him into drinking it," Richard said. "Or something like that. Look, gentlemen, this across-the-table sniping isn't going to accomplish anything. And we still have some legal issues to resolve. Such as whether Mary is really married, and if so, to whom, and if not, whether she's competent to handle her own affairs, or whether Paradise Beach falls into her nephew's hands."

"Nephews," Pete grunted disapprovingly.

Richard nodded. "Exactly. So, it's time to put our petty differences aside and do something constructive about this."

"And what might that be?" Ted asked.

Richard smiled. "It's time to settle this like grown-ups, Paradise Beach style. Where the cream rises to the top and gets churned into butter."

He paused for effect.

"Gentlemen, it's time to have a mob war."

"*What?*" Ted and Pete exclaimed in unison.

Erin choked on her coffee.

Mary rapped her cane on the table. "Perfect!"

"If you had suggested paving the streets of Paradise Beach with elephant dung, I couldn't have been more surprised," Erin said.

They'd driven back to check on her shop, and she was now making a show of poring over the books, checking on the sales Seana had made in her absence.

Richard gave her a satisfied smile. "Every once in a while, it's nice to surprise you."

"I wish you'd surprise me more often."

Ohhhh, do you? he thought. "I think I could find another surprise or two hovering in the back of my mind."

Erin looked at him, her eyes a mixture of anticipation and anxiety. "And what might they be, Richard the Third?"

He put his hand over hers, his thumb making tiny circles on the soft hollow of her wrist. "Perhaps we should retire to your place? Or mine?"

"Are you trying to seduce me, Richard?"

His thumb continued its maddening dance, even as his voice remained playful. "Your deduction of seduction is correct, Irish wench-goddess."

"Why, what do you have in mind, my rampaging pirate?" Her smile would melt steel, he thought. "You already tried kidnapping me. Life intervened."

His grip tightened on her wrist. "If at first you don't succeed . . ." He leaned forward until their lips met, drawing her lower lip into his mouth for a lingering moment, then finally releasing it. ". . . keep on sucking til you do succeed."

"A seduction of suction?" she offered with a giggle.

He tugged at her lip again. "A precise deduction."

Erin winced, then winked. "Might I recommend a reduction of suction?"

He backed away and looked at her. Another metal-melting, slightly pouty smile graced her lips. The fact was that her smile had been beckoning him ever since he'd announced the mob war at Mary's table. The kind of smile every man hoped to see just once in his life. The kind of smile that said *Come hither, now.*

"Okay, we're not going to fucktion . . . er . . . shit, now I can't stop doing it."

"Doing what?" she said, her fingertip tracing along his throat. "Making love like Dr. Seuss?"

He chuckled, even as the hair on his neck rose to her touch. "Would you, could you in the rain? In the tub, let's plug the drain?"

Now her tongue followed where her fingertips had been, dragging along his carotid artery, before she whispered in his ear, "I would not, could not in the rain. As for the tub, I'd not complain."

Her tongue was maddening, and he turned and placed a gentle bite on her earlobe. "But would you, could you with some pain?"

She let out a long, shuddering sigh. "Oh Richard dear, you fry my brain!"

Poetry yielded to rising passion as fingers and lips searched out new, ever more sensitive traces of skin to dance over. Richard let out a low moan. "Ummm . . . Erin, I don't think we're going to make it home."

"No, I don't think so. But we'd at least better lock the door. And maybe we should move into the back room. Unless you want us to drop out of sculpture and law and move into the live porn industry."

"We couldn't have that," he agreed. "I'll get the door."

And, for the second time in a week, he locked her door and flipped the sign in her door to Closed. This time, however, he wouldn't be driving her to Captiva. He wouldn't give either of them that much time to think about it. They both wanted . . . *needed* . . . this.

He walked into the back room and saw her sitting next to the pottery wheel, her shirt hanging open, the swell of her breasts rising and falling with every breath. He took a moment to admire her beauty. "Wow, you look delicious enough to eat."

Her knees slowly opened, the hem of her shorts rising a fraction. "So eat me, Mr. Pirate."

He moved toward her, slipping his polo shirt off and tossing it aside. She let out that indescribable shrug that sent her shirt tumbling off her shoulders and down her arms. By the time it fell in a puddle behind her stool, he was kneeling in front of her, his arms around her, reaching for the clasp of her bra while his lips sought out the heat at the hollow of her throat.

"Take me, Richard," she rasped. "Take me now."

He slid her bra off to reveal the breasts he had fantasized about for days. Full and creamy, with chocolate brown nipples that stood taut and erect within puckered areolae. His mouth slid lower, lower, into the hollow between her mounds, fingers still gliding over her back, tongue dancing at the first salty traces of perspiration that rose from those sheltered pores. He felt his own need surging, but this was a time to care for her, to take her as completely as a man could take a woman.

Her nails dragged over his back as he suckled between her breasts. "Oh please, Richard. Oh please."

The need in her voice egged on his teasing, and he began to kiss and nip in a wide circle around her left breast, his fingers mirroring the pattern on her right, circling, circling, knowing she needed him *there* and denying her that satisfaction, savoring the rising groans of raw sexual frustration that tore from her throat.

"Now, dammit! Now!"

He looked up into her smoky, lust-thickened eyes, the predator within him fully aroused now. "You said you wanted me to tie you to a mast and torture you. This is the best I can manage. So just . . . wait . . . deal with it . . . want it . . . need it . . . crave it . . . beg for it . . . until your soul shrieks within you . . . my captive goddess."

Her eyes flamed. "Oh yes! For you. Yes."

And he returned to her breasts, his other hand sliding down her belly, grazing around the curve of her navel, drifting lower until it grazed along the skin of her thigh beneath the hem of her shorts. His lips and fingers circled tighter, tighter, until they traced right at the edges of her areolae, that nubbed flesh dragging along the edges of his lips. And still he made her wait, as her hips rolled, her breath quickened, her hands clenched into fists at his back, her head fell backward, her eyes lolled open, her need pulsing and alive and consuming her whole.

Just as she must have thought he was about to settle onto her nipples, his kisses and fingers trailed up and away, to the soft skin of her shoulders, then slowly down her biceps, until the very tip of his tongue dabbed at the tender, hairless skin on the inside of her left elbow. The tip of his forefinger danced back and forth across her other inner elbow, knowing this was soft enough to almost tickle, forcing her to fight between the two sensations . . . tickling and raging sexual arousal.

Her fingers tightened in his hair. "Richard, you're making me crazy!"

He looked up at her face, his tongue still dappling on her skin. She was flushed with need, her eyes wild, lips parted, nostrils flaring. He winked. "Beg, darling. Beg for what you need."

"Oh Richard . . . please . . . *pleeaassee!*"

The smell of her arousal filled the room now, mixing with the smell of clay, both wet and baked, creating an intoxicating scent. He settled into the hollow of her arm and began to suckle at the skin, slowly, softly, not enough to hurt her, but enough that when he pulled away he had left behind the faintest pink mark, a perfect circle.

She tried to move her hand down to her pants, driven by raw animal lust toward a need that could no longer be denied, but he caught it in his own hand and looked up.

"Not yet, dear Erin. In my time. In my way."

He had never known such desires before. He wanted to take her completely, to control every nerve ending in her body, to make her scream with frustration before she screamed with ecstasy. And he could do it! The newfound power fueled his arousal like gasoline on open flame, one throbbing, pulsing, shuddering, rolling wave after another in his loins, and he realized he was hovering on the brink as well. That in teasing her beyond the point of all reason, he was doing the same to himself. He took a silent satisfaction in that as he knelt lower and began to kiss her calves, her thighs, her knees, feeling her leg muscles quivering around him, her entire body shuddering with unmet need and yet craving more, more, more.

Desire tore from her throat. "Ohhhh, Richard, I beg you . . . I'll do anything . . . *anything* . . . oh please . . . oh . . . now . . . please . . . I can't take any more . . . please!"

"Anything?" he asked, looking up into her eyes. His fingers continued their torturous dance on the backs of her calves. "That's a dangerous word, darling."

She looked at him, seeming to find a moment of focus. Her body stilled. Her face softened. "Anything, Richard. I. Am. Yours. Anything."

He smiled. "Stand up, sweetheart."

She shot to her feet, then wobbled, light-headed, and he held out a hand to steady her. Then, taking her shorts in his teeth, he slowly pulled them down, feeling the fabric slither over her long, trim, firm legs.

"Oh yes!" she growled, as his teeth now nipped at the front of her sodden panties and began to drag them down as well, slowly revealing the swell of her mound, nestled in the faintest wisps of curly hair, the pungent, musky scent of her arousal now released and filling his senses.

She stood naked, needy, her body alight with passion, making not the faintest attempt to cover

herself. She looked down, and her eyes locked
with his. "Richard Wesley . . . I . . . need . . . you."

Each word made him throb. "And have me
you shall, dear girl. Kneel, please, darling."

"Oh yes, *yesssssss!*"

She dropped to her knees over the stool,
breasts resting on it, thighs spread wide, hands
reaching back to part herself even further.

He pulled off his own shorts and underwear
and inched closer to her, his engorged member
pulsing with every heartbeat, already glistening
at the tip. Yes . . . take her he would . . . as the pirate she needed him to be. He felt the soft petals
of her outer labia on his tip, let her fingers steer
him for a moment, then slid into her. Slowly.
Teasingly. Knowing how much she needed him
by her attempts to thrust back upon him, but re-
straining her hips with his hands, forcing her to
accept it at his pace, until he felt the soft, pillowy
swell of her bottom against his belly.

"Mine," he whispered.

"Yours," she whispered back.

Their dance was languorous, not the frenzied
couplings he had known before or the full-
thrusting capture that she seemed to crave, and
which he in truth craved as well. He forced himself to take her slowly, feeling every slick, delicate moment, every pulse of her inner muscles,
every flicker of tension in her lower back and
buttocks as his hands glided over her skin. Seconds stretched into long, agonizing, blissful min-

utes as they rode together, her head thrown back with howls of pleasure, then turning to look at him with an incendiary blend of vulnerability and raw lust.

"Ohhh . . . touch . . . oh please, Richard . . . I need . . . touch me . . . there . . . please . . . I beg you . . . touch . . . your . . . woman."

Something in her words, her voice, her posture, her scent, her clenchings, her need pushed him over the last precipice of arousal. He reached beneath her, trapping that tiny nub between his fingertips and circling as his own passion exploded deep within her. Moments later, as the last blinding, numbing, light-headed tingles surged through him, he felt her flutter inside, each shuddering contraction mated to a ragged, gasping moan. Her joy lit him anew, and from somewhere deep within, a place he had dreamt could exist, he exploded yet again, his cries echoing hers, rising together, again and again, until his legs gave out and he lowered himself atop her, at the brink of consciousness, fighting for breath.

After a long, panting moment of skin slick against skin, he heard her whisper.

"Anything."

20

It seemed like hours later when she fully returned to planet Earth. It felt so *right* to be on her hands and knees, on the floor of her shop, propped over her stool, his body resting atop hers, listening to his breath. It was every pirate fantasy she'd ever had . . . captured . . . claimed . . . and yet cherished beyond all belief.

"Erin?" he whispered. "Are you okay?"

Okay? She was way beyond okay. "I could not be better," she sighed dreamily.

"I'm not too heavy?"

Ohhhh . . . wasn't that so like him. To take her this way, and yet to be so careful of her. "No, darling. You are just fine."

"That's good," he said with a soft laugh, his belly shaking against her back. "Because I don't think I can move."

"I don't want to move," she said simply.

She felt his hands settle over hers, his arms straightening a bit to support his weight, and for a moment she feared he would find a way to move regardless. A fear she would never have imagined swept through her. It was as if her body, her heart, her soul was not yet ready to break contact. She felt her wetness merged with his, trickling at the edge of her labia, and even then she did not want to move. She belonged here, with him, this way, and whatever else might be was simply part of being his.

Being his.

Yes, she was his. Totally. The thought both terrified her and filled her with incredible joy. To be . . . his. "Ohh . . . Richard."

"Yes, my Irish Valkyrie?"

"I have . . . never . . . ohhh . . . Richard."

He let out a soft sigh. "Neither have I, Erin. Neither have I."

As the endorphin rush of passion slipped away, she became aware of the hard floor beneath her knees, the hardness of the stool upon which her breasts were pressed by his weight. Part of her ached to be allowed up, and another part of her rebelled at the thought of asking him for release. His. Yes. His.

He seemed to sense her discomfort, however, and slowly made his way off of her to lie on the floor. She rolled off the stool onto the floor, curling in beside him, wanting to touch his face, to kiss him, to smother him in her love, yet wanting, needing him to invite that contact. She was his, and that need was . . . his.

"Richard . . . may I . . . I want to . . ." She couldn't finish the sentence. Didn't know how.

"What, darling?"

She blurted it out. "May I touch you?"

He smiled. It was a smile she could sink into for the rest of her life and feel totally, completely content. "Yes, sweet Erin Kelly. You may touch me."

Her heart leapt within her as her fingertips traced the curve of his smile, the relaxed softness of his face, the firm line of his jaw. Her lips sought out his and she sank into the kiss. Soft. Slow. Deep. Tender. Passionate. Giving. Willing.

A tiny squeak of a sigh emerged from her lips. "Oh. Thank you, Richard."

He looked into her eyes. "You're welcome, sweetheart. But . . . you can kiss me like that anytime your heart desires. Anytime."

Joy. She melted against him, her fingers roaming over his body, touching his skin for the first time. She giggled with delight when he arched at her touch to his nipples, and she settled her lips over them, kissing, tugging ever so softly. Her fingertips were entranced by the downy soft curls on his lower belly, trailing through them, combing, tousling. The hair of his inner thighs was finer, almost invisible in the semidarkness of the room, like tiny strands of silk caressing her nerve endings.

And his as well, it seemed, from the slowly shifting, rolling growth of his manhood. She looked up at his face, and saw . . . bliss.

"May I?" she asked, her voice lilting.

"Yes, you may," he whispered.

Her lips followed the trail her fingers had blazed, down over his flat abdomen, drinking in the scent from his tufts, until her lips touched the glistening tip of his stalk. Her tongue begin to flicker over it, knowing that she too could build his need, make him want, yet still wanting to please, to belong, to be in his strength. She dragged the first sighs from him before she took him in her mouth, tasting his salty essence mixed with her own musk, slowly drawing him deeper with firm, gentle suction, until she felt the first quivers in his belly.

"Erin?"

She scooted around and settled between his legs, then looked up at him. "Yes?"

His face hovered between loving sternness and dreamy bliss. "I like to be teased too."

She lowered her face and looked up at him, dark and sultry now, as her tongue dragged over his throbbing flesh. "Like this, Richard?"

"Ohhhh . . . perfect."

With his permission now, she set to the task of sharing his growing arousal, tongue flicking, then drawing the delicate flap of skin at the bottom of his cock into her mouth, soft nips around the head, then devouring him whole, then flick-

ing with her tongue again, never allowing any
sensation to continue long enough for him to
ride it.

She looked up again and saw his eyes closed,
brow furrowed, lips parted, and imagined what
she must have looked like mere minutes before,
when he was teasing her. He was . . . beautiful.
Her fingertips found that delicate skin beneath
his sac, and she traced her nails along it, down to
his rosebud, back up, back down, as her tongue
and teeth and lips worked their own magic up
above. She would push him as far as he wanted
to be pushed before letting him take her. For him.

Her own wetness reawakened, she pressed
her mound onto his knee, rocking gently to stir
her arousal as she teased, pleasured, touched,
shared. Finally his eyes clenched shut and his
head shook. His voice was a hoarse whisper.
"It's time, Erin."

She surprised herself by dipping her head in
obedience. "Yes, Richard."

She slithered up his body and straddled him,
carefully slipping him within her, leaning forward so as not to hurt him, clinging to him as his
arms wrapped around her. Their hips melded
and rocked together, kisses sprinkled at random
on whatever was available . . . necks, earlobes,
cheeks, chins, eyelids, hair, lips. Her nipples
dragged slowly over his as their passion
mounted. The orgasm crept up on her like a lion
in the brush, suddenly exploding into soul-

rending fireworks deep within her, her toes curling, lost once again to time and space. Distantly she felt him pulsing within her, and a fierce, willing pride spread through her.

She was his, yes. Totally.

But he was hers just as totally.

Together they rode the waves of passion until they had nothing left within them, reduced for the second time in an hour to limp, sated stillness.

"You are . . . amazing," he finally said.

She purred softly. "If that's true, it's because you bring out the amazing within me. What you make me feel. Oh. Wow."

His eyes glinted with piratical glee. "Yes, Erin. Oh. Wow."

They nestled together in the gathering darkness, immune to the hard floor, sheltered in each other's arms against a world once again turned mad by Mary Todd.

Even thinking of her name drew Erin out of her reverie. "Richard the Third?"

"Yes?"

"What are you going to do about this mob war?"

War councils have certainly changed since the old days, Pete thought. Not that he'd ever been to one. The Boss had never invited him. But he'd heard about them, second-or third-hand, from people who knew people.

Regardless, in the old days, what happened was that the Boss and a handful of senior under-bosses got together and decided they weren't making enough money, or they were simply fed up with being pestered by someone else's mob. They'd meet in the back room of a restaurant, or in a hotel room, with a couple of well-armed soldier guys outside to keep order. Once in awhile, there would be a turncoat in the meeting, and after a nice dinner they'd bludgeon him. Then they'd talk about who they were going to hit, and when, and make sure they had enough guys with guns. Every so often they'd need a specialist—an especially expert or vicious shooter, or someone who could wire up a car bomb, or whatever—but mostly it was just the Boss and his under-bosses and some soldiers outside the door.

Or so he'd been told.

What he'd *never* heard of was a council of war with *both* sides represented, and the mayor, and half the rest of the damn town, or so it seemed. Held in the front of a restaurant, with no soldiers outside. This wasn't a council of war. This was Apalachin, without the booze and the broads and the FBI to break up the party. Of course, he hadn't been at Apalachin either. By then he was out west, working for a guy who knew a guy who knew one of the senior under-bosses. That guy, he supposed, knew the Boss.

He dragged his mind back to the conversation. Now he was the Boss. At least the linguini was good.

"I don't want my town laid waste by a mob war," the mayor said.

The mayor had also ordered linguini with clam sauce, which was a lucky thing, because the drips of sauce flung by his clumsy attempts to twirl the linguini were slowly covering those hideous grinning flamingos on his cream-colored tie. How could a guy wear grinning pink flamingos with a canary yellow shirt under a purple suit? Come to think of it, how did a guy wear a purple suit at all? *He* would never be caught dead in a purple suit, *or* a canary yellow shirt, *or* a tie with grinning pink flamingos. There were limits.

"We're not planning to lay waste to the town," the lawyer said.

He had ordered the penne with prosciutto and shrimp. The guy had good taste, even if he was a lawyer. And a meddling lawyer at that. Why, Pete and Ted had been doing just fine. Ted had a lot to learn, sure, but Pete was the kind of guy who didn't mind teaching other people the right way to think. This, Pete thought, was progress. But the meddlesome lawyer at least recognized good food. The *a la page* look—navy blue suit, shirt, and tie—was a bit of a put-on, but he wore it well. And the guy seemed to have a head on his shoulders.

"What we're going to do," the lawyer continued, "is have a well-managed, safe, controlled war." He looked at Pete and Ted. "If Pete's mob wins, we all recognize his marriage with Mary, and Pete will act as trustee for her property. If Ted's mob wins, we ditch that phony marriage license, Pete moves out, Ted and Mary go on being . . . Ted and Mary . . . and we deal with Linus. That's the plan."

It was, Pete thought, an interesting plan. Mary liked it, which meant she had an angle in it somehow, but that was hardly surprising. Mary could find an angle in a puddle of olive oil.

"So okay," Pete finally wheezed, "how do we control this so nobody gets hurt?"

He'd never hurt anyone—the Boss had never wanted him to—and he didn't see any reason to start now.

"Yeah," the mayor added, twirling his linguini hard enough to camouflage another of those grinning pink monstrosities on his tie. "How do we make sure nobody gets hurt? And . . . what's in it for me?"

"There's another problem," Ted offered. "I don't *have* a mob."

"I'll go in with you," Dan said. "I have a couple of my guys here in town."

Pete suppressed a chuckle. Right. Now here was a guy with more than one iron in the fire. As a mobster, he wouldn't have lasted a minute. He was too damn obvious, for one thing, with the forties-look black suit, black tie, and black shirt.

He'd even found wide lapels. And he'd added a diamond stickpin in his lapel. Cubic zirconia, probably, but it looked impressive enough. At least he could screw up that sharklike look that the Boss used when it suited him, even if it was the look of a baby shark tagging around the edge of a feeding frenzy, waiting for the other sharks to drop a chunk of half-chewed tuna his way. Truth was, he was trying to impress that drop-dead-gorgeous Irish girl who was all the time hanging on him. That he'd managed to peel her off for the council of war showed more fortitude than Pete would have given him credit for. He was having the cannelloni formaggio.

Ted seemed to consider the offer the way a hungry man would consider a bowl of day-old squid. It was better than nothing, but jeez. Finally he nodded. "Sure. Thanks, Dan." He turned to the lawyer. "So that gives my side what . . . two guys?"

"Two guys," Dan agreed. "Plus me."

The mayor twirled his linguini yet again. "I think I could convince Colonel Albermarle to have the Paradise Beach House Guards join you, Ted."

Ted chuckled. "What are they going to do? Suck up Pete's guys in Dustbusters?"

"Actually," the lawyer said, "that's not a bad idea. For what I have in mind, Colonel Albermarle's men would do just fine."

"So that's what . . . ten guys on our side?" Dan asked.

Ted nodded. "Depending on how many of Albermarle's men are interested, yes. About that."

The lawyer turned to Pete. "How many guys do you have?"

Pete wheezed. This wasn't Apalachin. This was the Egyptians and Israelis at Camp David. "I can get eight or ten guys, if I make a couple of phone calls."

"They'll understand the rules?" the lawyer asked.

"They're good guys," Pete said. Truth was, the guys he had in mind were all retired and would welcome the opportunity to get some action. Six-Tooth Franco had always been up for a tussle, albeit with less than impressive results. Thus the six teeth. But hey, nobody was supposed to get hurt this time, right? "They'll do what I tell them to do."

"Okay," the lawyer said. "So that's eight or ten guys on each side. Now, the rules are, squirt bottles with ketchup. You get squirted, you're down."

"You've got to be kidding," Ted said, shaking his head.

Pete smiled. "I like it, Ted. My guys will play fair. Won't yours?"

"I can vouch for my two guys," Dan said.

"And I can't imagine the colonel's men having

a problem with that," the lawyer added. "They went after ghosts with Dustbusters, after all."

Ted threw up his hands. "Okay, sure. Squirt bottles with ketchup."

The mayor leaned forward, and his tie fell into his plate, erasing the last of the flamingos. "Just so nobody shoots me. I don't want to ruin my clothes."

21

Money.

That was what Linus told himself he was thinking about as he sat in the lobby of the Don Cesar waiting for Don Pete. He was thinking about money. Pete's mob was obviously going to win this war. And if Linus sided with Pete, then Linus would get a cut of the . . .

Money.

So said Sheila, and Sheila was the mayor's secretary, so she had to be smart. Smart enough to keep that dumb guy in office. Plus she talked smart. Plus she looked smart. He'd never in all his life seen a smarter-looking pair of . . .

Money.

That's what he was thinking about. This was all about the money. The rich, creamy, rising-with-every-breath, wiggling-when-she-giggled, Grand-Canyon-when-she-leaned-forward . . .

Money.

The secret of the mob war had lasted about as long as it took for the mayor to get back to his office and start making panicked phone calls. Within ten minutes, everyone in Paradise Beach knew about it. Linus, while not even in Paradise Beach at that time, had heard about it even faster, courtesy of Ms. Fall-Into-My-Pillowy-Softness-Forever . . .

Money.

Keep focused, he told himself. A white-uniformed waiter discreetly stepped over, and Linus ordered another Absolut and carrot juice—where *did* the nouveau riche develop a taste for these things?—and sipped/gagged on it while he pondered the possibilities. Pete wins. Ted agrees not to challenge Aunt Mary's marriage. Ergo, Pete becomes the trustee. The Floorsheim mob is out of the picture. And that leaves Linus . . . what?

Sheila had been kinda vague on that part. She'd kept leaning forward, talking about how it never hurt to go in on the winning side. That made sense. But if Pete became the trustee for Mary's land, where did Linus fit in after he was cut out? He didn't have any personal clout with that development company. Didn't have any—what was the term that college professor had always used—goodwill. The developer would follow the property. And Linus, having no goodwill, would end up shopping at Goodwill. Sheila would *not* be impressed with that turn of events. Then he'd have no chance to crawl into her heaving, straining-at-her-sweater, ever-so-slightly-freckled . . .

Money.

He took another sip from his drink, made a face, and stared into the odd, orange liquid. Someday, he'd be rich enough that he would *set* trends, and not have to follow them. Someday. That's what this meeting was all about. A business transaction. And business was all about . . .

"What a set of knockers, eh?"

"Ohhhhh yeah," Linus said, then realized he wasn't answering the voice inside his head. Unless the voice inside his head had developed an awful case of asthma.

He looked up to see Pete Lewis staring across the lobby at a vivacious young thang, obviously fresh from the beach, jiggling her way toward the elevators. Yeah, those were nice ones too.

He looked up again to find Pete still standing, looking down at him. Back in the dimmest recesses of his brain, a voice echoed from a long-ago etiquette class. He rose and extended his hand. "Linus Todd."

Pete looked him up and down, and grunted. "You're the nephew."

Linus nodded. "Yes, I'm Mary Todd's—"

"Just stay away from my blender," Pete said.

Linus started to answer, stopped, started again, stopped again, then furrowed his brow. "Ummm . . . okay."

"Good." Pete wheezed and sat. "So what is this offer you wanted to make me?"

Straight to the point. That was a good thing, Linus surmised. "Well, it's about this mob war."

"You've heard about it too?" Pete asked.

Linus tried an ingratiating smile. It might have ingratiated him in a room of unemployed televangelists. Maybe. If they were drunk enough. "I have connections," he said, with what he hoped was a conspiratorial nod. It was the kind of conspiratorial nod John Cleese might have used in the role of Basil Fawlty.

"I'll just bet you do," Pete said. "And what did these connections tell you?"

Linus leaned back, steepled his fingers beneath his chin, and paused for a moment. "My sources say there's going to be a mob war. Your guys and Dan Floorsheim's guys. The way I see it, you have . . . challenges."

"Do I?" Pete asked.

"Sure. For whatever they're worth otherwise, Colonel Albermarle's old coots do have connections in Paradise Beach. There won't be anywhere you or your guys can go that they won't hear about it."

"Perhaps," Pete conceded.

"And with that information, Floorsheim's goons will ambush your guys, and it's bingo, bango, bongo. Your guys get hit."

"Interesting theory," Pete said.

He was interested! Linus hadn't blown it yet!

Excitement began to bubble within him. If he could just close the deal, he'd be in on the winning side. He would get rich. He would get Sheila. And ordinary domestic light beer would become trendy.

"So here's my offer," Linus said, exuding his best let's-close-this-deal-before-the-muffler-falls-off charm. "I'll be *your* Paradise Beach insider. I grew up there. People know me."

That no one in Paradise Beach would give Linus a drink of water from a public fountain was totally beyond him. This was his big asset. He was a local.

Pete nodded and took a moment, either to nap or to think. Linus couldn't be sure which. Finally he looked up. "Assuming I brought you in on my side, what would you want?"

Now was the time to tumble the words out in a vocal equivalent of fine print. "You'll get Mary's property because she's been declared incompetent so you can do whatever you want with it and I already have connections with a developer who wants to build-and-I'm-not-talking-cottages-here so I get a piece of the deal."

Even Pete seemed out of breath by the end of the sentence. He also apparently didn't want Linus to repeat it, much to the relief of Linus's pulmonary system. He took another long thought, or a short nap, and nodded. "So you'll help me take down this Floorsheim gang in exchange for a piece of my action afterwards?"

"Exactly," Linus said, apparently not noticing that Pete had subtly changed the terms of the deal.

"I'll think it over and let you know," Pete said. "Where can I find you?"

Linus thought about that for a moment. His actual address was somewhat less than impressive. And he had no posh office. Appearances were everything. He looked around the lobby, as if an answer might be found in the fronds of the potted palms. The idea was out of his mouth before he had time to think about it. "You can leave messages for me at the desk here."

"You're staying here, are you?" Pete asked. He seemed impressed.

Linus smiled. "I make do."

And the first thing he'd have to make Sheila do was charm the desk clerk into holding messages for him. She could do that. She could charm anyone into anything, with those sweet, soft, luscious mounds of . . .

Money.

It was all about . . .

"Damn, what a rack she has," Pete wheezed, now looking at a white-clad tennis buffy bouncing out of the elevator, racquet over her shoulder. Pete rose, still watching her stride across the lobby. He let out what might have been a sigh, thirty or forty years ago, but now sounded like a jet turbine winding up. "I tell ya, Linus, it's almost enough to make a man forget his common sense."

"Yeah," Linus said. "She sure is worth it."   .

"Worth it?" Pete asked. "Nah. When you get to my age, Linus, having to put coal in the furnace an hour ahead of time at sixty bucks a pop, it's enough just to look."

"It's all about the money," Linus said.

Pete clapped him on the back. "A man after my own heart. I'll be in touch."

Linus pumped his hand. "A sound investment is always breast."

That boy Richard definitely has a mind, Mary thought with a silent chuckle. A mob war! Brilliant, and in so many ways. Most of which the poor boy probably hadn't considered, but that was fine. Mary was a strong believer in bringing out the full potential in other people's ideas. Even if that potential had nothing whatever to do with what those people were thinking when they came up with their ideas. Even if they didn't like what she added to their ideas. It was for their own good, anyway. Usually.

Take Richard and Erin, for example. From the flushed glow on Erin's face, it was obvious that the two of them had finally gotten down to some blissful romancing. Which was fine, so far as it went. But blissful romancing only went so far. True love—the kind of love that endured—

thrived in the fires of crisis. If theirs was true love, a crisis would only strengthen it and assure them that they were truly meant for each other.

Enter Mary Todd, CEO of Crises R Us.

Of course, she had her own crisis right here in her living room. With the advent of the mob war, Ted had—for the first time ever—suggested a meeting of the Hole in the Seawall Gang. The good Reverend Archer and Hadley Philpot had been only too delighted to get involved. The problem was, Pete lived here.

Ordinarily, Mary would simply nudge Pete out the door. But at this particular moment, Mary needed to talk to Pete, so she needed him here. Moreover, she didn't especially want to let slip that her mind was fully functional, not even to the Hole in the Seawall Gang. It wasn't that she couldn't trust them. They'd kept bigger secrets, which was quite a feat in Paradise Beach. Rather, it was that she still needed them to believe she was depressed. This was essential to *her* plans, and she saw the larger picture.

So, here she sat, trying to look glum and despondent, even as her mind whirled behind her dark eyes, all the while waiting for the meeting to break up so she could talk to Pete and put her own schemes in motion.

Not that looking glum and despondent was all that much of a stretch. Reverend Archer, Ted, and Hadley had taken up residence in her living room, where Pete was watching a documentary special on manatee rescues. Pete was no nature lover; his idea of conservation was saving the leftovers for lunch the next day. He was simply being obstreperous. Needless to say, his presence was putting a damper on the discussion, but the gang always met in Mary's living room, and Ted refused to budge, not even to retire to the den or the dining room.

Thus, the conversation was limping along.

"We need to talk to . . . you know . . . Jillie's husband," Hadley said, referring to Chief Blaise Corrigan. Jillie Corrigan had recently had a bouncy baby boy, who, in other circumstances, would have been the talk of Paradise Beach. But these were not other circumstances.

"That's right," the reverend intoned. "Otherwise someone might . . . you know . . ."

"Exactly," Ted agreed.

And so on, for an hour now, communicating via a code-in-progress, with varying degrees of success.

"So you think . . . you know . . . we used her last Thanksgiving . . . maybe?" Ted asked.

"Huh?" the reverend replied.

"You know . . . the"—Ted inclined his head—"neighbor."

"Which?" Hadley asked.

"The . . ." Ted now nodded left, then right, then left again with a shrug, then dipped his head and raised it back to the right. It would, Mary thought, make an interesting aerobic workout for a turtle, but it didn't communicate worth a damn.

Finally, after what seemed like days but was only an hour or so, Ted gave in to frustration and suggested that the gang move to his living room. Mary sat glumly in her chair as they said their good-byes, then let out a laugh after they'd gone.

"What was that for?" Pete asked.

Mary waved a hand. "Oh, just that Ted is finally blooming into the ringleader I always wanted him to be. I've only been working on him for forty years."

Pete let out a wheezy huff. "He's a straight arrow. No fun at all."

"Not totally," Mary said. "Besides, a straight arrow is easier to control. It goes where you aim it."

"Maybe. But you need someone with spunk. Someone who can match your Machiavellian tendencies."

"You're saying I need you," Mary said, turning her gaze on him.

Pete smiled and shrugged. "Well, I'm here, aren't I?"

Mary's face turned glacial. "Yes. You are most definitely here."

Pete sat for a moment and studied the TV. Now they were rescuing baby harp seals. He turned to her. "You're still mad about St. Louis, aren't you?"

Dammit, this was not the time. "Don't even mention St. Louis."

His face softened. "It was sixty years ago, Mary."

Mary rapped her cane against the arm of her chair. "Sixty-five. It was sixty-five years, four months, and eight days ago."

Pete nodded. "I did what I thought was best. If I had it to do over, I'd do it again."

She glared at him. "I'd bought a wedding dress, Pete! I was *wearing* it! At a *church*! Waiting for *you*!"

"Yes. You were beautiful."

What? She turned away. "You weren't there, remember? That's how *I* remember it, anyway, and despite what Judge Dipshot says, my mind still works just fine."

He reached out for her hand, but she pulled it away. "I had to have one last look at you, Mary. I was in the old Commerce Building, two blocks away, looking out the window. It was a bright June day, under a blue sky the likes of which I've never seen since. The sun glistened off the river, so bright I had to shade my eyes while I looked for you, waiting for you to come out of the church. And then I saw you, in the dress, Mary. You were beautiful. Beautiful."

If he'd meant to ease the pain, he hadn't. Instead, he'd ripped away the scar tissue. Her heart felt like an open, burning sore. "*Why*, Pete?"

His eyes met hers, and for a moment she saw the softness that had once drawn her to him. "Mary, you were the riverboat queen. I'd never seen anyone like you, and I've never met anyone like you since. There was a fire in your heart, a flash in your eyes. Like a schoolgirl in a toy shop, and yet seeing it all with the cool savvy of an adult. The boat made money because of you, Mary Todd. They came and put their money on the table just to be near you. Most of them didn't even care when they lost, so long as you'd given them one of those flirty kisses on the cheek, or draped your arm around them."

She remembered those days. She'd been a cigarette girl with a wardrobe full of saucy dresses, which hadn't been easy to find, even if the depression was finally lifting. Halfway around the world, a madman had started a war, and while the United States wasn't in it yet, the country was already lifting its collective head out of an empty soup bowl, looking outward with drive and purpose. For the first time in her life, poverty and sorrow were not the dominant themes in her world, and she'd exploded into that newfound sunshine like a bird taking wing.

He looked at her and smiled. "And you *loved* that, Mary. I could see it in your eyes. You were the one they all wanted, and you made yourself just *almost* available, without ever letting them really get anything. You played that game with passion and skill and *joy*, and that's what made

Pride of Vicksburg the hottest steamboat on the Mississippi. The sharks bought thousand-dollar trays just to sit at a poker table . . . and be next to Mary Todd."

He paused and looked down. "And I couldn't take that away from you. If you'd married me, you'd have settled down and had babies and you wouldn't have been the riverboat queen anymore."

Mary nodded silently. "I'd have willingly given it all up for you, Pete. I would have."

"And you'd have resented me for the rest of your life. I couldn't do that to you. So I left you the papers to the boat, watched you come out of the church in your wedding dress, and walked over to the recruiting station to sign up. I shipped out four days later, and next thing I knew the Japanese were bombing Pearl Harbor and I was on my way to boot camp."

More surprises. "You went in the army?"

"That's right, Mary. Army Air Corps. I figured I'd get some action, die for God and country. I ended up counting flies on flypaper in Arizona, because some damn clerk somewhere, as a joke, made up a flypaper efficiency form."

Poor Pete. No matter how hard he'd tried, the Boss never wanted him near the action. She sighed. "I wasn't on the river by then, Pete. It wasn't the same without you. I sold the boat."

He nodded. "I knew you'd sold it. Did she at least get a good price?"

Mary pointed out the window, across the boulevard, toward the dunes and the gulf beyond. "Enough to buy this island. I didn't get you, Pete, so I came back home and bought a sandbar called Pelican Key. I renamed it Paradise Beach. Sold enough here and there to let the town build up, staked some people I liked to businesses, gave a nudge here and there in town elections, and my little island grew into a Florida vacation spot. I couldn't have you, so this town and its people became my lifelong love."

"And Ted?"

"He came about five years later, just after the war."

He smiled. "That wasn't what I meant, Mary."

"I know."

His hand had found hers, and held it softly. "Have you ever told him you love him?"

Her eyes met his. "I haven't said those words in sixty-five years, four months, and eight days. Being left at the altar once in a lifetime is enough."

"That was me, Mary. And it was a long time ago. Ted is here and now, and it sounds like he's been here and now for a long, long time."

Mary looked down. "He's a straight arrow."

Pete chuckled. "And you've finally found a way to bend him a little, with this whole Linus mess."

Damn him. He always could see right through her. He was the only man who ever could.

Maybe that's why she had loved him so. A long, long time ago. "We'll see."

Pete nodded and patted her hand.

She hadn't meant for it to go like this. But now it had. And maybe that would make things easier to arrange. She turned to him. "Pete, I have a favor to ask . . ."

22

Dan looks even more edible than ever, Seana thought as she watched him brief Colonel Albermarle. So this was what he did. It was a bit frightening, and thrilling, all at the same time. But it was only a tiny bit frightening, because he'd explained the rules they'd worked out for the war. It had seemed odd at the time, although she couldn't honestly say she wished they were using real guns and real bullets. But he'd explained that Pete was old, and besides, he'd rather not get the Feds coming down on him over a real war. This, he explained, was why people weren't hearing so much about the mob anymore. A low profile, he'd said.

It made sense, to a point. Although squirting ketchup on each other in public hardly struck her as keeping a low profile. She'd certainly never read about ketchup melees in the newspapers. It seemed like the sort of thing that would tweak a reporter's attention. But he obviously knew what he was doing.

"Six-Tooth Franco is down on the beach every morning at five," Dan said. "But that's not the place to go after him. There's no cover. Instead, wait until he walks up to Benny's for breakfast."

"Right-oh," Albermarle said. "My men will deploy in the palm trees beside the walk, and lay an ambush. Classic commando tactics. We've drilled them for years."

Seana laughed and twirled the straw in her soda. "Why do I think you're not kidding, Colonel?"

Albermarle looked at her. "Young lady, eternal vigilance is the price of liberty." Turning back to Dan, he nodded. "My men won't let you down, sir. I'll reveille the men at zero-three-thirty and take up our positions."

"Very well," Dan said briskly, almost slipping into Albermarle's crisp diction.

It was a habit of his, Seana thought, mimicking the speech patterns of foreigners, as if he wanted to add them to his repertoire. She could tell Albermarle had picked up on it as the colonel rose and snapped his heels together. He snapped an open-hand salute to his right eyebrow.

"To the glory of Paradise Beach, sir."

"To the glory of Paradise Beach," Dan echoed, returning the salute.

It wasn't very mobster-esque, to Seana, but it

seemed to motivate the colonel. He strode out, leaving them alone in Seana's kitchen. Erin was out with Richard, again, as she had been most of the past few nights. They'd been inseparable since the announcement of the mob war, on the very thin pretense that Richard had to protect her. The truth, quite simply, was that they had tumbled over the cliff for each other. Regardless, Dan had begun to spend more of his time at the Kelly sisters' place, and the kitchen had turned into a command post.

A detailed map of Paradise Beach was taped to the wall, and the table beneath it was covered with scribbled scraps of paper of all shapes, sizes and colors. The citizens of Paradise Beach had clearly made their choice—for Ted and the colonel, and thus for Dan—and it seemed as if hardly a half hour would pass without someone walking furtively up to the door and sliding a note through the mail slot. Timmy "Reno" Kerrigan had been spotted at the mayor's bar on Tuesday night, and again on Thursday and Friday. Benny "String Tie" Johnson played bingo at the Reverend Archer's church on Monday night, always playing five cards, always arranging them in a precise line on the table. As the reports accumulated, Dan sorted them by target and time, and Seana put sticky notes on the map. Dan probably knew more about where Pete's men were than Pete did. A decided advantage, Seana thought.

For the moment, though, she simply wanted

to curl up in his arms, feel his hard muscles against her, and have him pay attention to her. All she wanted was just a little bit of that exhilarating focus he was applying to his war.

She moved her chair closer so their thighs touched. Dan looked at her, tried to force a thin smile, and returned to sorting through the notes.

He looked so confident about the mob war, and for good reason, and yet lately he'd seemed more distant from her. The mystery simply drew her closer to him, wanting to open up his secrets and live in his thoughts.

"Dan?" she said.

"Yes, darling?"

"Could we get some quiet time for awhile?"

He looked up. "I would love that, Seana. But . . ."

Why had she *known* there was a "but" coming? "Yes?"

"Well, there's a war on, honey. I owe it to Ted to do my very best."

Seana nodded. It wasn't the answer she was looking for, but it was as much of an answer as she was going to get. She made an effort to smile appreciatively, then got up to root around through the fridge for some veggies to stir-fry. Maybe food would loosen him up. Nothing else had lately.

In fact, here in the midst of the most exciting events that had ever occurred in her young life, all she wanted to do was cry. Erin was totally preoccupied, barely speaking to her. She was hopelessly involved with Richard the Third, who, despite talking about rules and regulations and all that mumbo-jumbo stuff that had the men all hot and bothered, still managed to look at Erin with eyes hot enough to dwarf the midday sun. It was beautiful to see her sister so happy, and yet it left Seana aching.

But Dan didn't look at *her* that way anymore. His eyes always seemed to be looking just past her, or through her. Or skittering away from her, as if he were afraid of what he might see.

Catching her reflection in the side of a shiny stock pot, she paused and looked. She hadn't grown horns, or warts, her teeth hadn't turned green, and her roots weren't showing yet. Her clothes still fit exactly right, so she was the same shape and size that had appealed to Dan only a short time ago.

Biting her lower lip, she sniffled and blinked away a lone tear. Then, annoyed at herself, but mostly at Dan, she pulled the wok out of the lower cupboard and slammed it on the stove.

She glanced over at Dan to see if she'd gotten his attention, but he was still poring over the little notes. This time she sniffed, a distinctly different sound, but he didn't notice that either.

Cook for this man? Cook for this unappreciative, distant, rotten, scum of a crook who'd forgotten she existed? Why should she mess with hot oil and the mess that stir-frying invariably made all over the stove and the counters, to please him?

No way. Angrier still, she shoved the wok back into the cupboard. Feeling both vindictive and foolish, she opened the fridge and pulled out a diet protein shake. She could subsist on this stuff, even though she didn't think *he* could. And she didn't even offer him a can, either.

Sitting down with her two hundred and fifty calories of protein, vitamins and ungodly chocolate flavor, she waited for him to get hungry.

He glanced her way, his eyes going no further than the can in her hand. "That stuff's not good for you. Hey, you're not dieting, are you?"

"No." Inwardly pleased that he seemed aware of her, she still refused to smile. "I just don't feel like cooking."

He nodded. "That's okay. Hey, have you got another one of those?"

She wanted to bean him with the can but decided that five to ten for battery wasn't an experience she wanted to have. Even if it would put her firmly on Dan's side of the law. She slammed the can down beside him, hoping he would at least jump.

He didn't. All he murmured distractedly was, "Thanks."

Now in a total huff, Seana took her can and

stepped out onto the small balcony that over-looked the gulf. She and Erin shared a tiny condo at the south end of Paradise Beach, on the fourth floor of a high-rise. The building had originally been meant to house time-shares for people who wanted a Florida getaway for a few weeks a year, but time-shares had stopped selling, and quite a few of the units were rented out now as apartments.

It was a great view of the shore, the water and the streamers of red cloud as the sun settled in the west for the night, but Seana hardly noticed it. She'd be going back to college soon for the fall semester, back to the small apartment she shared with three roommates during the school year, and she didn't want to go without a commit-ment from Dan.

She tried to reason with herself, the way Erin had often tried to teach her, but reason wasn't working. She wanted Dan. She'd never felt this way about anyone before in her life. Oh, she'd thought she was in love before, but those feel-ings didn't hold a candle to what she felt for this man. They didn't even come close.

He was a crook. A criminal. A member of the mob. The worst sort of person. Once Erin got wind of Dan's occupation, she'd probably hit the roof.

In fact, now that she thought about it, she wondered how Erin could have gone so long in ignorance. Everybody in the whole town seemed to know who Dan Floorsheim was. How had Erin missed the news?

Turning, she looked back through the open sliding glass door at Dan, who was still hunched at the dinette, muttering to himself as he organized his mound of sticky notes.

Maybe, she thought, *nobody has told Erin*. No, wait. Erin *had* to know. After all, Richard the Third was organizing this mob war. Erin had to know who the players were. Besides, Erin had been talking to Dan at the sporting goods shop when Seana had met him. So Erin had to know.

So why wasn't her sister threatening to hog-tie her and send her to a convent in some desolate, remote, unmapped region of . . . say . . . Antarctica? For the first time, that question truly bothered her. Erin should be fighting this relationship tooth and nail. So far she hadn't done much except voice a small protest.

Maybe Erin was too caught up in Richard the Third. Maybe for once in her life, Erin was so involved with someone else that she was hardly noticing her sister.

The thought didn't make Seana feel too good. Everybody seemed to be ignoring her right now, and she wasn't used to being ignored. But . . .

Hmmm.

She had a brainstorm. A brilliant idea from her soon-to-be *summa cum laude* mind. She suddenly knew how to handle the whole thing.

Sashaying her hips provocatively, even if the idiot at the table didn't notice, she returned to Dan's side, swung the chair around, and straddled.

"Hey, kemo sabe," she said.

He looked at her, his eyes vague.

"I wanna play, too."

Dan's gaze focused on her then. He was really seeing her for the first time in what seemed like forever. She preened a little, having gotten what she wanted.

Even if he *was* looking horrified.

Erin's life wasn't going a whole lot better at the moment. Richard, too, was preoccupied with the mob war, mainly because Pete's cronies were considerably more bloodthirsty than Dan's henchmen.

Oh, they didn't want to use guns or anything. They weren't crazy. All of them were getting up in years, and none of them wanted to spend their retirement in one of the Spartan condominiums known as the Federal Penitentiary System. Hell, they had heard Florida was a terrible place to do time. No air-conditioning! No expensive cigar dipped in Chianti after dinner. Untailored sacks to wear without even a belt to boast a diamond-studded belt buckle. And all these guys dripped diamonds. The thought of doing without their pinkie rings was enough to send them into a tailspin.

So no, they didn't want guns. In fact, they repeatedly checked to make sure that *nobody* was going to have real guns, or even anything that *looked* like a real gun. Cops could get nervous about that.

But colorful squirt guns were another matter. Super squirt guns to be precise. Those big soakers that could spray almost as much as a fire hose.

Richard watched benevolently as they tested one of the top-of-the-line models to see how much ketchup it would hold. Two of those jumbo-sized plastic bottles from the discount warehouse? No, better yet. Three of them. Plenty of ammo.

Of course, they were a little hard to pump up. . . .

But Vinnie got it pumped up, and the resultant spray, covering the wood privacy fence outside Richard's house, to the consternation of two birds and a cat, who went squawking and howling to a safer locale, satisfied everybody.

"Yeah," said Leon, blowing a cloud of cigar smoke. "Almost as good as a tommy gun."

"But hard to pump up," Vinnie said, panting a little. "Once you got it pumped, it's okay, but getting it there . . ." He shook his head.

"Well," suggested Richard, making the fatal mistake, "you could water down the ketchup a little."

"Water it down?" Leon wailed. "It's my *ammo*."

"Yes," said Richard reasonably, "it is. But as long as the other guys get splotched, it doesn't matter if the ketchup is a little runny."

"True," wheezed Pete, who was supervising from a lawn chair, a glass of single malt whiskey in one hand, and a for-sure Havana cigar in the other. That alone, thought Erin, was probably enough to get someone arrested. But she was growing philosophical about the whole idea of getting arrested. Exactly why, she couldn't say. Maybe it had something to do with the idea of Richard defending her in a courtroom. At least then he'd have to pay attention to her.

As soon as she had the selfish thought, she scolded herself for being immature. The important thing now was to rescue Mary . . . although, as she thought about it now, she couldn't exactly remember how this was going to rescue anyone. Oh, yes. The gentlemen's agreement between Ted and Pete.

An agreement she frankly wasn't sure either one of them could be held to. But at least this wasn't *her* idea.

On the other hand, watching Richard stride around the yard in white slacks and an open-throated white shirt, his feet bare . . . well, that was worth the price of admission. He was looking more piratical by the hour. Strap a heavy leather belt on him, slap a scarf on his head, hand him a cutlass . . .

And maybe they could wind up in Captiva again.

"Just add some water and see if it isn't easier to pump," Richard ordered.

It was kind of thrilling to watch him ordering his "crew" about, especially when she thought about how these guys had once been dangerous mobsters. Maybe *were* still dangerous.

Vinnie obligingly poured out some of the ketchup, and Leon held the hose to refill the squirt gun.

"Hey!" Vinnie yelped, when the hose splashed him. "Watch it, you joik."

"Sorry," said Leon, with amazing meekness.

"Those two," sighed Pete, sounding like an asthmatic steam whistle, "have been at each other for the last forty years at least. Something to do with a piece of desert. I kid you not, a piece of desert. It's still a piece of desert. Useless."

"Why did they want it?" Erin asked.

Pete shrugged. "They wanted to build another Las Vegas."

"Why didn't they?"

"Because the idiots got told to cut it out."

"Oh." She supposed one or the other had found a horse's head in his bed. She looked at the two men and actually felt a twinge of sympathy for them. Right now they were shaking the squirt gun to mix the ketchup and water.

"Okay," said Richard, holding up a hand. "Try it now."

Vinnie started pumping and soon was red in the face. "It's not any easier."

"No," agreed Richard, "but look what the spray does now."

Vinnie looked at him, looked at the gun, shrugged and squirted. The spray went even further this time, and hit Leon so hard that he yelped and jumped Vinnie. The sight of two men of Social Security age rolling on the ground like a couple of scrappy ten-year-olds almost made Erin laugh out loud.

"Cut it out!" Pete yelled, sounding like the quitting-time steam whistle at a factory. "Quit acting like idiots. We got serious business here." He covered his heart with his hand. "My whole future is at stake."

Vinnie spat out a piece of grass. "Yeah, but mine isn't. *That* turkey's future is at stake." He jerked his head toward Leon, who looked rather ridiculous covered in grass stains and watery ketchup.

Richard helped the two men to their feet. "No fighting among yourselves," he ordered sternly. "If you can't behave, the Floorsheim mob is going to win."

Erin suddenly wondered why Richard was helping Pete's gang anyway. Didn't he want Mary to have the man of her heart?

Of course, the whole world was going crazy

anyway, so why should Richard be exempt? And he did look dashing.

"Okay," said Richard, "the watered-down ketchup goes farther and hits harder. What's more, that means you can hit more people with less pumping."

Vinnie suddenly brightened. Even Leon looked appeased. "Yeah," they both chimed.

Then the awful thing happened, spawned by Richard's innocent suggestion.

Pete tapped ash from his cigar into an old coffee can Richard had found for the purpose. "You know," he said, "if we're going to water down the ketchup, we ought to water it down with something that will count."

Richard stiffened. Erin held her breath.

"You know," said Pete. "Something that will stink. Or sting. Like . . . maybe . . . garlic juice?"

23

Six-Tooth Franco Plantaro—he was born Frank Planter but changed his name when he thought it might be an advantage in the old days—liked the beach in the early morning hours. It was dark, for one thing, which meant he didn't have to worry about sunburn. What's more, there was nobody else on the beach at this hour, so he had the time to himself. And despite his reputation as a brawler, Franco had always enjoyed time to himself.

Truth was, he hadn't really been in a fight since grade school. He'd watched a lot of fights, and his overall impression had been that, far more often than not, both guys came out of it the worse for wear. He'd been *around* a lot of fights. That much was true. And when it happened he'd usually arrange to shove a shoulder here or there. A confederate's, if possible. They would assume he'd been jostled into them in the melee and were less likely to swing back. As the fight started to wind down, he'd find someone who had been less circumspect and bump into him to get the appropriate soilage on his shirt. He'd come out of it the battle-hardened hero, with nary a scratch.

Well, except for the time he'd stepped on a broken beer bottle. Now *that* had left a scratch— a gash, really. In the old days it wouldn't have happened, but this fight happened in the seventies. In the old days he'd have had on proper footwear with sturdy leather soles, and the bottle wouldn't have penetrated. Certainly not as deeply. But this was the seventies, when running shoes were all the new rage, and Franco always liked to look trendy. So, slick as you please, that broken bottle cut right through the rubber sole of his running shoes—he didn't even run, for crying out loud, unless he'd eaten too much of Ginny's goulash and the bathroom was too far away—and left an inch-deep slice in the bottom of his foot.

That in itself wouldn't have been too bad, except he'd done the ordinary, reflexive, manly thing, and doubled over to howl in pain. And as it turned out, he'd been standing next to a pool table, and *that* had become the real problem, when he'd slammed his face onto it and put most of his teeth in the corner pocket. All rumors to the contrary notwithstanding, and he'd fueled some of those rumors himself, that was how he'd become Six-Tooth Franco.

And the good thing about the beach at five in the morning was that a man could think about such things, wince at the memory of the bottle and the pool table, laugh at the memory of the rumors, and nobody thought he was crazy. A man could remember Ginny's goulash, even Ginny herself, and think about fifty years with a woman who had never made a single major mistake outside the kitchen. He could talk to her as if a bout with the flu hadn't taken her away three winters ago, and remember the way she'd giggled in the emergency room when he'd told her about that fight. She was the only person he'd ever told the true story. He could never lie to her, not even now that she was gone.

Take this war, for example. Truth be told, this was likely to be the most fun he'd ever had as a mobster. The old ring-kissing, finger-pricking days were over, and good riddance, to his mind. There had been too damn many fights about too damn little. All he'd ever really wanted was a way to bet on the Packers games. He'd gotten in because he got a better deal on the vig as an insider—call it professional courtesy—and for a lot of years that'd been a good thing, because the Packers had gone in the tank after Lombardi left and hadn't resurfaced until the nineties. But when they'd come back . . . well, let's just say

Favre & Co. had built Franco a tidy nest egg, which he and Ginny had intended to share into their golden years. But there had been too damn much stupidity to go around, all things considered.

This was the way things ought to be. Get together and arrange some sensible rules, like grown-ups, and use squirt guns. Hell, from what he'd been told, there was even a worthy cause involved. All in all, it was a major improvement.

And it was during that thought—with the sky beginning to shift from a deep, nighttime indigo to a lighter shade of violet—that Six-Tooth Franco decided it was time for his usual breakfast of light toast with butter and a grapefruit half, and headed toward his destiny as the first victim of the Paradise Beach Mob War.

He heard the rustle in the bushes a half-second before a stream of ketchup accompanied a squirty sound that reminded him once again of Ginny's goulash. The ketchup caught him flush in the nose.

"Well shit," he said, as a man stepped out of the bushes to tuck a swagger stick under his arm. "Now I'm going to want eggs for breakfast."

"I say," Albermarle said, nodding across the alley, "jolly good shot, Prentice! Damn fine show!"

Linus had taken to slinking in doorways. When he'd agreed to toss his lot in with Pete, he hadn't considered that he would become a target. And it certainly never occurred to him that the citizens of Paradise Beach would have taken any possible excuse to make him one, even if he hadn't joined Pete. He'd simply made it easier for them, and two of Albermarle's men had already taken potshots at him, not to mention the two elderly women who had thrown ketchup-drenched French fries at him while he was trying to scarf down a fast-food burger. No one had hit him yet—the Floorsheim gang hadn't upgraded to mega squirt guns—but instead of gleaning important information about the comings and goings of Dan's goons and Albermarle's coots, Linus was reduced to hiding in doorways.

It was from such a vantage point, peering out across the alley, that Linus kept watch as Vinnie and Leon walked down the alley back-to-back—Vinnie walking forward, Leon walking backward—with squirt guns at the ready. Vinnie threw an elbow after Leon stepped on his heel, but otherwise they managed to look only mildly ridiculous until they reached the back door of Erin's shop.

There they had a brief but heated discussion about who would go in the door first. Leon protested that he was tired of walking backward, and that he was sure Vinnie would let the door hit him in the back. Vinnie argued that the Boss—as Pete now insisted on being called—had told them to watch each other's backs, and they couldn't do that if they were both looking the same way. They batted that around for a moment, before deciding to shuffle in sideways, still back-to-back.

But the door was too narrow.

Even when they sucked in their stomachs and held their squirt guns over their heads and smushed their backsides against each other, they couldn't fit. What they could manage, and did, was to get stuck. Thoroughly. Inextricably.

So much for the element of surprise, Linus thought. Watching these old incompetents bumble around, he found himself wondering why he'd been so afraid of the mob to begin with. If what he'd seen in the last three days had been any indication, he had nothing to worry about.

"Hey, pinhead!" Leon called.

Linus looked around and saw no one else in sight, probably much to the relief of Vinnie and Leon, then looked back at them.

"Yeah, you, idjit!" Vinnie said, leaving no doubt as to whom they referred. "A little help here?"

"I'm the lookout," Linus said. "I'm looking . . . out."

"Well look out from over here and shove this lard-ass past me," Leon said.

"Who are you callin' a lard-ass," Vinnie objected, trying to throw an elbow but managing only to look like an infant trying to bat at a crib toy.

"I ain't the one who had eggs this morning," Leon said. "I had a bran muffin."

"I didn't have no eggs," Vinnie said. "That was Franco who had the eggs."

"Franco don't eat eggs. Says the cholesterol isn't good for him."

Vinnie tried to throw another elbow. "You think I don't know this? Of course I know this. But Franco, he got hit this morning. So he had eggs."

"He had eggs because he got hit?"

"It was the taste of ketchup. He always had ketchup on his eggs in the morning, back when Ginny was around."

"Well that's no surprise," Leon said. "You ever eat Ginny's cooking? You *had* to drown it in ketchup."

"I liked Ginny's cooking," Vinnie argued. "She made a great chicken Limburger."

"That was *supposed* to be chicken Parmesan, you moron. She ran out of Parmesan, and Franco, he didn't want to go out and get more, so she made it with Limburger instead."

"I *know* that!" Vinnie said in exasperation. "Point is, I liked it!"

"Point is," Leon countered, "it smelled like cow shit. And it looked like cow shit. It even *felt* like cow shit."

"But it tasted good," Vinnie said.

Leon shook his head. "I never tried it."

"Point is, it was good," Vinnie said.

"No," Leon demurred, "point is, Franco hated it. That's why he put ketchup on everything."

"No," Vinnie pressed on, "point is, that's why Franco wanted eggs this morning, and all I had was a slice of watermelon, and I am *not* a lard-ass."

"I don't care if you ate nothing but boiled air," Leon said. "You're still a lard-ass."

At which point Vinnie turned to Linus and asked, "Is my ass big?"

Linus, having no idea what the right answer to that question might be, decided instead to answer their original plea, and to break cover to shove them through Erin's back door.

And that was when two of Albermarle's men, who had been watching the entire episode from the roof, dropped a giant water balloon. Linus saw it falling and, looking up, tripped over a rock and toppled sideways, taking him out of the splatter zone as the water balloon exploded in a spray of diluted ketchup. He then stumbled into Vinnie and Leon, which shoved them through the doorway and into a pile of Erin's clay.

Vinnie climbed off of Leon and rose to a sitting position, picking clay from his hair. He glared at his partner and whispered, "I do *not* have a lard-ass."

Leon simply pointed toward the doorway, which gave out to the front of the shop, where Erin looked down at them.

She laughed. "Hi, guys!"

"Hi," Vinnie replied with a wave. "The Boss told us to kidnap you."

Erin sighed. "Let me get my purse."

All things considered, Richard was pleased with the motion he'd filed. It was a novel legal theory, but not as novel as the time he'd had to prove that his client—who had tumbled across an abandoned boat in Tampa Bay and relieved it of a radio, three life preservers, and its GPS system—was not a burglar but was instead a salvor, and that rather than prosecution was entitled to either the return of the items rescued or a salvage fee from the state. Of course, he'd been satisfied when the state attorney had simply dropped the charges. But he had gone out on legal limbs before, and won. And this wasn't too much more of a stretch.

The germ of the idea had been born while he was riding over the Skyway, listening to Erin's confession. She'd asked an actor friend to impersonate a mobster, hoping to get Mary's blood pumping again. Where but in Paradise Beach would a scheme that serpentine be hatched? Add to that the spark of a memory from a college psychology class, where the professor had asserted that much of what we call "mental illness" is socially defined, and another spark of a memory from a law school class on the First

Amendment, where obscenity must be judged by contemporary community standards, and it had all come together.

And thus was born his motion: that mental competence must be judged by community standards, that Paradise Beach was not a normal community, and that Mary Todd was thus "competent by community standards." Exhibit A, a mob war between two clans of geriatrics, being fought with ketchup, on the streets of Paradise Beach. If that wasn't enough to prove that Mary was no nuttier than the rest of this town, nothing would be.

In the normal course of things, Richard would have called Dipshot's judicial assistant for a hearing date, probably two or three weeks hence, filed the motion, and waited. He didn't feel like waiting, so he'd applied a bit of oil to the machinery of justice by driving the motion over to the courthouse, filing one copy at the clerk's office and hand-carrying another up to Dipshot's office. There he had charmed one Eleanor Dixby—quite a feat, as anyone who had ever met Eleanor would attest, given the fact that she had both the looks and temperament of a startled rhinoceros—and scheduled a hearing in three days. By the end of the day, he'd delivered a copy of the motion and notice of hearing to Linus Todd's attorney, and had been feeling fat and happy as he'd driven over to Erin's house for a night of romantic recreation.

His mood had fallen a bit when he'd found that she wasn't home. It had fallen a bit more when he'd called the store and gotten no answer. Still, he was only mildly concerned and still feeling pleasantly recreative when the phone rang.

"Wesley?" the caller asked, in an accent that dripped memories of the Dodgers . . . before they'd moved from Brooklyn to Los Angeles.

"Hi Leon," Richard said. "What's up?"

"This ain't Leon," Leon said. "This is a guy who works for the Boss. And the Boss has something you want. Say hello, sweets."

There was a pause before Erin's voice came on. "Thanks, Leon," she said. "Hi Richard. Guess what? I've been kidnapped."

"Again?"

"Yeah," she said wearily. "First you and now these guys. I'm going to start keeping an overnight bag with me. Anyway, I'm supposed to tell you that I'm okay, and they haven't hurt me, but I'm really scared, so do whatever they tell you to do."

Richard's heart jumped for a moment. "*Are* you really scared, Erin?"

She laughed. Oh, that laugh! "Hell no, but I'm supposed to say that. So I said it. Anyway, do whatever they tell you to do, unless you don't want to."

There was another pause, and Leon's voice returned. "The Boss says you're supposed to do whatever he tells you to do, and it doesn't matter whether you want to or not. She messed up that part."

"Ahh," Richard said. "I thought she might have. So, Leon, what does Pete want?"

"He wants you to convince Ted Wannamaker to be alone on the beach in front of Mary's house at 10 P.M. tomorrow night, so we can whack him."

"And if I don't?"

"The Boss says we'll start by sending you a lock of her hair, then fingernail clippings."

"And if I still don't?"

"I dunno," Leon said. "I guess toenail clippings."

"*Nooooooo,*" Erin cried dramatically in the background. "*Not my toenails! Save me, Richard!*"

"Yeah, okay," Richard said. "I guess I'll talk to Ted about it and see what he thinks. How do I get back to you with an answer?"

"Oh, we're with Pete at Mary's," Leon said, then paused and grunted. "Ummm, the Boss says we'll get in touch with you."

"Okeydokey, Leon," Richard said. "Tell Pete and Mary I said hi, and I'll talk to Ted."

"Thanks," Leon said. "Have a good day."

"You too. Bye."

"Oh, before you hang up!" Leon said quickly. "Where can I get some decent barbecue around here? This is the south, right? There has to be good barbecue."

"Maxie's is pretty good," Richard said, and

gave him the address. "Get the ribs. They're amazing."

"Got it," Leon said. "Thanks again, and do what you're told and all of that stuff."

"I wouldn't risk Erin's toenails."

Richard hung up the phone with mixed emotions. On the one hand, he really was looking forward to some romantic recreation. On the other hand, Paradise Beach just kept getting crazier and crazier, and that was good for his client. So all things considered, it could be a lot worse. Or that's what he told himself as he turned on a cold shower.

24

Freddy Dipshot was bored. He'd had just as much of people's problems as he could stomach for one day, especially when his stomach was already rolling from the shrimp scampi with extra garlic he'd eaten at lunch. Besides, either Richard Wesley had gone totally round the bend, or he'd raised an interesting legal insight. Either way, he wasn't really listening as yet another marginal lawyer, working for some miscellaneous plaintiff, whined piteously about some trivial wrong committed by some equally miscellaneous defendant. He brought the gavel down with a crack.

"I've heard enough," he said.

"But Your Honor," the lawyer whimpered, "I haven't even called a witness yet."

"Don't bother," Dipshot groused. He pointed at the defendant. "Even if that idiot did misalign his sprinkler so it sprayed your idiot's precious petunias, there's no way you can prove the damage was caused by his sprinkler, and not by the severe thunderstorm that swept through the county that very same afternoon. Complaint dismissed. I'm outta here."

The lawyer continued to whine as Dipshot rose and scooted back to his chambers. "Eleanor, I'm going over to Paradise Beach to see if it's as loony a bin as Wesley says in his motion."

Eleanor pursed her lips, which at least drew his attention from her wide-set, beady eyes and the wart on her nose. The courthouse rumors were right. She did look like a rhino. "Are you sure that's wise, sir?" she said in a voice that left little doubt that *she* didn't believe it was wise at all.

"It's either that, or I throw my gavel at the next damn lawyer who walks an idiot into my courtroom," he said. "Consider it a service to the legal community."

"Shrimp scampi for lunch again?" she asked.

He looked down at his tie. No, there was no evidence this time. "Yes. How'd you guess?"

"It wasn't difficult," she said. "Okay, sir, should I reschedule the hearing on *Stippins v. Flopley*? Intentional trespass, personal injury?"

"The one about the neighbor kid who supposedly trained his dog to shit on Stippins's front step, so Flopley's wife would fall on it?"

"That would be the one," she said.

"Yeah, reschedule it. For a morning. I don't think I can handle dog shit on a full stomach."

"Yes, sir," Eleanor said.

Thirty minutes later, Dipshot was cruising along Gulf Boulevard, wondering how such an island of insanity could exist in an otherwise normal world. He'd barely reached the business district when two old men in black shirts, shorts, and pith helmets burst out of the car in front of him and opened fire with squirt guns on another pair of old men in bowling shirts that had "The Boss's Hosses" embroidered on the back. The bowling shirt duo didn't even have time to bring their own massive squirt guns to bear.

"Dammit, this was a *clean* bowling shirt!" one of the men yelled.

"Right-oh," said the driver of the car, as he climbed out and snapped a swagger stick against the hood. "That makes six for us, against one of them. Damn fine show, chaps!"

This place wasn't a loony bin. That would be an insult to loony bins. This was pandemonium on the hoof. Mary Todd's bomber episode looked more and more like a movie title: *One Flew Over the Cuckoo's Nest*.

Maybe Wesley's motion wasn't so off the wall.

Desperate times call for desperate measures, Richard thought. Not that he was *that* desperate. It had only been two days since he'd held Erin in his arms. But it felt like two years. Here he was, supposed to be concentrating on his arguments for Mary's court appearance tomorrow, and instead he was thinking of the way Erin's green eyes glittered like starlight in his heart.

He wasn't worried about Pete's threats. He'd mentioned the kidnapping to Ted, who of course had already heard about it through the Paradise Beach grapevine. (Was it even remotely possible to keep a secret in this town?) Everyone knew who had taken Erin, and where she was being kept, and what the ransom demand was, down to the details of what time Ted was supposed to be on the beach, and where. As covert criminal enterprises went, this wasn't. But it was having the desired effect—Mary Todd's desired effect, Richard had no doubt—and he was more and more on the spot.

"Haven't rescued her yet, old boy?" Albermarle asked him over lunch. Then, with that oh-so-British cluck of his tongue, Albermarle pointed to the chalkboard on the wall, where the seafood house normally listed its daily specials. Instead, the chalkboard looked like a football pool, with the townspeople having placed bets on whether Richard would effect a successful rescue. Albermarle clucked again. "My quid says you're a mudder, chap. Not the horse to bet on a fast track, but when the going gets sloppy, you'll pull through."

"Ummm, thanks," Richard said. "I think."

The colonel drew himself even more ramrod straight, if that were possible, then leaned forward from the hips and tapped the table with a fingertip. "We Brits know our sport, son. And we know what it means to be mudders. It's our tradition . . . Wellington . . . Montgomery. Keep your powder dry, laddie, and you'll do fine."

And thus had gone the day. That afternoon, his secretary had slipped a copy of *Miracle at Dunkirk* onto his desk as she'd delivered the mail. When he'd asked her about the book, she'd simply smiled and walked away. The mayor had waddled in—blinding in an electric blue suit, purple shirt, and a tie covered with blooming hibiscus— to say he'd put a ten-spot on Richard making a rescue, and of course Richard knew how the mayor felt about losing money, didn't he?

The kicker, however, came when Seana met him in his driveway as he got home from work. She was carrying a garment bag, and had an I-will-*not*-take-no-for-an-answer look on her face. "Do you love my sister?" she asked.

Richard considered the question. *Love* was a very, very big word. Was this love, or simply a merging of hormones? He certainly enjoyed Erin's company, and not only when they were slipping against each other in bed. She had a face he could watch forever, savoring every emotion that flickered across her features. She was smart and funny and fun, and there was a depth in those green eyes as well. She'd overcome much to find her way in life, and she seemed to have overcome it with grace and beauty. Was this a woman—*the* woman—that he could wake up next to every day for all eternity?

The answer, he supposed, lay in how he'd felt these past two mornings, when he'd rolled over, still half asleep, to that spot that had come to be hers. A deep, aching aloneness.

"She is beauty," he answered simply.

Seana smiled and held out the garment bag. "Then it's time to get your lover back, Mr. Pirate."

She handed him the bag, turned, and walked away without another word. He carried it into the house, hung it on the hook on his closet door, and zipped it open. The laugh virtually burst out of him.

An Errol Flynn costume.

Of course. This *was* Paradise Beach, after all.

Erin looked at the growing pile of chips in front of her. Leon and Vinnie were nice enough guys, for retired gangsters, but they were awful poker players. Leon had a habit of scratching his eyebrow when he had a good hand, while Vinnie made a little grunting sound at the back of his throat whenever he bluffed. She was taking candy from babies. Fortunately, they were only playing for chips, or she'd be leaving with their Social Security checks.

Assuming she left at all. She had already determined that if Richard didn't get his piratical posterior in gear and rescue her, she was walking away from the relationship. It wasn't like there was any real *risk* involved. Leon and Vinnie knew the rules, and they were willing to play by them. Why, Richard had taken more of a risk filing that motion than he ever might in a rescue attempt. If he didn't care enough to come to her aid now, what would he do if there was *real* trouble?

"Oh, stop fretting," Mary said. "He's always been late. That boy will be late for his own funeral."

"As long as he's not late for his own wedding," Erin said, then caught herself. "I mean, if he ever met someone who . . . you know . . ."

"Balderdash," Mary announced, tapping her cane against the table. As well as Erin was doing at the game, Mary was doing better. She hadn't forgotten much from her riverboat days, as the neat stacks of chips in front of her attested. "You meant exactly what you said, girl. And he will be on time for that, if I have to have him hog-tied and delivered like a package."

"Assuming it ever happens," Erin said. She glanced at her cards again—it was still only a pair of fives—then at Leon. "I'll see your five and raise you five."

"I'm out," Vinnie announced.

"I'm in for another five," Leon said, scratching his eyebrow and tossing another red chip into the pot.

Mary rapped her cane again, although if there was any significance to that, Erin hadn't figured it out yet. Mary rapped her cane against the table every time she reached for her cards, every time she looked at the pot, every time she reached for her chips. It was as if, by focusing on that one tic, she had avoided any others that might give away her thoughts. She pushed a pair of chips into the center of the table.

"I'll see the five and raise another ten."

"Oh hell," Erin said. "I'll see the ten."

Leon stopped scratching his eyebrow. Erin watched the thought form in his eyes in the instant before he turned his cards down. "When you two women start throwing blue chips like you're flicking lint off the table, it's time for me to fold."

Truth was, Leon's hand would have almost certainly beat Erin's. But that was the thing with poker. It wasn't so much the cards you held as how you played them. A lot like life, she thought. And love. And she was calling Richard's hand.

"I'll call," Mary said, putting out her cards one by one, three of hearts, four of diamonds, five of hearts, six of spades . . . and the ten of clubs.

"You win," she said, before Erin could turn her cards.

"How did you know?"

Mary chuckled and was about to answer when she glanced out the French doors.

Desperate times call for desperate measures,

Richard repeated again to himself as he tied the
rope to the tree behind Mary's house. He looked
and felt absurd in black pantaloons, an open-
necked white shirt with bloused sleeves, and a
crimson sash tied around his waist. But Erin was
worth feeling a little absurd over. It was time to
buckle his swash. He slid the black eye patch
down into position, climbed the tree, took aim at
the French doors on Mary's patio, and let himself
swing.

In the instant he left the branch, he thought,
This is not a good idea. What if the doors were
locked? What if he hit the glass and cut himself?
He had time for a dozen more what-ifs in the
half-second it took to swing down. The old seventies song "The Things We Do for Love" was
playing in his mind. He scrunched his eyes shut.

Mary moved with a spry speed that surprised
everyone in the room, and opened the doors.
Richard tumbled into the room, skidding and
rolling across the floor, his voice hardly a heroic
yell, but instead more of a panicked "Waaaaaah!"
Still, Erin thought he was beautiful.

Vinnie and Leon, who had left their squirt
guns across the room, were slower to react. They
scrambled as best as their aging, aching joints
would allow. Richard flailed with his arms and
legs, trying to right himself, and tripped the two
just as they reached their weapons. For a moment, they were little more than a tangled heap

of "Oh shit" and "Hold still, dammit!" When the three finally found their footing and stood, Erin started to laugh.

"What's so funny?" Leon asked.

"Yeah," Vinnie said. "We're tryin' to fight here. Show some respect."

Mary chuckled and pointed to their chests. "I think the fight's over, boys."

Vinnie and Leon looked down. In the tumbling melee, they'd shot each other.

"Well, don't that figure?" Leon said, glaring at Vinnie. "You shot me."

Vinnie glared back. "You shot me first!"

"And how would you know that?" Leon demanded.

"Because . . . because . . ."

Richard held up a hand. "Ummm, guys, I hate to interrupt, but I have a damsel to rescue here." He turned to Erin. "How are you?"

She smiled and looked at the table. "Fine. I was winning at poker."

"Should I come back another time?" Richard asked, a rakish smile on his face.

"Not if you know what's good for you," she said.

With that, he swept her into his arms and carried her up the half-staircase that led to Mary's sunroom, then took her out onto the deck. "Wait here. I'll be right back."

"What's this about?" she asked.

"If I'm going to rescue my Irish Valkyrie, I'm going to do it in style."

With that he ran back down the stairs and out the door, grabbed the rope, and held it up to her. "Hold onto this for a moment?"

Erin leaned over the railing and took the rope, a smile forming on her face. Vinnie, Leon, and Mary had come outside and were watching the goings-on with evident amusement.

Richard dashed back inside, up the stairs, and out onto the deck, where Erin handed him the rope. "Hold on tight," he said.

She wrapped her arms around him. "Gladly."

He wrapped one arm around her and looped the rope around his wrist, then scissored his legs over the railing and swung off. Erin let go as they landed gently on the ground. But Richard held on too long, and learned firsthand why tying the rope to the tree was not such a great idea. Picking himself up at the base of the live oak, he turned to hear the tinkle of Erin's laughter.

"Richard, darling? I was hoping for Errol Flynn, not George of the Jungle."

He strode across the lawn and took her in his arms. "I guess I'll need more practice, then."

"*Lots* more practice," she said with a giggle, and kissed him fiercely. "*Lots* more practice."

25

Seana watched as Dan pumped up his squirt gun. "Are you sure they're going to let you bring that into the courthouse?" she asked. He hadn't had time to prepare before they'd left for Mary's hearing, so here he sat at a red light, getting his weapon ready to fire.

"Well, I guess we'll find out when we get there," he answered, straightening his white tie.

He was back to the monochromatic, black-on-black look, save for the white tie, and a white fedora with a black band. She wondered if there was a special clothing store for gangsters, although in all honesty, he didn't really look all that much like a gangster anymore. Oh, he still played it up when he was strolling around Paradise Beach, but in private he seemed afraid to say more than a few words in succession. She told herself it was the stress from the mob war, but her intuition told her it was something more than that.

"So are you back to New York after this war is over?" she asked.

He shrugged. "New York, L.A., wherever the work takes me."

"I thought you guys were more territorial. I mean, from what I've seen in movies and stuff."

He looked out the window at the condo canyon that was what Gulf Boulevard had become farther north on the barrier islands, and what it would become in Paradise Beach if Linus had his way. "Don't believe everything you see in the movies," he said absently.

"You don't like movies?" She was desperate for anything to keep a conversation rolling.

"Oh, I do. I like the way you can take an idea, turn it into a hundred or so pages of screenplay, turn that over to a director who chops it up into five- and ten-second shots, turn those over to actors who have to be totally real for those five or ten seconds at a time, and turn that over to an editor who weaves it all together into a story that seems seamless. When it's done right, anyway."

That was more words than he'd said in nearly a week. It was obviously a subject that fascinated him. Maybe he was like the loan shark in *Get Shorty*—a frustrated film producer at heart?

"You know a lot about how movies are made," she said. "I hadn't really thought about the actors having to work in such short bursts. I guess I just assumed it was kind of like filming a play."

Dan laughed and shook his head. "Everyone assumes that. I guess because acting *looks* like acting, whether you're doing it on stage or on screen. But it's actually very different. Half the time a film actor will only say two or three lines at a time, for a specific shot. Or be standing on a sound stage in front of a green screen, having to think and feel as if there's a torrential flood roaring down behind him. That's the hardest part, I think."

Something clicked. Seana knew, even then, even if she wasn't sure she knew. She knew. "Why the green screen?"

"Oh, that's called matte photography. Blue-green is the natural color of undeveloped film. So the actors work in front of a huge blue-green screen, and the effects are photographed separately. Then the lab merges the images, blurs the edges a bit, digitizes some foreground effect, and by the time the process is done, it looks like the actor is standing in the middle of a flood."

"Fascinating."

He smiled. "Yeah, it's pretty cool."

"You've seen it done," she said. It wasn't a question.   •

Dan looked across at her. Her eyes flickered over for only a moment, but there was warmth there. Would there still be warmth when she found out he'd been lying all this time? Was there even much to lose? After all, in a few days this gig would be over, and he'd be off to the West Coast to film the series pilot—if the producer had come up with the money—and the next time she saw him, it'd be on her television. She could curse him then and he wouldn't even know it. Or wouldn't he?

He'd read somewhere about people who were so emotionally connected that they could sense each other's feelings, even miles apart. Men and women who woke in a fright or suddenly felt an emptiness in their chests, *knowing* their lovers or parents or siblings or children had just died at that very moment. Or the countless stories of people who found themselves thinking of a long-lost friend or lover, only to answer the ringing phone and hear the other person's voice. Was he that close to Seana? Would he feel her anger and sadness as she saw his face on the screen and switched the channel with an angry push of a remote button? Would the thought of how he'd deceived her haunt him like the spectre of a murdered boarder, clanking around in the empty attic of "if only"?

The hollow ache in his chest answered the question better than any rational analysis could have. Yes. If he didn't tell her, it wouldn't matter whether she forgave him *in absentia*. He'd never forgive himself.

"Yes, Seana. I've seen it. Firsthand. It's what I do for a living." There, the dam was open, and the words tumbled out like a river now. "When I'm not pretending to be a mobster as a favor for an old college friend. Erin and I went to theatre school together. She thought it might pull Mary out of herself. But I never meant to . . . what we've done wasn't . . . Seana, the only *honest* thing I've done in the last few weeks is fall for you."

It was the kind of yes-I-was-lying-but-I-wasn't-lying-about-*us* scene he'd avoided at all costs when he was looking at roles. They had always seemed so hokey in a script or on the screen. Now he was living it in real life, and however hokey it may have seemed, it was as if the entire universe rested on the next words she would say, the next expression on her face, the next flicker of thought, the next beat of her heart.

She smiled. "So I wouldn't end up having to visit you in prison, or being swept away with you to some tiny town in Idaho as part of the Witness Protection Program?"

It was as if a boulder had been lifted from his chest. "Not unless they make acting a crime."

Seana laughed, a tension-breaking laugh. "Some of the acting I've seen *ought* to be criminal!"

Dan joined in the laugh. "Some of the acting I've *done* ought to be criminal. God, when I look at the tapes from back when I was on the soaps. Lock me up and throw away the key!"

She swatted his thigh. "Stop it. You couldn't have been *that* bad."

"Trust me, I was," he said, taking her hand. "I knew nothing and I thought I knew everything. That's not a good combination."

"Well, Dan Floorsheim, or whatever your name really is, you've learned a lot since then. You fooled everyone in town, and we Paradisians pride ourselves on being able to see through people's facades."

"O'Doole."

"Hmm?" she asked.

"That's my real name. Daniel Fitzpatrick O'Doole."

Now she guffawed. "You *would* be Irish! Who but the Irish could shovel such blarney?"

He found a space in the courthouse parking lot, then turned the key and shifted to face her. "So you're not disappointed that I'm just an actor?"

Seana leaned over and kissed him full on the lips. "Daniel Fitzpatrick O'Doole, how could I be mad at you? I got the thrill of being a gangster's moll without the risk."

"And now?" he asked, hopefully.

"And now," she said, "we need to help Richard win Mary's case, and help Ted win this mob war. Then we can think about us, and our future."

Those last two words were, he thought, the most beautiful sound he'd ever heard. *Our fu-*

ture. He got out of the car and tucked the giant squirt gun under his arm. It was time for battle.

"In re: Mary Maxine Todd," the bailiff announced.

This time, Mary thought, the courtroom was more to her liking. Linus sat at the petitioner's table with his anal-retentive hyphen of a lawyer, and behind him sat Pete Lewis, all alone, casting furtive glances across the aisle at Ted and Dan, both of whom were holding bright green and orange squirt guns in their laps. Oddly, or not so oddly, they were color-coordinated with the mayor, who had spared no expense to look like Bozo the Clown on a bad hair day. Colonel Albermarle and his men were seated at attention, still in their black khakis, their pith helmets on their laps. Behind her, Erin and Seana stifled a giggle as Judge Dipshot surveyed his domain and rolled his eyes. This, Mary thought, should be fun.

"We're here on respondent's motion for rehearing," Dipshot said. "Mr. Wesley, you may proceed."

Richard rose and nodded. "Thank you, Your Honor. May it please the court." He turned to Linus's table, leaving no stone of protocol unturned. "Counsel." He paused for a breath—or for effect—and continued. "As the court is aware, Miss Todd has filed a motion for rehearing, raising new legal and factual issues which have arisen since this court's decision."

Dipshot nodded. "I've read your motion, Counselor. Is there any precedent for your legal theory here?"

"Yes, your honor. The respondent cites *Lemon*, a United States Supreme Court decision which established the test for obscenity. Specifically, the Court held that obscenity was a question of fact, to be judged according to contemporary community standards. The respondent argues that both obscenity and competence—as challenged in this case—are questions of normal versus abnormal behavior, where 'normal' is socially defined. That is, where 'normal' is defined by contemporary community standards. Behavior that might seem absurd to the point of incompetence in one setting might be perfectly ordinary in another."

Mary smiled. Now *this* was the Richard she'd known all of these years.

"Consider," he continued, "how out of place a stockbroker would be in a jungle tribe. Where the community might be focused on hunting, gathering, spinning, weaving, and the like, a man who worried about flickering numbers on his PalmPilot might seem . . . incompetent. By contrast, the jungle tribesman would be dismissed as a vagrant at best, and perhaps even arrested, but certainly deemed incompetent, were he hunting, gathering, spinning, weaving, and the like . . . in Central Park."

"Objection," the hyphen said. "We're not talking about Manhattan versus the Amazon here. We're talking about a beach community in Florida, in the United States. Surely counsel is not arguing that the residents of this community spend their lives ... what was it ... hunting, gathering, spinning, weaving, and the like?"

"If it please the court," Richard said, layering on politeness the way a French chef spreads white wine sauce, "I am prepared to demonstrate that Paradise Beach is indeed a unique community, with its own customs and mores."

Dipshot grumbled and waved a hand. "Sit down, Mr. Colan. Proceed, Mr. Wesley."

"Your Honor, the respondent is prepared to present witnesses." Richard paused and waited for Dipshot to nod.

This would be the difficult part, Mary remembered. Richard had told her that Dipshot hated to hear from witnesses, who, he thought, merely cluttered the issue with facts. However, Dipshot nodded, and Richard continued.

"Your Honor, the respondent calls Daniel O'Doole."

Dan rose and walked up to the witness box, still carrying his industrial-sized squirt gun. Judge Dipshot eyed him warily. "Mr. O'Doole, I can't let you have that thing in here."

Richard cut in. "That will be evidence, Your Honor. I'd ask the court for some leeway here."

"Objection!" the hyphen said. "No foundation."

Richard smiled. "Oh, I'll present the foundation, Your Honor. Believe me."

The judge let out a weary sigh. "Okay, but I'll hold onto it here at the bench. Bailiff?"

The bailiff took the gun from Dan and placed it on Dipshot's bench as Dan was sworn in and took his seat. Richard gave him a moment to settle.

"Please state your full name for the record?"

"Daniel Fitzpatrick O'Doole."

"And what is your occupation?" Richard asked.

Dan looked at Seana and smiled. "I'm an actor."

Linus's jaw dropped like a buxom geriatric's bosom. "What?" He turned to the hyphen. "What?" he said again.

Dipshot rapped his gavel. "Quiet, Mr. Todd. Proceed, Mr. Wesley."

"And what brought you to Paradise Beach, Mr. O'Doole?"

"An old college friend," Dan said with a glance at Erin. "I was asked to play the role of a gangster."

"Did your friend give a reason for this?"

"Objection, hearsay!" the hyphen said.

Dipshot glared. "Oh, just shut up! I'm being inducted into the Columnade Club at lunch. I'm not going to be late for gumbo because of a bunch of legal mumbo jumbo! Understood?"

The hyphen nodded. "Good! Get on with it, Wesley."

"Mr. O'Doole?" Richard asked. "Do you need me to repeat the question?"

"No, that's fine. Yes, I was told the reason for the performance was to help someone who was depressed."

"Are you a resident of Paradise Beach, Mr. O'Doole?"

"No," Dan said. "I live in New York, mostly. Also on the West Coast. I was home between jobs when Ms. Kelly called."

"Did this strike you as a 'normal' thing to do?"

Dan laughed. "Normal for New York? Normal for Los Angeles? Or normal for Erin?"

"Normal for what you're used to."

"Mr. Wesley, I'm used to theatre and movie people. Paradise Beach is like *théâtre en vie*."

"Huh?" Dipshot asked.

"The theater of life," Dan said, turning to the judge. "The whole town is a stage, and everyone in it a player. It's a lot of fun, actually."

"Okay," the judge said. "But try to keep the testimony in English."

"My apologies," Dan said.

Richard nodded to Dan. "Now, Mr. O'Doole, why are you carrying a squirt gun?"

"Self-defense," Dan said. "We're having a mob war."

"Excuse me?" the hyphen said. "A what?"

Dipshot picked up the squirt gun and aimed it at the hyphen's table. "You heard him, Mr. Colan. Now sit down and shut up."

"And how did this mob war begin?" Richard asked.

"We had a meeting. It seemed like the best way to resolve a dispute between Ted and Pete."

"That would be Ted Wannamaker and Pete Lewis?"

"Yes," Dan said, pointing at them. "They're both in love with Mary Todd."

"This is *absurd*!" the hyphen said.

Dipshot aimed. "One more word!"

"That's entirely the point," Richard said calmly. "Paradise Beach is an ongoing theatre of the absurd."

"Right!" Dipshot said. "That's his point."

"But—" the hyphen began.

Dipshot squeezed the trigger, and a blast of ketchup shot across the courtroom, spattering the table, Linus, the hyphen, and the floor. "Damn!" the judge said. "Nice gun, Mr. O'-Doole!"

"Thank you, Your Honor," Dan said.

Richard turned to the hyphen. "Your witness."

"This is how court *ought* to be!" Mary whispered to him as he sat down.

Richard suppressed a chuckle. "If only the county seat were in Paradise Beach."

The judge looked over at Linus's lawyer. "Any cross?"

The hyphen was still trying to wipe ketchup from his shirt with a legal pad. "Uh . . . no, Your Honor."

"Next witness?" Dipshot asked.

"The respondent calls Ted Wannamaker."

Ted was carrying a smaller, more gentlemanly weapon, as befit his regal stride to the witness stand. He handed it to the bailiff, raised his other hand, and said "I do," when prompted.

"Mr. Wannamaker," Richard began, "would you explain your role in this mob war?"

"Surely," Ted said. "I'm in love with Mary Todd."

Mary gasped. He'd never said that before. But he'd sworn to tell the truth, the whole truth, and nothing but the truth . . .

"And?" Richard asked.

"And I intended to arrange our prior marriage to protect her interests. I remembered her mentioning an old . . . connection . . . and I flipped through her diaries until I found a name."

"And who was that?"

Ted pointed. "Pete Lewis. I then talked to some of my . . . connections, located Mr. Lewis, and called him to arrange the prior marriage."

"And did he?"

Ted shook his head. "Not the way I'd planned. He arranged it, but married her to him instead."

Pete wheezed. "But we *were* married!"

"No, we weren't!" Mary said. "You left, remember?"

"I have the paper!" Pete said, rising.

Dipshot took aim and let fly again, this time spattering Pete, as well as Leon and Vinnie behind him.

"But we were already dead!" Leon said.

"Yeah," Vinnie added. "No fair shooting us again."

"And you just lost the war, Pete," Ted said with a smile.

Pete looked down. "So I did." He paused, then looked at the judge. "Your Honor, we're not married."

"Of course not," Dipshot said. He gave Pete a querulous look. "Why would I marry *you*?"

"No, I meant—"

"Objection!" the hyphen said. "The witness hasn't been sworn."

"Order!" Dipshot cried, now rising to his full height, Dan's gun in one hand, Ted's in the other. "Everybody shut up *now* or I'll hose down the lot of you!"

"Not me!" the mayor said. "It'd ruin my suit!"

Dipshot turned on him, and the mayor scrunched down behind the front bench. "Anyone else?"

Ted nodded to Richard. Richard turned to Mary. "Yes, Your Honor. The respondent calls Mary Maxine Todd."

"Well?" Ted whispered in her ear as he returned to his seat.

What is Richard up to? Mary wondered. She

shook her head, but he pressed on, pulling a photocopied page from his briefcase. "You're busted, Mary. It's time."

Mary wanted to argue the point until she studied the paper he was holding. Behind her, Erin chuckled. *Well damn*, Mary thought, *I taught her well*. Mary slowly rose from her chair and made her way to the witness stand.

"It's about damn time," Judge Dipshot said, glancing at his watch.

Mary rapped her cane against his bench. "Be patient, young man. You'll get your lunch soon enough. From the looks of you, you could skip a meal or three and not suffer for it."

Dipshot opened his mouth to speak, but instead Mary turned to the bailiff. "Of course I'm going to tell the truth," she said. She glanced back over her shoulder at the judge. "Doesn't that prove it?"

The bailiff looked at the judge, who looked at the hyphen, who simply buried his head in his hands. "Take your seat, ma'am," he said.

"Mary, have you ever heard of Timothy Herschfeld?"

"Of course," Mary said. "You mentioned his name in the last hearing. The developer, right?"

Richard smiled and shook his head. "And?"

"Yes," she said simply.

"Huh?" Dipshot asked.

She turned to him. "*I* contacted Herschfeld back in December and suggested he call my nephew about some property."

"Huh?" the hyphen asked, looking up.

"Your Honor," Mary continued, "there comes a time in a woman's life when she has to know what's real and what isn't. Ted and I had bobbed along for forty years, and I've always kept him at arm's length." She turned to Ted. "Because you're too damn ordinary. So I figured I'd set up my nephew and see if *that* would push you off the bubble."

"Huh?" Linus asked.

Richard smiled. "So this whole thing . . . the bomber, your refusal to testify in the last hearing, the faked depression . . . all of it was—"

"A test," Mary said. She smiled at Ted. "And you passed, my love." Then she rapped the judge's bench again. "So who's so crazy now?"

Dipshot raised his hands. "Anyone who crosses you. The prior order of this court is reversed." He grabbed the squirt gun as the hyphen rose. "Don't even think about it, Mr. Colan. Petition denied. I'm going to lunch."

Albermarle and his men broke into a chorus of "Men of Harlech." Mary hugged Richard. Richard hugged Erin. Dan hugged Seana. Ted shook Pete's hand, then turned and, for the first time in forty years, kissed Mary Todd.

The mayor peeked up over the back of the bench.

"Is it safe to come out now?"

EPILOGUE

"Welcome to Cactus Bottom," Pete wheezed to Linus. "I promised I'd set you up, and I have."

Linus looked around the barren Nevada landscape. He'd agreed to go back west with Pete on the promise of his own hotel and casino to run. Instead, he was here, in the middle of nowhere, with only two buildings in sight. One was an abandoned gas station so old that the posted prices were in single digits. The other was a ramshackle, clapboard dump with a faded sign over the front door that said Rooms. Linus suspected the last people to stay here had never yet heard of radio, let alone television or computers.

"It's a fixer-upper," Pete said.

"At the very least," Linus answered. "Anyone live around here?"

"Only rattlesnakes and jackrabbits right now," Pete said. "But this is gonna be the next Las Vegas. Without all the smog and the big money running everything. And you're in on the ground floor, boy. I'm making you a partner in the business."

Linus took a second look around. They were only an hour from the interstate. And it was nice to be able to look up and see stars. With the right planning, it could work. It needed a point man. A man with business savvy. A man who could pull a deal together.

"What do I do?" he asked.

Pete walked him over to the side of the building and pulled back a tarp to reveal dozens of buckets of paint, and rollers. "Start with the outside," Pete said. "I'll be back in a couple of days to see how it's going."

"What?" Linus asked.

Pete expelled a wheezy laugh. "Like I said, son, you're getting in on the ground floor."

"We should go to Ted's," Mary announced from the comfort of her deck chair, looking out over the sunset on the gulf.

"Your house has a better view, love," Ted said, patting the back of her hand.

"Balderdash!" she said, pulling her hand away. "I'm not talking about your house, young man. I'm talking about your island!"

"His island?" Dan asked, snuggling Seana closer to him as seagulls dipped and danced in the last rays of twilight.

"Didn't you know?" Erin asked. "Ted has his very own Caribbean island."

"An ideal honeymoon spot," Richard announced. He looked at Erin, then gave her another rakish smile. "Well, you have a choice. You can marry me, or I'll kidnap you."

"I've done kidnapping," Erin said with a disdainful wave. "That's old hat."

Richard caught her hand in midair. "Everything's old hat to you now. I still can't believe you rifled through Mary's diary that way."

"All's fair in love and war," she announced with a laugh. "Isn't that right, Mary?"

Mary rapped the leg of Erin's deck chair. "You learned well. Sometimes it takes a war to build a love."

"Like ours?" Ted asked.

Mary snorted. "Oh, enough with the mushy-mush, Ted. You've chased me for forty years, but you wouldn't know what to do with me if you caught me."

He leaned across to kiss her cheek. "Well, I think I could figure it out from watching Dan and Seana."

The two blushed at the mention of their names. They'd been inseparable since the hearing, in more ways than one.

"I can't help it," Seana said, burying her forehead in the curve of Dan's neck. "He's perfect. And I won't have to marry him in prison!"

"Who said anything about marriage?" Dan asked with a playful swat to her bottom.

"I did," Richard cut in, laughing, then turned to Erin. "To you. Would you?"

Erin's eyes flashed green gold in the last wink of the sunset. "I will. If you promise to kidnap me after."

"Again?"

She smiled and held up a pair of handcuffs. "Yeah. I could get used to being your captive."

Mary put her hand over Ted's eyes as he watched in rapt attention.

"Absolutely not, Ted."

He couldn't see her wink.